THE IRON
CHRONICLES
Book II: IRON ZULU
Brad R. Cook
Second Edition
I0645553

THE IRON CHRONICLES

BOOK I:

IRON ZULU

Brad R. Cook

Second Edition

Book Cover
Designed by Brad R. Cook
Milli-Train Illustration by Jennifer Stolzer
Border and other images from Pixabay.com

Interior
Sparrowhawk, Milli-train, Iron Horseman, and Black
Knight illustrations by Jennifer Stolzer
JenniferStolzer.com
Scrolls and frames from pixabay.com
Layout by Brad R. Cook

More of Jennifer's amazing Iron Chronicles art
at bradrcook.com

Iron Zulu, Book II of The Iron Chronicles
was originally published by
Treehouse Publishing Group in 2015

For

My Family

"I fear not the army of lions led by a sheep, I fear the army of sheep led by a lion."

Alexander the Great

Map of the Iron Zulu adventure

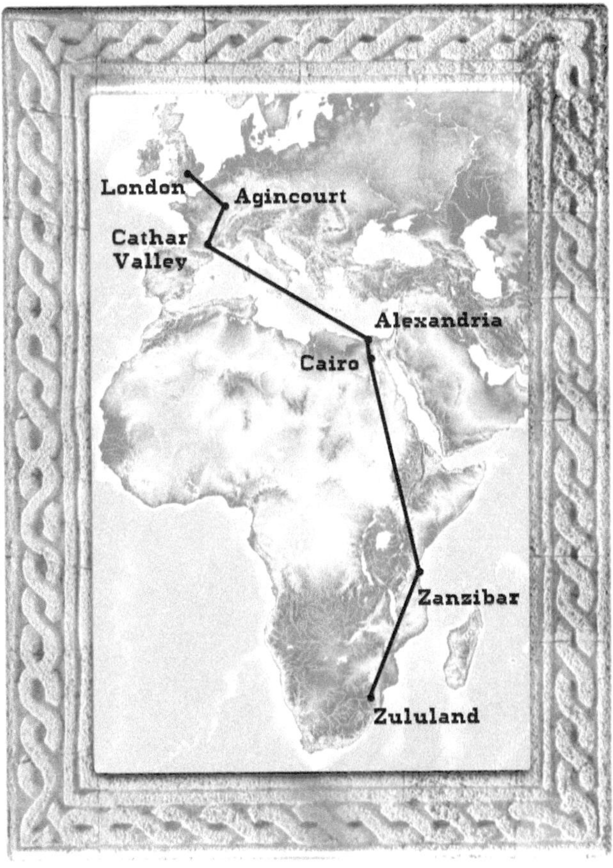

London 1882

Second chances are rare. I know this—when they arise, seize them. So, unlike before, when my nerves were rattled, this time, I intended to make the most of my second chance.

As I stood beside my father, the wind whipped around me, and pinned my overcoat to my sides. We waited for Genevieve and Baron Kensington to arrive. I hadn't seen her or her father, since they'd left for his convalescence in Egypt.

An overnight dusting of snow covered the cobblestones and blanketed the airships that had docked overnight. I shuffled back and forth trying to stay warm. I should have a gift for Genevieve, like flowers, or candy, or an overcoat. The London weather would be an adjustment, I'm sure, for both of them. But no, they probably knew that already. So what? Jewelry. A gentleman would have jewelry. I sighed. Maybe I could get a third chance.

"Alexander, stop fidgeting." My father pressed his hand against the back

of my arm. "You look like your being attacked by bugs."

A tremor rumbled inside, and I closed my eyes. Instantly, it was as if a swarm of insects—every vile thing that crawled or flew—surrounded me. As they twitched their legs and beat their wings, scurrying over every inch of me, visions of last year's Battle of the Thames resurfaced. Some of the events of that day had stayed with me, filled my nights and haunted my lonely daytime moments. The buzzing intensified, and drowned out all other sounds. Instinctively, I grabbed my arms, and swatted the bugs as they nipped their way inside.

I opened my eyes. No bugs. Nothing surrounded me but the cold wind. I sighed and let the tension slip away.

"Alexander?" my father asked with concern.

"I'm just cold," I said, and hoping to warm my heart, I thought back to when Genevieve and I were in Gibraltar, the sun shining off the white stucco and Spanish tile roofs.

Father squeezed my shoulder. "We shouldn't be here much longer." He let go and shaded his eyes. "But you have to be on your best behavior."

"I promise I won't say anything to upset the baron."

"He's not returning today," he said, as if this as if I should have known this.

I cocked my head sideways and glowered at him. *That might have been something you could have mentioned before making me stand in the cold for an hour.* Sensing my disapproval, my father added, "Baron Kensington decided to stay in Egypt for the winter. I recently sent him a cable suggesting several archeological sites to see while he's there."

Then why was I standing here? And why did it not

occur to him that I might have even had something to say in the cable—to Genevieve? And if we weren't here to greet her and the baron, who was on this airship? I tried not to think about Genevieve's absence. I shouldn't think of her at all. She was betrothed—to the Duke's son, no less. I was nothing more than a penniless boy. Why couldn't life be fair? Just once.

What if Genevieve's stuck in the desert, longing to get back London? *Yeah right.* Not cold and dreary London. She was having a blast in the beautiful summery weather of the Mediterranean, while I was stuck here in a bitter and perpetually gray world.

Before I could ask my father who we were waiting for, he returned his gaze toward the sky and pointed as an imperial airship gently slipped through the clouds. "There they are." The vibrant blue canvas hull trimmed in gleaming gold stood in stark contrast to the dirty, snow-dusted London streets. Even the snow was not pristine in this city.

As the airship landed. My father ignored my question and strode briskly toward the gangplank. I scampered to keep up. Just as the door opened, the Duke, dressed in a long, red jacket with gold buttons, stood out against the dreary landscape.

The Duke glided along the walkway with ease. Did all nobles go to some tutor to learn to move with effortless grace? Had I somehow missed that class at Eton College? He did not even shiver as a cold wind whipped around us. I tugged the stiff collar of my jacket, wanting nothing more than to leave, until my father jerked my arm back down.

As the Duke arrived on the dock, he stopped, abruptly forcing everyone behind him to stop as well.

He thwapped his swagger stick against his palm. "Why, Professor," he said, "whatever are you doing here?"

My father stepped forward and whipped his hat off. "I was sent to welcome our guest."

"Ah yes, the savages. How nice of you, but all you need do is pass them off to the queen's ministers."

Savages? *Savages* was a word the nobles used to mean anyone not from the brick-laden civilized world. He'd probably call me a savage, too, for my outbursts.

The Duke glanced down his nose at me and said, "I see you brought the pup. Still as insolent as before?"

"Wh…?" Furious, I balled my hands into tight fists. My father checked my outburst with a tight squeeze of his hand on my shoulder. My face hardened as I clenched my jaw and gnashed my teeth, and my nails cut into the palms of my hands.

"Ah yes, I suppose some pups just need a stronger hand," he sighed.

As he turned my father said, "Good *day*, Your *Grace*." The Duke paused at my father's harsh tone.

A voice broke through everyone backed up on the gangplank. Then, working his way through the crowd, I saw a young man flanked by two other young nobles. From his annoyed expression at the slow-moving attendants, I assumed he was someone of importance, too. He stood taller than me, though not by much. And his poufy hair added an inch or two.

When the young man approached the Duke, he quipped, "What is the hold up, Father?"

The Duke rolled his eyes and said, "Patience my son; patience."

My eyes bulged. *Son?* Genevieve's betrothed. Prince Charming in all his finery. And here I am in my school uniform. *Perfect.* Well, he may be charming, but at least I didn't have a long thin nose like a mosquito.

With this, our first meeting, I wanted—had to—make an impression. Or at least not totally screw it up—so I could at least make a much better second impression. I sure didn't want him to see me as a 'pup', too.

Be bold, I told myself, like Captain Baldrich. Have the presence of the Templar Grand Master Sinclair. So, I puffed up my chest and stood as straight as possible waiting for the Duke to introduce us. But he didn't.

Instead, he sidestepped us and walked briskly toward a waiting carriage, and said "Richard, hurry along."

Richard, I snarled. Probably named after Richard the Lionheart. Like being named after somebody important meant something. Then I paused—I was named after Alexander the Great.

As Richard approached me, I stuck out my hand to welcome him, but he just whooshed by. He didn't even look my way. Just like when I'd first arrived at Eton College. I was invisible then, too.

In moments, the entire entourage was gone. Still, we stood there as my father bowed to several other dignitaries disembarking from the airship. Another young man, about my age, appeared at the airship's doors. Dressed in a fine suit, he walked down the gangplank. Behind him, stood a rather large-bellied man, his western suit snug around the middle They were African.

Excited and intrigued, I smiled. Even though I'd never been to Africa, the Dark Continent fascinated me. Tales of exotic animals—lions, giraffes, massive herds of zebras, and especially, the ancient cultures filled me with wonderment.

My father, too, shifted with excitement. "Chief

Zwelethu! Welcome to London. I'm John Armitage, a professor at Eton College and a friend of Baron Kensington."

The chief, who had the darkest, richest skin color, I'd ever seen, gently prodded the young man to the end of the gangplank. "Thank you. We are excited to be in your … wait, your accent, are you American?"

"Yes sir, we are."

"Ah, how exciting. I have always wanted to meet one from your country. We will have to speak of your people while I am here." He then motioned to the young man in front of him. "Allow me to introduce my seventh son, Owethu."

Owethu bowed. "It is an honor to meet you, sir," he said to my father, while he eyed me with a questioning gaze. When I continued to grin, his smile grew wide, too.

My father gestured to me. "And this is my son, Alexander."

They both bowed to me and I returned the gesture, for once, feeling like a noble myself.

Looking past them at the airship, I said, "Did you enjoy your flight? It's my favorite."

Chief Zwelethu turned and glanced at the airship. "It was an interesting way to travel."

"I really liked it," Owethu added. More and more, he didn't seem like a noble. I nodded, and grinned. His expression held the unrestrained joy of one who had burst through the clouds and wouldn't come down for weeks. I knew the feeling well, all I'd ever dreamed of was gliding along the air currents, and soaring through a starry sky.

My father escorted us over to the steamcarriage. Finn waited, running his fingers through his bright orange hair, he opened the door to the steamcarriage and said, "Lord Marbury will be your host while in London. I've been asked to take you there."

Chief Zwelethu nodded and we all climbed inside. Finn closed the door and jumped up to the driver's perch. He pulled the lever releasing the brake and grabbed the steering column connected to a series of gears. The steamcarriage lurched as the engine at the back belched white smoke.

Chief Zwelethu, with concern etched on his face, glanced over his shoulder at the steam engine as we chugged through the streets of London. Owethu, pressed against the window unable to hide his excitement. And neither could I.

2
A Meeting
Before Dinner

The steamcarriage rolled onto the lane leading to Lord Marbury's sprawling country estate nestled among the forests outside London. My father pushed his glasses up on his nose. "Lord Marbury and his staff will assist in your meetings with her majesty's ministers, and arrangements have been made for your son to participate at Eton."

"Excellent," Chief Zwelethu said with a nod. "I am eager to speak with them. Especially Lord Sinclair."

"I'm certain he'll be in attendance," my father nodded. "If there is anything I can do, Chief, please let me know. And as Alexander attends Eton, if your son has any questions, myself or Alexander would be happy to answer them."

I nodded. I had a ton of questions about Africa all of which Owethu could answer, or at least I hoped he could.

Curling up the circle drive to the manor, we stopped under a large stone archway, and two of Lord Marbury's footmen rushed up to greet us. They opened the steamcarriage's door and bowed as the chief stepped out first. Trumpets

blared. Not expecting it, I jumped and grabbed my chest. A lively ditty followed and might have been a little out of place, but then, Lord Marbury always tended toward the dramatic.

Owethu stepped out next and joined his father. I slid out ahead of my father and servants lined themselves alongside the front steps, while Lord Marbury stood stiff and regal at the large double doors.

Chief Zwelethu marched forward, inspecting the staff on either side as if he were an air-captain inspecting his crew. My father and I followed behind Owethu, and all of us—except the chief—bowed when we reached Lord Marbury.

Lord Marbury nodded and ushered us inside to a long, narrow, stately room, exquisitely furnished. He, Chief Zwelethu, and my father took their places in chairs and began to discuss the protocol and schedule for his visit with the queen's dignitaries. But my brain numbed until their voices became nothing more than mumbling. I was intrigued by all the paintings.

Paintings covered every inch of the walls. Most were portraits, but a huge painting of Lord Marbury's manor hung above the fireplace. I walked over to study it. Stretching from the left edge of the canvas, a king sitting atop his stead, and followed by his entourage traveled toward the house. Frozen in a unseen wind, the flags atop the manor snag my attention. Below the Marbury family banner lay the white flag with the distinctive red cross at its center. The Templar flag.

Owethu joined me in front of the painting. He looked up, and then to me. "Is that one of your grandfathers?"

"No," I said, "I'm not of royal blood." I pointed to

the estate in the painting. "That's this house, though."

"I see this. The spires are the same." Owethu pointed to the king's entourage. "The lord of this estate must be important if the king comes to him."

"It was tradition. The king would travel around the country visiting the estates of his noblemen and force them to host him. It was very prestigious. In America, too, the president travels to greet the people—when it's time to get elected."

"In my country, the people travel for days to see the chieftains." Owethu smiled.

"Where are you from?"

"Zululand."

I spun on my heel and faced Owethu. "You're a Zulu?"

Owethu eyes hardened. "Do you have a problem with this, too?"

"No. I think it's fascinating! Why, Shaka was the greatest African king since the pharaohs."

His stance eased. "How do you know of the Zulu?"

"I study a lot. If my father isn't making me study some old, dead language, then he's making me read about another culture—for which I will have to study their language shortly after."

"I heard that," my father said from the other side of the room.

"It's true," I chuckled. We moved on to another painting, a portrait of one of the former ladies of the manor. Templar crosses of gold hung around the necks of many people in the paintings. In fact, over half of the art in this room had a Templar cross somewhere within.

Seeing all the Templar crosses brought back a flood of images, sounds, and smells from last year's battles between the Order and the Knights of the Golden Circle. The memories of the labyrinth on Malta, the horrors of the fire, and the Horsemen hearts, all threatened to consume me. I could still taste the sulfur burning the back of my throat, still hear the cracking rock as it crashed down around Genevieve and me. Her scream as Hendrix smashed the antidote to the baron's poison remained like the return of a distant echo.

To push back the nightmares from my adventure, I turned to Owethu, "Tell me about your homeland. Are you on the great savannah or do you live in the desert lands?"

"My home sits high on the rolling plains."

Thoughts of lying around the grassy English moors brought pleasant memories, and eased my anxiety. Realizing Owethu was staring at me, I said, "That would be the relaxing on a sunny day."

"No," Owethu smiled and shook his head. "There are lions nearby."

"Oh." I'd forgotten about the predators who also made the savannahs their home. England didn't have any exotic animals to fear. They barely had any snakes. All I really had to worry about were bugs.

My father crossed the room. "You boys need to get changed for dinner. Finn has a suit for you, Alexander."

"Yes, Father," I said, and started toward Finn who stood in the doorway carrying a bag. As I passed Lord Marbury, I noticed him wringing his hands together and staring off into the distance. He shifted nervously, and his agitation was never a good sign.

Lords, dressed in fine suits, and ladies, adorned in elaborate gowns, paraded into the house in a regal precession, just as the lord and his attendants did in the painting. Leaning against the polished wooden railing, I watched from the top of a grand staircase as they filed through the foyer into the ballroom, and gestured to their friends and the other important guests they were here to impress.

Grand Master Sinclair, head of the Templar Order, entered using his cane to aid him. I hoped the baron, and Genevieve, would walk in behind him, but I knew it wouldn't happen.

Sinclair handed off his top hat and cloak to a waiting attendant, but instead of entering the ballroom, he turned and entered a small chamber at the base of the stairs. I wondered what that meant. A secret Templar meeting, maybe? Perhaps the Knights of the Golden Circle had returned.

I knew one thing for certain, though; this presented the perfect lurking opportunity. If Genevieve were here, she'd agree. I slipped down the stairs, staying close to the banister. Then I rushed to the door and pressed myself against the wall. The door opened into the room, so I peered around the edge of the doorway. Noblemen and women were still arriving in the ballroom, but a large blue and white porcelain vase blocked me from their view.

Inside, Grand Master Sinclair greeted Chief Zwelethu. I cupped my ear to better hear the conversation. His deep Scottish accent filled the room. "Thank you for coming to London, Chief Zwelethu."

"Your queen wishes to award me," the chief stated. "But in truth, I come to speak with your warriors."

"I know. But there are too many ears to speak about it now."

I snapped back. Was Sinclair talking about me? The old guy must have eyes in the back of his head, but what kind of crazy Templar magic could he be using.?

Sinclair continued, "We can't be too careful. Lord Blackthorne is here."

Not me. I breathed a sigh of relief.

Chief Zwelethu remained stern. "I would like to speak of this matter before the ceremony."

"Most definitely. Lord Cobblefield will speak with us after the main course."

The chief's face hardened and his hands curled into fists. "Why him?"

Sinclair's voice softened. "I know you two have a history due to the war, but I can tell you when it comes to our enemies, you both are in agreement."

Common enemies and tense allies—now that sounded interesting. Something was afoot. Of course, I would have to find them later to hear that conversation. As they stepped into the ballroom, Sinclair patted the chief's back. Chief Zwelethu turned his head to look at the hand, disturbed by the gesture.

With the two men gone, I snuck back up the staircase and settled back on the landing. My father stepped out of the ballroom and looked up and down the hall. I didn't know if he was looking for me, but he didn't see me with my elbows perched on the railing. When he turned to go back inside, I hurried down to the main ballroom doors, where two footmen ushered me into the grand room.

Heads spun around as I entered. Their faces were a mix of, "Who is that?" followed by, "Oh, no one important." I quickly shuffled to the table where my father sat.

"There you are." He pointed to the chair. "Don't make me glue you down."

"What's this party for?" I asked.

"We are welcoming Chief Zwelethu to England."

"I just saw him in the hall."

"That's nice," my father said dismissively as he craned his neck to find the chieftain and his son over the heads of all the noblemen.

"But …" My father wasn't listening. Right now, I knew whatever I said would only receive a half-hearted, 'That's nice'. So, I said, "Old books smell like dusty mold."

He glanced over at me, a quizzical look on his face. *Really? This one time he's paying attention?* I raised my eyebrows and shrugged. My father leaned in. "Yes, he's here to meet with the Order, but we've talked about this, Alexander." he reminded me. Then without any warning, he grabbed my face and kissed my forehead. I scrunched up. "You're not to get involved until after your studies are completed."

I rolled my eyes, but nodded in agreement.

He tousled my hair, and returned to staring at the Zulu over the nobles. Bored, I stared down at the plate in front of me and ran my finger around the edge of the gold and porcelain charger plate with the Marbury family crest in its center. I don't know why I needed a plate for my plates. Of course, Father would tell me, "It's the proper way."

The smell of roses snagged my senses, as a slender hand reached out and tapped my shoulder. Before I could turn around, Genevieve's sweet English accent filled my ear. "Hey Sky Raider."

"Genevieve!" I jumped up, and almost knocked over my chair. "They said you weren't coming back." I started to reach out and hug her, but she stepped back and her eyes grew large, so I froze mid-gesture. I realized, as did she, where I stood—in a ballroom full of noble born—and if I hugged her, I would seriously break decorum.

She stepped back away from me, and said, "We slipped into the city. My father didn't want to make a big deal about coming home."

"That's magnificent!" I shifted as if the world wobbled on its axis. "I mean ... welcome back."

"Thank you," she said, with her sweet expression that lit the room, and caused me to sway, unsure if I'd eventually give in to my wobbly legs.

My mind reeled. I wanted to tell her a thousand things. Everything I'd been through, everything I felt while she was away, but the words bunched up in my throat and I choked on them. They wouldn't budge. I'd spent every day since she left, thinking of the perfect question to ask upon her

return, but I hadn't prepared for the scent of rose petals, or the surprise at hearing her sweet voice again. I had an entire script memorized, to ensure I was cool, calm, and collected when I saw her again. But that vanished, along with every language I knew, leaving me with only a panicked expression, and oddly, thinking in Gaelic. So, all that came out was, "Is your father feeling better?"

Idiot.

She nodded. "He recovered quickly in the dry dessert air." Tension slipped from her shoulders. "He hardly rested. We dealt with grave robbers and a mummy while in Egypt."

All my boring stories of Eton, my father's office, and freezing in my drafty room fizzled in my throat. She'd been living a life of adventure, and I'd been stuck in my studies. Not fair! "Did the mummy attack?"

"Kind of." Her brow wrinkled. I couldn't tell if she was serious or not. Could she have been attacked by a real mummy, just like I'd heard in stories? I was about to ask her more questions, when a voice from behind stopped me cold. A shiver zipped up my spine and I tensed. Prince Charming.

"Genevieve, how wonderful you've returned." The silky, condescending voice of the Duke's son slipped over my shoulder as he glided around me and took Genevieve's hands into his own. "I'm so very sorry we kept missing each other in Alexandria."

They were in *my* city. Together. The city founded by Alexander the Great. My namesake. Every muscle in my body trembled. My blood boiled, but then as I looked at Genevieve, I realized something. She wasn't happy to see him. Genevieve had avoided him. I envisioned her fleeing his lecherous pursuits like Cleopatra from Octavian.

"Richard." Her smile tensed but remained stoic. "It was unfortunate."

"We were delighted to hear about your mother's return."

Genevieve hardened. Nothing more than a flash across her face, which was quickly replaced by her stoic grace. "Thank you. We are delighted."

What? I wanted to ask. That can't be. Genevieve told me her mother had passed away. She'd shone me the locket she wore around her neck with her mother's picture. A remembrance. Hundreds of questions ran through my mind, but the pain in her eyes silenced me. She didn't want to talk about it.

"Father decided to return to London," she said to Richard. "I suppose the Empire needs him once more."

"My dear Genevieve, I try to stay out of such things." His smile looked contorted as he leaned down to kiss her gloved hand. "I was delighted to see that your father seemed in better spirits when we met in Cairo." Genevieve's betrothed took another step toward her, brushing in front of me. "By the by, that night at the pyramids was magical."

My heart dropped into my shoes. *Stupid.* I knew I should have run off to the desert, instead of staying here. She'd already been to my city, and seen the pyramids, too. I should be the one looking into Genevieve's eyes, saying those things to her. Not … not *him.*

Genevieve's cheeks flushed. She pulled her hands from his grasp and toyed with the silver locket around her neck. "I … I must not have found the sandstorm as magical as you, Richard."

He let out an uneasy chuckle, while I smiled. The moment had turned incredibly awkward. Mr. Perfect wasn't so perfect after all. Still, I wanted to punch him, or at least stomp on his perfectly polished boots. Anything to wrinkle his perfect façade.

A whirling gear shattered the moment, as a winged automaton struck a bronze gong and the room reverberated. Everyone turned. Lord Marbury motioned for us all to sit. Smiling at his guests, he said, "You'll have to indulge me. I acquired that magnificent piece on a recent trip to India."

Genevieve grasped my forearm. I turned to her, but her eyes remain fixed on the double doors. A woman, elegant, unescorted, entered the room. She walked into the ballroom with the grace and charm of a noblewoman. Immediately, I was struck by the beauty of her short, auburn hair, a style I'd never seen on noblewoman before. She bowed her head, a soft smile parting her lips as she made her way through the crowd, seemingly not noticing the whispers spinning up as she passed. When she reached the baron, she extended her hands out to him and kissed him passionately. Some guests gasped, but most faces held large smiles. Without a word, Genevieve released my arm, stepped away, and joined Richard, the Duke, and her family.

Three long tables filled the room in a 'U' shape. I sat at the end of one arm. Genevieve sat in the middle, and although we weren't that far apart, in terms of the blue-blooded society sitting in front of me, we were worlds away from each other.

I didn't listen to much of what Lord Marbury said. My focus was on Genevieve. As if she knew I was staring at her, she looked over and her eyes lit up, igniting a fire within me. I smiled back. Without taking her eyes from me, she leaned into her father, who whispered in her ear.

Then I saw Richard staring at me. A cold, devilish look, earmarked with a disgusted turn of his chin. He didn't approve. My smile faded. I returned his stare. I didn't approve of him, either.

The doors swung open and servants entered with the first course of cold soup. Soon they brought out tiny pheasants with barely enough meat on the bones. I started to wonder if anything I would actually eat might be placed in front of me tonight.

After the main course, while a bard sang tales in center of the hall, Grand Master Sinclair stood up and headed in the hall. He was followed by Baron Kensington, the Duke, and Lord Marbury, who escorted Chief Zwelethu through the side door.

This was it. The secret meeting was about to take place. I thought about Genevieve. I knew she'd want to listen, but she was surrounded by nobles, and it would be rude of me to interrupt. With my father locked in a debate with the gentleman next to him, I saw my chance. Not wanting to miss a word, I got up and slipped into the hall, and watched as Lord Marbury walked into a parlor room and closed the door. I pressed against the wall looking back and forth to make sure no one followed me. Inside, muffled voices talked over each other.

With no one in the hall, I slid up to the door and crouched down to spy through the keyhole. My vision was limited, but the baron pacing back and forth, while Sinclair and a man I didn't know sat across from Chief Zwelethu, who had deep scowl on his face. The other men, too, appeared anxious. *Must be serious.*

Footsteps. The hard-heeled boots of the house guards echoed behind me. Another step and they'd catch me for certain. I stepped back and my elbow bumped a large porcelain vase. I ducked behind it and held my breath.

The house guards continued on, but the door I'd been spying at swung open, and someone thundered by. I stayed behind the vase, but the footsteps moving down the hall sounded soft, padded, like bare feet. I wanted to peek from behind my hiding place, but didn't dare. There'd be no way to explain my presence here.

The hard heel of a boot followed and Genevieve's father called out, "Chief Zwelethu! Wait, please come back. We still have matters to discuss." Then after a brief pause, he added, "He didn't mean it."

The chief stopped. "I will not." He spoke softly, but his tone was harsh. "Never put that man in the same room with me again, for I will kill him."

Resigned, the baron replied, "I understand."

"No, I do not think you do," Chief Zwelethu said. "But you are a better man than most of the lords I have met."

I peeked around the vase as Chief Zwelethu headed off. Lord Marbury stepped out of the room next to the baron, and was followed by Sinclair. In his Scottish drawl, Sinclair asked, "Now what do we do?"

Lord Marbury sighed. "Do as he said; keep Lord Cobblefield away from him."

"We can do that." Sinclair pounded his fist against his palm. "Did Lord Cobblefield fight in the Zulu Wars?"

"I believe so," Baron Kensington said. "But it shouldn't matter. Did the man have to use the word 'savage'?"

I waited as the men wandered down the hall, their voices growing ever softer. When I couldn't hear them any longer, I poked my head up over of the vase.

Stepping out from behind it, I returned to the ballroom. Searching the room for Genevieve, I quickly took my seat at my table, I saw everyone but Chief Zwelethu. Lord Cobblefield had returned, too. He looked annoyed. He sat down and immediately gulped down his drink.

Lord Cobblefield coughed and twitched, a look of surprise washed across his face, and then he dropped his goblet. He clawed at his throat as he gasped for air and jerked up out of his chair. He grabbed the woman next to him, she pulled away and screamed as Cobblefield crashed forward onto the table. Several nobles covered their faces and gasped.

My father, along with the baron, Grand Master Sinclair, and Lord Marbury entered the room and ran to his aid. The baron and my father pulled him up off the table and laid him on the floor. By the look on their faces, it was too late. Lord Cobblefield gargled one last horrific cry, and with one final exhale, he died.

Panic erupted throughout the ballroom. Except for the four men standing around the body—an honor guard amidst the chaos—the room cleared quickly. Seeing me, Genevieve resisted, but Richard swept her up and escorted out of the room, too. I hadn't moved from my chair. And no one noticed.

"Damn it. What the hell just happened?" Grand Master Sinclair snarled as he smacked the head of his cane against his palm. "Check the glass." Baron Kensington pointed to the overturned goblet. "Perhaps he was poisoned."

"But we all drank the wine," Lord Marbury said, fidgeting. "You don't think it could be dark tribal magic, do you?"

The baron whipped around. "I don't want to

hear that kind of talk. Chief Zwelethu and his people are Zulu, honorable warriors, knights of their land. I don't know what this is, but we can't jump to the wrong conclusions."

My father leaned into the body. "He was definitely poisoned." He pointed to the man's face, still twisted in a final scream. "His tongue, those dark veins, they don't look natural."

"Then the murderer was here at my party," Lord Marbury said.

Grand Master Sinclair straightened up and fixed his vest. "Gentlemen, we have a killer among us. We must focus our efforts on finding him."

A mystery. *Could it be the chief?* He had threatened to kill the lord if they were in the same room again. Maybe I was wrong, but the chief didn't seem the type of person to poison someone—more like the challenge-you-to-open-combat type.

I twisted around in my chair and knocked my glass over, and it clinked against my plate, spilling the contents. All four men spun around, the baron and Sinclair with their hands on the hilts of their sword canes.

"Alexander!" My father sounded relieved. "You shouldn't be here."

"But I—"

Father walked up to me and turned me around. "No. Head upstairs. We will be staying here tonight."

**4
The Colonist
and The Savage**

The next morning, I dressed in my school uniform and headed down to meet my father. When I reached the front hall, I found him with Owethu. As usual, my father had his notebook open, the place he wrote down all his translations and whatever alphabet he was working on at the time.

Owethu looked over at me as he tugged at the starched collar of his Eton College uniform. He looked even more uncomfortable in the tailed coat and striped wool pants than I did. I gave him a sympathetic nod.

My father lifted up his head. "Ah good, Alexander. Good morning. I have to be at Eton early for a meeting, so you'll have to pick up something to eat there."

"Will we be coming back here tonight?"

"No." He tugged on his glasses. "Owethu will, but you'll be back in your own bed." My father ushered us out to the steamcarriage.

I nodded with a half-smile. The bed had been really comfortable, but Lord Marbury's home felt more like a museum than a house, and I didn't like that I couldn't touch anything.

I waved to Finn,

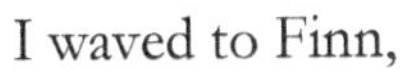

who waited by the steamcarriage. "I would have thought you'd be driving the baron around."

"The baron sent me here, wants to make certain the chief's son gets to Eton in nice right shape." He leaned in to me. "Did you see yet who's in town, Master Armitage?"

"We spoke last night at the party."

My face must have betrayed my thoughts because Finn grinned and winked. Then he pulled off his hat, letting loose his wild orange hair, and poked me in the ribs. "She asked about you."

Before I could ask him what she said, my father's voice came from inside the steamcarriage, "Alexander, don't dawdle." Finn laughed, plopped his hat back on his head, and ushered me into the steamcarriage

What had she asked? I wanted to know. Even though Finn couldn't tell me, she'd asked about me, which was promising.

Owethu stared out the window as the steamcarriage sped down the road. He fidgeted a lot—more than me, and that wasn't easy. He kept shaking his feet and I noticed he wasn't wearing socks. It felt rude not to say anything to him during the ride, so I asked, "What division are you in?"

His wrinkled brow let me know he had no idea what I meant. This was common when talking about Eton, which wasn't like any school I'd attended in America.

"It's like a grade level," I said, but Owethu's brow didn't ease. "Eton doesn't have teachers or classes, or school years, or principals. Well, we have them; we call them by different names. Eton College is three hundred years older than the United States."

Owethu relaxed and nodded. "I have a teacher who

has taught me all I know. Well, my brothers taught me to hunt, and my father taught me how to fight."

Finn stopped and let us out in front of the school. My father turned to the two of us. "Alexander, make certain that Owethu gets to the right building. I want you to show him around."

I nodded to Owethu and said, "Of course."

"Good. At the end of the day, you two can stop by my office."

"Will do." I pointed toward campus. "Come on, Owethu, the building you need is this way."

It didn't take long for the staring to start. My fellow students, who on a normal day would have welcomed the colonist to class, now stared and whispered to each other. A couple of kids even followed us down the hall. Three more blocked our path. They'd trapped us. I looked around for an escape. Flashbacks of the pirate armada I'd faced with the Sky Raiders raced through my mind. Only this time I didn't have the cannons for a broadside.

I wasn't afraid, but I knew what was coming. I hoped they'd just pick on us, but the wild look in their eyes, said differently. I wish I had my Thumper strapped on, but my father wouldn't let me carry it at Eton, even though I told him how much I needed it.

And ... Richard was with them. Could this get any better?

Standing behind us, Thadeous, Lord Blackthorne's son, cut off our escape as Richard circled like a predator. "They'll let anyone in here, won't they?"

"Just let us pass," I said. "We're not here to cause trouble."

Richard stopped so close, his hot breath enveloped me. "Then why walk around with a savage?"

I cringed at the venom in his words. Rage pulsed

within my veins. I could only imagine how Owethu felt. I looked over at him. His jaw was tight and he'd curled his hands into fists, but oddly, he looked calm.

Thadeous Blackthorne bumped our shoulders as he pushed between us. "I can't believe they let either of them in here." He turned to me, and though he stood a head taller and loomed over me, I had no problem locking his stare with mine. I'd stood next to Sky Raiders. Fought the sky-witch, Zerelda, and defeated the Iron Horsemen. Noble-borns' didn't scare me. "Fitting that the savage and the colonist are friends."

I puffed up my chest like Captain Baldrich and said, "He's a better man than you, Blackthorne."

Blackthorne's eyes widened in rage and his lip curled. I could tell he wanted to hit me, but something was holding him back. He'd had no trouble last year. So, what had changed? Thadeus' lips curled, "Pathetic. The colonist thinks he can challenge the empire."

"I might not be a blue-blood, but Owethu is, and he's ranked higher than the likes of you. He is the son of the chief."

They both laughed, and Richard put his arm on Blackthorne's shoulder. "That's nothing, but I wouldn't expect a commoner to understand such things."

I'd walked into that trap. I needed to ask Owethu more questions after this, but for the moment I had to think of a comeback. I couldn't let them win this encounter, leaving me like the smoking airship wreck, barely hanging in the sky. What would the Sky Raiders do? Punch them in the face. But that might not be my best option. I'd never win with the administration in an argument against the Duke's son.

Owethu shook his head. "I see nothing but

pompous Englishmen fighting over nothing. None of you would last a night in my country."

Richard stopped laughing. "I've been to your country. You're all the same."

"Just like all you pompous blue bloods," I said, stepping between Owethu and Richard. I knew calling a royal any inappropriate name was a bad idea, might even lead to a detention, but I couldn't let our guest stand alone.

Richard eye's spat fire, just like Zerelda's had when she saw her airship about to fall out of the sky. I'd cut the straps holding her ship to the air tanks one by one, until it listed so badly, she had to retreat. I needed to cut a few more of Richard's straps and he'd retreat, too. I bet I was the first person to call him a name in years. Maybe ever. I smiled.

"Do you know who you are talking to?" Richard poked my chest with his finger, digging in the same spot with each word he spoke. "*I* am eleventh in line to the throne. *You* are nothing but a Master's brat." My skin burned with each additional jab, but I didn't budge. Then pointing at Owethu, he added, "And he is the son of a murderer. It's only a matter of time before Scotland Yard proves it was the Zulu."

I wanted to punch him, in the face, for which, I would *definitely* be caned. But right now, I didn't care.

The brash voice of my history professor, Mr. Baker, shattered the tension, "Is there a problem, lads?" He crossed the end of the hall and stopped, observing us over the rims of his glasses.

Richard flipped on his bright, wide smile, and spun on his heel. He threw his arm around my shoulder. "Just a couple of old chums discussing Wellington's masterful defeat of Napoleon."

I grabbed his arm and pushed it away from me. "Come on Owethu. We don't want to be late for class."

Owethu eyed the boys around him. They stepped aside. We walked slowly away, but then he stopped and turned around. "Shaka's blood is in my veins, and he would have defeated your Wellington." He spun back to me and we rushed past Mr. Baker. Once we'd turned the corner, I raised my hand to Owethu and said, "Nice comeback."

After school, and after the sun had set, Owethu and I ascended the stairs to my father's office. Finn would be coming soon with Chief Zwelethu and the baron to usher them to Lord Marbury's estate. As my hand reached out for his door, I paused. Gone was the long crack that started my adventure and still haunted my nightmares. The whirl of Col. Hendrix's gears sent shivers up my spine faster than any nails on a chalkboard. My stomach wrenched, twisted in agony. Could anxiety cause this? My father couldn't be mad enough to cause this feeling of danger. Nothing had doubled me over since … last year. Something … something was wrong.

"Alexander," Owethu said with a tinge of concern, "what unsettles you?"

"Trouble." I gripped my stomach.

Owethu spun around like a warrior. "I see nothing."

"Get into my dad's office." I pushed the door open and fell in, stumbling over my feet. I ran into the shelves stacked with artifacts and old manuscripts and steadied myself. Owethu followed me into the dark wood paneled office.

"Alexander," my father said as he pushed off from his oak desk, "what is the meaning of this outburst?"

I looked up to find the baron standing beside my father. Concern etched on their faces. I tried to stand straight but the knot in my guts wouldn't unwind.

"Is it like before?" my father asked.

"Kind of," I said, still hunched over.

The baron rushed into the hallway. A loud crash echoed through the hall. We followed, and Owethu squatted, putting his ear closer to the floor. He turned his head from side to side. "That way."

"Let's go." I tapped Owethu's shoulder and we ran off toward the sound. I heard my father's protest, but I ignored them as the baron joined us. The pain in my stomach eased with each step. I hadn't felt more like myself since last year's adventure.

We reached the end of the hall, and Owethu pointed down a stairwell. My feet moved feverously from one step to the next trying to reach the bottom. Professor McCafferty's workshop lay ahead, the door half open with a sign dangling from one chain that read 'Keep Door Closed'. A piercing scream stopped us, and I didn't need anyone to tell me it had come from the workshop.

Two years ago, I would have run screaming for my father, but now I didn't even hesitate. I rushed into the workshop and heard a clatter from the back. Owethu and I rushed behind a large tank, and found Professor McCafferty crumpled over, gasping in agony. One last gasp escaped and his struggle ended. I froze. My father and the baron rushed past us and laid the portly man on his back. The professor's eye's bulged open as if the horror of his final sight had been forever captured on his face. His mouth was agape, forced open by a large, black swollen tongue.

Glass shattered outside. The baron rushed after the noise. My father turned to Owethu and me. "You boys stay here, and don't touch anything. I have to alert the faculty."

"Understood." I said, looking at Owethu, who studied the scene with the sharp narrow eyes of a hunter.

Father hesitated, but rushed off.

Owethu and I stood in silence for a moment. Neither of us taking our eyes off the grotesque face lying in front of us.

"Maybe, we should see if we can find what he was working on."

Owethu nodded and nodded, "Yes, yes. That would be better." Owethu studied the room for a moment and pointed to one of the tables across the room. "He was working over there, and stumbled here."

"How can you tell?"

Owethu pointed, "The knocked-over canisters, and the shattered tea pot. He must have bumped them as he struggled. And there is a dent in this cabinet, where he fell. See?" Owethu passed his finger over the impression, then quickly wiped his finger on his striped pants.

I was impressed. Even though I looked at the same scene as Owethu, I didn't see any of that. "That must have been the noise we heard."

Owethu nodded.

As we walked over to the professor's desk, I studied the rest of the workshop, which held rocks of every kind. Large geodes sat on top of filing cabinets, along with a huge slab covered in purple amethyst crystals. Equipment had been jammed into every nook and cranny. We stood behind the boiler powering his smelter, a small oven with such intense heat that it melts metal ore.

At first Professor McCafferty's workbench didn't look like much, but as I inspected it in more detail, nothing made sense. Where was the notebook of scribbled pages with the quill still dripping ink? No unbroken rock or papers to be graded. So, if he wasn't working, why was the smelter glowing bright orange? In truth, I didn't know much about geology. But I'm sure I would have, if my father studied rocks, rather than dead languages. Still, the professor must have been working on something. The table was in disorder, and tools lay in a heap, not neatly laid out like a nearby shelf of categorized rocks.

I laid my hand on the top of the workbench. The warmth I felt meant something had set here, recently.

Owethu stepped over to the fireplace beside the smelter. Several trophies sat on the dusty mantle. "One is missing." He pointed to an oval outline in the dust.

"But why take a trophy?"

"I do not know." I walked back over to the body and looked for a trophy. There was none. I thought back to the automaton serpent that had attacked the baron. Maybe this was another automaton. I bent over to get a better look at the professor. Deep purple marks followed along the veins of his neck up to his ear. There, poking into his skin was a small, wooden sliver. It looked like a dart. "Owethu, I think I found something."

He walked over and leaned down. I pointed to the professor's neck and looked back at Owethu. His eyes bulged and he backed up.

"What is it?" I said, realizing that seeing the dart affected Owethu more than the dead guy lying in front of us.

Before he could answer, Baron Kensington returned, breathing hard, but still standing with stoic grace. "Are you boys alright?" We nodded.

"Did you catch them?"

"No, I lost them in the fog."

"Then you got a look at them?" I asked.

"I did." The baron diverted his eyes away from Owethu. "I'm … not sure what I saw." He popped his cane again his palm, and turned to Owethu. "Actually, that isn't true, I know what I saw, but I don't understand, nor do I believe it."

With that kind of buildup, I had to ask, "What did you see?"

The baron hesitated before he answered. He put his hand on Owethu's shoulder. "A cloaked Zulu."

Owethu stared at the baron. "That isn't possible."

"I know. But I also know what I saw."

"The dart … is it African, too?" I asked.

Owethu barely nodded, but it was enough to confirm my thoughts. I shook my head. "But that's impossible! The only two Zulu in London are …"

Owethu finished. "My father and I."

What dart?" the baron asked.

I pointed at the professor's neck. "I think the professor was killed by a poison dart, and I think the killer took whatever he was working on."

"An excellent deduction," the baron smiled. "I see time away from the Black Knight hasn't dulled your senses."

"Never."

We didn't remain in my father's office long after the authorities arrived. Neither Father nor Baron Kensington were interested in the investigation, deciding to leave the details to Scotland Yard. Finn drove us back to the baron's London house in the steamcarriage. This time, however, Owethu didn't enjoy the ride. And neither did I.

Back at the estate, I sat in the blue room with Owethu. Mrs. Henderson brought in a teapot and two teacups, set it down, and then wound up a small automaton knight sitting on the table. She departed with a nod, and I turned to my new friend.

"You have to see this, Owethu," I said as the knight, with a plume of red hair spouting from its helmet, poured the darkened liquid into the two cups.

"It is a machine?" Owethu stood up and circled the automaton as it settled back into a resting pose.

"Inside, it is nothing but gears and springs."

He nodded. "My people have cast off the notion that magic rules this world."

"I wouldn't be too quick to ignore magic."

"I agree, but the Great Elephant taught us that it is we who make our destiny here on earth. Magic is a tool, and if one is not careful, will become a crutch."

"Shaka was wise."

"He was angry," Owethu added. Like you, those of his same age did not want him around."

"Was he an outsider?"

"No. His brothers were chosen over him. But he was the one destiny called on."

I nodded and handed him the cup of tea, taking the other for myself. "Do you think a Zulu is committing these murders?"

"No." He sipped the tea.

"I don't either. But I think someone wants to make everyone think it is your father." I drank the Earl Grey, letting the warm liquid warm my insides.

The door whooshed open, and as the stillness shattered, our teacups rattled on their saucers. Genevieve rushed in, but held the door with her fingers as she slid it silently closed. Owethu looked worried, but I jumped up, and asked, "Hey, what's up?"

She stopped as if my words had built a wall. "You are rushed into my house in the middle of the night and ask *me* what is up?"

I wanted to kick myself. Still, her country's customs refused to come easily to me. I should have greeted her formally and presented myself. But I was an American, who, as my classmate's constantly reminded me, insisted on doing everything all at once.

Owethu stepped forward. "I am Owethu, son of Zwelethu, one of the thirteen chieftains under King Cetshwayo, ruler of Zululand. We are here to advocate his reinstatement and end the warring of my people." He bowed.

Genevieve curtsied. "Welcome to my home, Owethu."

I set my tea down on the tray. "There was another murder at Eton tonight. Professor McCafferty."

Her eyes lit up. "That's horrible." She paused and then asked, "Do you know who killed him?"

"Your father saw a Zulu running away," Owethu said. "But I do not want to believe it."

"Oh," was all she said. "My father and your fathers are in the conservatory, along with Sinclair right now. Maybe we should …"

I sprang toward the door. "Agreed! Let's go lurking."

The three of us slipped down to the conservatory where the adults had gathered. Sinclair's boisterous voice boomed against the baron's aristocratic tone as they spoke. Then I heard the unmistakable voice of Chief Zwelethu. His deep, stoic words filled the air, but even more voices lay within. The Duke. His snooty voice broke through the others and everything grew silent.

"I believe our culprit is evident," the Duke said. "Multiple witnesses saw a Zulu leave the scene. Perhaps we should be pressing the chief for more answers."

The baron quickly replied, "Your Grace, we should examine all the facts before reaching any conclusions. I fear someone is trying to reignite the war between England and the Zulu."

"Or perhaps they are using our hospitality to eliminate their enemies."

"I don't think that is what is happening," the baron replied. "Chief Zwelethu was with me during one of the murders, and you yourself brought the only delegation on your airship."

"I do not accuse the chieftain of committing these murders, but our experts on the Dark Continent are dying." The Duke's words dripped with sarcasm. "A little too convenient, wouldn't you say?"

"Is this true?" Sinclair asked.

"Cobblefield and McCafferty were Britain's leading African anthropologist and geologist. Both were involved in the Zulu conflicts."

Chief Zwelethu's deep voice silenced the room. "But the Zulu are here to talk to the great mother, not fight with her."

"Please, Chief Zwelethu, understand that we do not suspect you," the baron said. "We, too, seek an end to the conflict between our people."

"We need to focus on who could carry out this kind of an attack," Sinclair added.

The Duke replied, "Well, then, if not the chief, has anyone asked about his son's whereabouts?"

Chief Zwelethu laughed. "Is this what you call English hospitality? Accusing my son?"

Owethu's shoulders slumped and my heart did the same. How could they think such things? My new friend was fascinating, and I knew I'd just scratched the surface of who Owethu was inside, but I was certain he was an honorable man, not an assassin. So many questions and no answers. Listening to the bickering in the next room, it didn't sound like they had any answers, either. Genevieve shook her head as concern chased her smile away. The tension pouring out of the room, sounded like war might break out at any moment.

The three of us continued to hover outside the room. I wanted to storm in like I had last year when the order decided who would replace the baron in the Iron Templar, and put them all in their place, but I don't think I would silence the room like before. Instead, I'd be the spark that would light the powder keg.

Finn stepped around the corner and stopped when he saw us. He shook his head as he walked up. "Now what are you scamps doing here? Go on, back upstairs before someone sees yah."

I pointed toward the room and whispered, "We're curious about what's going on."

"Trouble that's what. You know what curiosity did to the cat. You best leave this one alone, laddy."

"Okay, we will," I said as we shuffled toward the stairs.

I turned as Finn walked into the room and heard him say, "Pardon the interruption, gentlemen, but my Lord, I've been sent to fetch you."

Still at the bottom of the stairs when they began to file out of the room, we rushed upstairs. Once back in the blue room, Genevieve spun around and said, "I, for one, am not giving up. Trouble means we're on the right track."

Owethu nodded.

I started to protest, to remind everyone that people were dying, but the words choked up in my throat when I looked at Genevieve. She wouldn't like a guy who'd back down in the face of danger. Besides, I was a knight. Sort of. If people were dying, then it was my duty to stop whoever was doing it. "So, what do we do?"

She propped her hands on her waist. "We need to figure out who is next."

Calling on the skills my father had taught me, I said, "Then we must find the common thread between them. We have two victims. Lord Cobblefield, an African explorer and anthropologist, and Professor McCafferty, a geologist. Your father said both men had been involved in the Zulu Wars."

Genevieve's hand went to her chin and the other supported her elbow, the same stance her father often made. "There has to be something else. Tomorrow at Eton, see if you can find out if any other people might be connected to Africa."

Owethu's shoulders slumped. "I do not think I will go tomorrow. The students will have heard about the murders."

He was right. They'd be merciless. Even those who ordinarily weren't mean, would walk down other hallways, or press against the walls on seeing Owethu.

"I have an idea." I ran my fingers through my hair. "And Owethu, I think it will help our standing at school."

At Eton the next day, Owethu and I walked through one of the large carved archways. We passed Thad Blackthorne and couple of my classmates. They rushed off, so I knew the game was afoot.

"A quarter says they ran off to get Richard," I said. Owethu looked puzzled.

"American money, you know, like a Shilling."

Owethu nodded but didn't have the same sense of glee that I did. I hadn't told him what I was planning, although Genevieve didn't let me leave the breakfast table until I told her. At first, she didn't look amused, but after explaining everything, she couldn't help but showing her excitement as the light filled her eyes.

"Come on, we need to be somewhere more public for this encounter."

I grabbed Owethu by the arm and we darted off for The Cloisters, the tails of our coats streaming behind us. Inside, we found throngs of students getting ready for class. Everyone turned and stared at us as we entered. I immediately thought of the encounter with the pirate armada. As in

those skies, we were surrounded. Outnumbered. Trapped. Only this time, I had them right where I wanted.

I smiled and nodded to Owethu. His puzzled expression joined with his unease of being the center of attention. I wanted to tell him what was about to happen, but I needed his reactions to be genuine. I took a deep breath. I was ready. Now, I just needed our opponents.

Richard, Blackthorne, and three other noble-born sauntered into the hall, like kings. They each locked eyes on us. As they crossed the room, Richard paused to say hello to some students sitting nearby, and waved to those too far away. With each step toward us, their smug smiles grew.

Blackthorne stopped in front of me. "I'm surprised, colonist, that you'd still stand next to this *savage*, given his father's nighttime activities."

I spoke up so the whole room could hear. "Chief Zwelethu is a great warrior, as is his son, Owethu." I put my hand on Owethu's shoulder. "You should apologize, Blackthorne. All of you should apologize." I didn't know if the chieftain could fight or not, but this wasn't a time for facts. I was a Sky Raider, and this was my battlefield.

The entire hall of students erupted in one unifying "*O-o-o-o.*"

"Scotland Yard told my father they think it's a Zulu, given the poisoned used." Richard kept his gaze on me. I couldn't tell if he was ignoring Owethu on purpose, or just focused on my words.

Owethu grabbed Richard's coat sleeve and pushed him around until they faced each other. "We do not poison our enemies. *If* I wanted to kill you, I would do it with an Iklwa."

A gasp rippled through the crowd. Every student

had heard tales of the fearsome Zulu short spear created by Shaka, to wage war on his enemies.

Richard yanked his arm back and brushed it off. "I would kill you first with a sword."

I stepped between them. "You're right! We need a duel." Both Owethu and Richard pulled back. I think they thought I was serious. "I propose a test of wits."

The students cheered. One called for a game of riddles. Two others boys announced a wrestling match, and when a third cried out for a math problem, I raised my hand. The room fell silent.

"I suggest a hunt." I walked into the middle of the crowd. "For missing treasure."

The cheering got louder.

Richard's eyes narrowed, but he curled his lip in contempt. "I know. Last week, a painting was removed from the Lupton's Tower. Discover its whereabouts within the hour and be declared the winner. He nodded to Blackthorne.

I shook my head. "No. Undoubtedly you already know where it is."

Richard sneered, but it quickly faded. "Well, we can't trust you to choose something. How do we know this whole thing isn't a setup?"

"We have not set this up," I boasted. Which technically, wasn't true. I was setting all this up, but not just to best Richard. That was a bonus. By the end of the day, everyone would know Owethu like I did, and maybe we'd find the next victim.

"There's no way to prove that," Blackthorne said.

I had to think of something, and quick. "Well then, we'll just have someone else choose the treasure."

"I suggest Thad–"

I cut Richard off. "Of course you would." The crowd of students, stone silent, were hooked on my every word. "No, it has to be someone independent. Someone to make the hunt fair. Even the odds." I looked at Richard and Blackthorne. "Something I'm not certain *y'all* are familiar with."

The crowd hissed.

"So," I said jumping up on a nearby table, "I turn it over to the group." I pointed my finger at the crowd. "As Aristotle said, 'At his best, man is the noblest of all animals; separated from law and justice, he is the worst'. What say you, good men? What has gone missing that must be found?"

The room remained silent. I wasn't sure if my speech hit its mark, but then Lord Carter's son spoke up. I didn't know him well, but he'd never given me trouble. "I heard the Head Master talking about the Cricket Trophy in Master McCafferty's workshop. It was missing. Apparently, he'd been making repairs to the base before he was killed."

A murmur rippled through the crowd of students like a whirlwind. The trophy was the prize we'd won over our greatest rivals at Harrow School.

"Then it's settled. A game of wits to find the Cricket Trophy."

My classmates erupted in cheers again. Lord Carter's son stood up on a chair and rallied others to him. "The teams are Alexander and Owethu, and Richard and Thad. The rules are simple. You have one hour to find the trophy. Ask anyone a question; but you can't ask for help in finding it."

"Agreed," I said with a chuckle.

Richard and Blackthorne, now stoic, nodded, and the crowd roared. Richard backhanded Blackthorne's shoulder, "Come on, Thad. I know just where to start looking." They ran off and half the students followed.

I turned to Owethu. "Why don't we start in the workshop, since that's its last location."

"Good idea."

The door squeaked as I pushed open McCafferty's office. No one had been allowed in after Scotland Yard took over. Several students who had followed us, pressed their faces against the glass, but no one else entered. Inside, nothing had been moved. The chairs remained toppled over, a small table lay on its side, with the shattered remains of a tea set scattered around the floor.

I tried not to focus on the where the professor had fallen, but I couldn't take my eyes off that spot on the floor.

"It sat above the fire?" Owethu walked over to the mantle above the fireplace. He studied the area. His focus pulled me from the where Professor McCafferty had died to the perfect oval left by the trophy in the light layer of dust. Two other trophies sat on the shelf but looked untouched. Just the one had been taken. The most valuable one.

While Owethu studied the mantle, I took a moment to search for more clues about why he died, and who might be next. I checked the drawers and all the papers on his desk. I don't know what I was looking for, a note, or maybe, a Templar cross.

"Normally, I'd say someone from the Harrow School might have taken it, but then why didn't Master McCafferty tell someone it was missing?"

"Agreed. It was a tall man with thin feet."

I spun around on my heel. "How do you know that?"

"I see it."

I stared at Owethu, who still stood close to the fireplace, trying to see what he saw. "I don't see it," I said as I walked over to him.

Owethu leaned over and pointed to the marble step in front of the fireplace. "Tracks." Outlined in soot, a footprint on the stone. He continued. "See? They are long; so he is tall. They are thin, so he is not a large man."

Amazed by Owethu's deductions, I asked, "How do you know it's a man?"

"The shape. The women of your land have strange footprints with a tiny heel."

I couldn't argue with that. His logic was flawless. To him, it was like reading a book on the ground. I thought about how my father would analyze the marks on a parchment to determine its age. Studying how the paper had weathered, the binding, or the way the ink had been applied. Owethu was a genius.

I lifted my foot and looked at the sole of my own shoe. It had a distinctive guitar shape, nothing like the footprint on the ground. "Well, it isn't a student. We all wear this same loafer." I crouched down and stared at the footprint. Owethu left my side, but I wanted to see if there was anything else I could add to our information. Maybe he favored one leg, or had cane. I searched for a mark, but saw nothing.

"Alexander, come here. I found his trail." I rushed over and Owethu pointed to another black mark. "He favors his left side."

I nodded, wishing I'd been the one to see this. "So,

how does this tell us where the trophy is now?"

"We track the prints."

Owethu tore out of the lab and I ran behind him. The students watching us turned and chased us. Our fervor ignited their anticipation. As we all followed Owethu, I heard them call other students to follow, and several yelled, "They've found it!"

We hadn't yet. But all we had to do was track those shoeprints. They would surely lead us to the culprit who had the trophy. My mind raced over all the Masters at Eton who might fit Owethu's description, as well as the people who worked here. Fortunately, it was a short list: three teachers, a librarian, and one of the groundskeepers.

Owethu stopped, knelt down, and ran his fingertips over the ground. He then smelled his fingers and looked off toward the building on our right. "That way," he pointed.

We ran toward the library, past the statue of Henry VI. Glancing over my shoulder, the crowd had swelled, and now half the school ran behind us. As we entered the library, Owethu stopped. I paused right behind him, but the students, caught up in the excitement, crashed into each other.

Owethu pointed. "He changed direction."

I walked around and looked at the floor for another clue. Owethu joined me and the entourage of students formed a semi-circle around us, watching and waiting.

"The soot is fading. We will lose the trail soon," Owethu said.

"That's okay, I think it's here."

Two librarians rushed over and pushed their way through the gaggle of students. The first, his mustache twirled to fine points, said, "You are disrupting the library.

I demand to know the meaning of this gathering!"

A voice from the crowd called out. "They're solving a crime!"

The librarians spun around and said in a loud whisper, "Who said that?"

I stepped forward, "Sir, allow me to explain."

A murmur rippled from the back of the crowd and the students parted to make way. Richard and Blackthorne entered with the other half of the student body. "Just a simple game of wits," the Duke's son said. "Apparently Alexander and his friends were also able to figure out that the trophy was here in the library."

The man shook his head and spun his fingers on his mustache. "I object, Your Grace. This institution would never be involved in a crime."

The assistant librarian twitched. His foot shifted as he said, "All of you … you need to break this up and return to your studies."

The man matched Owethu's description: thin, almost frail, and tall. His gangly body made me wonder if he could even be a criminal. He looked more like a bookworm, which made me rethink why the statue had been taken in the first place. Maybe it had been recovered? I looked down. The man's narrow feet stuck out several inches from his trousers. It was him. He was the culprit.

My heart pounded. I had the answer. Well, half of it.

Richard, standing there, looked so smug, as if he owned the room. The problem was, he did. I knew he was up to something. He was too certain of himself, maybe even who had taken the trophy. But I was not going to let

Mr. Perfect win. I needed to find the trophy—the actual prize—and I had to act before my adversary.

Like Captain Baldarich, I stepped forward to claim the room. "He's right, no crime has been committed," I said, looking directly at Richard, who scowled at me. I continued, "We are just here to locate the Cricket trophy … as a matter of honor, sir. And return it to its rightful place."

The head librarian twisted his mustache. "Mister Armitage, you are making less sense than your classmates. Explain yourself."

"Allow me," Richard said, stepping in front of me. "You see, the colonist here, is about to tell you that Mr. Scuttlebore was seen leaving Master McCafferty's study. And now I say, he is going to tell us where he hid the trophy."

"This is preposterous," said Scuttlebore as he wagged his finger. "These allegations are completely unfounded!"

A chorus of whispers swept through the students around us. Richard's crooked grin was for me, but my attention went to Owethu, who used the distraction to scan the room for the trophy. He spotted something, and his eyes narrowed. I followed his gaze to a black smudge at the base of a cabinet, and he turned to me with large smile crossing his face. I raised my hand and the room went silent. "We do not accuse you, sir. I know where the trophy is … and the reason you recovered it."

Richard spun around, and glared at me with burning eyes. I could tell he didn't have a clue where the trophy was. I crossed the room, and Richard charged over to the librarian like he was going to rip the information from him, but I addressed the students. My real judges.

"Owethu, will you please reveal the trophy using your amazing skills of deduction."

"I would be happy to, Alexander."

Owethu knelt down and studied the ground. He got really low, and held his ear just above the floor as if it had something to say. Then he proudly moved to the cabinet door. Mr. Scuttlebore tried to rush forward, but the students blocked him long enough for Owethu to throw open the doors, revealing the trophy. The students cheered as Owethu raised it in triumph.

Everyone turned toward Mr. Scuttlebore who screeched, "I did not steal it!"

"He's right." The crowd went silent and turned back to me. "The shelf in the professor's study was dusty, but this trophy sat on the dust, and when it was moved, there was dust underneath."

"So?" one of my classmates shouted.

Richard looked at me and shook his head. "It means the trophy had been put there recently, lending credibility that it was Master McCafferty who took the trophy and Mr. Scuttlebore who returned it."

"McCafferty was commissioned to repair it," Scuttlebore said, still nervously twitching. "But he'd won the trophy when he attended Eton, and wanted it for his office. When I came to retrieve it, he refused. I decided not to tell anyone, to avoid embarrassing the man. I figured after it was repaired, I could sneak it back and no one would have to know."

Applause and cheers filled the library, which was when the two librarians cleared us from their building. The hero treatment for Owethu and I continued in the quad. I doubted it would last long, but for a moment we'd shown them all—the Zulu weren't savages and even a commoner could best a nobleman.

I wish Genevieve had been here to see this. I couldn't wait to tell her.

BOOK II: IRON ZULU

With the sun setting on my triumphant day, Owethu and I walked back to Father's office. Our prize had once again been placed in its proper display. I'd bested my rival, but in the fading light, it felt like a hollow victory. Genevieve and Richard were still betrothed. And he'd found the culprit, too; so it was hardly a routing. But a victory, *any victory*, should be celebrated. I'd learned that flying with the Sky Raiders.

"We should have ice cream tonight for dessert," I said. "I think we've earned it."

"Why do I want frozen cream?" Owethu shook his head in distaste.

"It's cold and sweet, and dare I say, ice cream is one of the greatest foods ever created by human hands."

Still Owethu shook his head, so I searched for a way to describe the bliss, but all that rolled out was, "It's almost frozen cream that's sweet."

His brow gathered in another puzzled look.

"Trust me, its good. The Greeks called it ambrosia—food for the gods. Food for kings. And sons of kings. And common people, too."

When we reached my father's building, I grabbed

the door handle and my stomach, like before, twisted into knots. I grimaced in pain and Owethu put his hand on my shoulder. Before he could say anything, though, I snapped up and threw open the door.

Without waiting for him, I ran as fast as my feet would traverse the stairs. My heart pounded against my ribcage, so hard I feared it would burst. Panic whipped through my veins, pushing me down the hall. Again, something was wrong. Something was very, very wrong. I didn't know what, but it lay ahead of me. And I knew it came from my father's office.

"Faster," I said between labored breaths.

With each step, my mind flashed back to the horrors of a year ago. Would I find Hendrix and his thugs inside? Would they again kidnap my father? Even though Genevieve and I were successful, with the help of the Sky Raiders in rescuing him before, I couldn't bear the thought of losing him again. And this time, I didn't have a weapon. My Thumper. Father refused to allow me to carry it at Eton.

Owethu hadn't asked a single question, or even give me a look of confusion. He just ran at my side, and together we rounded the corner. My father's office door sat at the end of a narrow hall. I stopped short, and held Owethu back.

Father's door stood open, but was blocked by a cloaked figure. One dressed in a tight black suit and adorned with native Zulu jewelry. With their back to me, all I saw was his hand, which held a brass, segmented pipe the size of a fountain pen with two thin, silver tubes running along one side.

The assassin didn't see us from behind. Over the shoulder of the cloaked figure, I saw my father buried in a book, oblivious to the threat behind him.

As I rushed forward, with Owethu close behind, I cried out, "Dad!"

He looked up, confused by the sound of my voice, and even more so when he saw the cloaked assassin. He jumped up, and raised the dusty leather-bound tome he'd been studying as the cloaked figure raised the silver and brass device. With a burst of air the dart shot at him,

I screamed, "No!" But the dart sank into the cover.

"Alexander, no!" my father screamed. "Run!"

But I didn't. I couldn't. This time I was not going to let anyone take him from me. Owethu and I set shoulders and prepared to smash into the assassin like jousting knights, but mere steps away, the slender leg of a … a woman, emerged from the cloak. With the agility of a jousting knight, she pressed one foot against the doorframe, and sprang to the top of the thin door. Owethu and I stumbled into each other and tumbled to the floor. The lady assassin loomed above us, and locked eyes with me. The intensity of her dark eyes sent chills through me. The rest of her face was obscured by a brass gas mask.

"Alexander! Owethu! Run!" my father screamed again.

She raised the pneumatic dart gun, and we scrambled toward my father as another dart stuck into the floor where we'd laid.

The assassin dropped silently to the floor. Never taking her eyes from us. My father dug through his desk drawer. For what I didn't know. She raised the pneumatic blow-dart gun and aimed it right at my father.

Time slowed as my heart pulsed faster, reverberating through me like an electrical impulse. I didn't have a way to stop her.

Then my father yelled, "Here it is!" He stood up with a revolver in hand. He spun around and pulled the trigger barely aiming at the lady assassin. He screamed, but it wasn't from fright. More like a wild battle cry. Owethu and I covered our ears.

She twisted as he fired again and again.

The first bullet struck the wall and the second tore through her cloak. She reached into a leather pouch on her hip and pulled out a small glass vile, smashing it against the floor. She turned and charged down the hall. Yellowish vapor rose to form a noxious cloud around the three of us leaving us gasping for air. My father ran into the hall still firing his gun. Owethu and I followed, coughing and trying to force fresh air into our lungs.

As she reached the window at the end of the hall, she pulled a small, pocket-watch-like disk from her pouch. She hurled it at the window. A high pitch, sonic pulse shattered the glass. Pulling her cloak around her, she crashed through the broken wooden frame and disappeared.

Instinctively, I cried, "No!" We were on the second floor. Along with Father and Owethu, I ran to the ledge and peered down at the ground. The lady assassin popped up as if nothing happened, and ran to a waiting carriage. She leapt up onto the back wheel, threw her legs over the side, and landed in the open seat. A cloaked figure sat on the seat facing her, facing us. My father raised his revolver and pulled the trigger but it only clicked.

Terror seized me. The passenger lifted his head and removed the hood of the cloak. A face half-covered in bronze plates stared back at me. His one eye sparking with electricity. Even from the second floor, I heard the inexplicable, intricate gears and sprockets spinning—the one's that had haunted my dreams since returning home. Then the *snick* as they locked into place. I couldn't move as I watched the man lift his Stetson. Colonel Hendrix.

During my previous adventure, I hadn't paid attention to the sound, but afterward, it haunted my nights. Colonel Hendrix tipped his Stetson with his mechanical hand and leered at us. I looked over at my father; his eyes were trained on the carriage, but his face held a haunted far away stare as if he weren't there. He lowered the gun barrel slowly, until it rested on the window sill.

The revolver was empty, and I recognized the look on my father's face. It was the same as mine when I heard Hendrix's gears.

Hendrix threw back his head and laughed. Removing his hat, he stood and bowed as the carriage pulled away.

Without a word, Owethu bolted for the stairs. I ran after him. I heard my father protest, but I didn't listen. Once out the door, we rounded the building, but the carriage had sped away.

We followed them onto Slough Road, but my legs burned and I had to stop. I doubled over, each breath searing my lungs. Owethu kept running and followed them to the bridge. He returned at a full jog. He didn't even look winded.

"Did you see which way they went?" I asked between gasps.

With concern on his face Owethu asked, "Alexander, are you wounded?" He put his hand on my shoulder and leaned closer. "Did one of those darts hit you?"

"No … just out of breath."

"Good. No, I didn't see where they went. I will never catch them. Nothing leaves tracks on this stone."

Finally able to stand straight, I said, "The man in the carriage, we know him. Colonel Hendrix. The Knights of the Golden Circle. They are the ones behind these murders."

"Who?"

"They kidnapped my father a year ago. To help them decipher an ancient text that led to the hearts of the four horsemen. Then they tried to destroy and enslave the world."

"Oh, I see. They are using my people; how do you say?"

"As a scapegoat," I said.

"Ah, yes. To blame us for their savagery."

"They are bad news." I ran my fingers through my hair. "But who was she?"

"I do not know, but now I understand why the killer is dressed like my people."

"I was her next target," my father said as he stepped up behind us.

"What have you been working on?" I asked. "Were you working with Professor McCafferty?"

He adjusted his glasses. "Nothing together, but maybe we were separately on the same case."

Owethu asked. "What do we do now?"

"I've summoned the baron and Grand Master Sinclair. We're handing this over to the Order."

I spun around. "But—"

"No." Father held up his hand. "I do not want you getting involved. If the Golden Circle has returned, then I want you as far away as possible."

"But…."

"No, Alexander. I'm not budging on this. Last year was a one-time event. And Alexander—" He made sure I was looking him in the eye. "I don't want you running off. Understand?"

Great, now he's treating me like a baby, and in front of my new friend. I couldn't look at Owethu.

"I won't," I groaned. "Can't anyway," I mumbled under my breath. "You won't let me build an airship,"

"Thank you." He gripped his shoulders as the wind rushed by. "Okay, boys, let's get inside."

Soon everyone was buzzing around us. Scotland Yard asked me and Owethu questions. The baron and Sinclair, too. But I couldn't say anything more than I had seen Colonel Hendrix, and the woman dressed like the Zulu.

I couldn't get Hendrix's laugh out of my head. Even now his exhaled grunt was like a distant echo.

BOOK II: IRON ZULU

9
The
Sparrowhawk

I traced the cool panels of hardened liquid glass on my father's office window with my finger. Replaced the previous year after the baron had crashed through to save us from Col. Hendrix, and yet not a mark of that day remained. At least not on the window. A few Bobbies and Eton officials moved about outside, but I sat transfixed on the warped reflections of the members of the Templar Order and other people darting in and out of the office.

Owethu sat in my father's chair answering Scotland Yard's questions over and over again. I wouldn't want to be in his seat. However, none of the Templars asked me. They all talked to my father to see if I was unhurt. Again, it was as if I was invisible.

Through the blur of fine suits and uniforms flashing across the glass, I saw Genevieve. She looked like a painting, in a deep-blue dress, her hands tucked inside her fur muff, framed by the doorway. Her small, bronze dragon sitting majestically on her shoulder, creating the kind of portrait that hung in every manor in England. I didn't want to turn around. She looked beautiful, and I

was still dressed as a schoolboy. Maybe she wouldn't see me, and I could avoid the embarrassment, but all I wanted was to speak with her.

Rodin soared across the room and landed on my shoulder. He'd grown very little in the last year, still the size of an eagle, or raven. He rubbed his horned nubs against my cheek as he tucked in his wings and wrapped his tail around my other shoulder.

"Hi, Rodin." I rubbed under his chin, and his eyes narrowed to slits as the softest coo rumbled within his belly.

Genevieve crossed the room, and I turned as she approached me.

"Are you unhurt?" she asked, as she reached up to push back my hair. "My father said you fought the assassin."

I managed to stutter a quick, "Fine," out of my ever-tightening chest.

She smiled, and I melted into a puddle of goo on the floor, blabbering like an idiot. I spun sideways, so that Rodin was between us. In front of me was one of the many shelves holding artifacts. What could be more boring than shards of ancient Greek pottery to distract me from my feelings? I sighed, and finally spoke like I made sense. "We didn't really fight her. She was too good."

"*She?* It was a woman?"

"Yeah, and she was European, not African. It's not a Zulu."

"Thank goodness it can now be proven."

I paused, but had to tell her. "Hendrix is back. He waited for her in a carriage. They fled after trying to kill my father."

"Hendrix." Her voice hardened. "The Golden Circle is causing all these deaths."

"It looks that way." I turned back to the window. "And now they're getting away."

"My father has people checking the docks," Genevieve said.

"We need to go. We have to find them."

She paused, smiled, and said, "Agreed."

Owethu slipped between two Bobbies, and stepped beside Genevieve, "But how?" he whispered.

I tried to think of a way, but knew it would take a miracle. Outside, a white horse rode up to the building. I watched with increasing curiosity, as a messenger jumped off and rushed through the doors. We all turned as the man entered my father's office and handed the baron a folded piece of paper. The baron thanked him and read the note. He nodded. "They've arrived at the air docks and await our arrival, professor."

"Who?" Father asked.

"The Sparrowhawk."

I nearly jumped with joy.

My father protested. "But my classes."

I burned at his passiveness. We'd been attacked, nearly killed, and he was worried about his classes? I never understood why my father insisted on burying himself behind a wall of books.

"Don't you want revenge for what they did to you?" I stared at my father, but before he could answer I pounded his desk with my fist. "We have to defeat the Knights of the Golden Circle once and for all."

"Alexander, there is no we. I've told you; you are not going anywhere! And neither am I."

The baron shook his head. "Your son is right,

Professor. You are perhaps the only one who has any clue what's going on. You said it yourself: there might be a connection between the three of you. And until we figure that out, you aren't leaving my side. Her Majesty's orders."

My father stepped forward, his finger raised, "Don't pull that 'For queen and country stuff' with me."

The baron gave my father a look, not of anger, but of understanding. Finally, my father nodded and the two men shook hands. Baron Kensington nodded, and held up the note. "Be ready in an hour. Our transport awaits."

"I will," my father said, "but, what about Alexander?"

"Mrs. Hinderman will look after him until we get back."

I shook my head. "Wait! That's not fair. I …" I motioned to Genevieve and Owethu, "we want to go, too."

Both men turned, and in unison, said, "No!"

My father wrung his hands together. "Alexander, we already discussed this." *Actually, you discussed it,* I wanted to say, but didn't.

The baron pointed the paper at his daughter. "We will not repeat our earlier conversation."

She hardened, but said, "Yes, Father."

I spun around, grabbed Genevieve's arm, and pulled her over to the corner. I motioned for Owethu to follow. Her puzzled expression turned to surprise as I leaned closer to her ear. When she turned her face to me, my senses dulled at the scent of roses. She was intoxicating.

"Captain Baldarich is taking them," I whispered. "I just figured out how we're going."

Her eyes lit up, but she said nothing.

I leaned over to Owethu, "We're going after the

assassin. Want to come?"

He grinned and nodded.

"Grab whatever you think you'll need and meet back here in twenty minutes."

Genevieve raised an eyebrow. "I thought we had an hour."

"We're not going *with* my father. We have to get there first."

They nodded and we split off from each other.

I waved goodbye, but my father was too busy to notice. I ran to my house which sat within a stones throw from Eton. I had to get there before he did.

I dumped the books and papers from my bag onto my bed, and quickly rifled through my room, collecting clothes for the journey. Then I slid a drawer from beneath my bed. Under a sweater lay my Thumper, my knife, my father's telescope, and the leather strap I'd bound myself with. I tucked them all into the bag, grabbed my tooth brush, and ran out the door. But I heard my father in his room just down the hall.

I wanted to stop and tell him I was ready to go, that he might need me, but I knew there was no reasoning with him. He'd never agree. He didn't like to talk about last year. Another in a long list of topics we didn't discuss.

I crept to the front door, but hesitated. He'd ground me for certain when I saw him again. I exhaled and silently opened the door. I slipped out of the house and across the empty quads at Eton. Some things were worth getting in trouble for.

10
Stowaways

I sat outside my father's office waiting for the others, wondering if any of them would even show. I knew they wanted to, but what if Owethu told his father? Or Genevieve couldn't get away from Mrs. Hinderman? A few deep breaths and the panic growing within eased. Genevieve, I told myself, could easily escape her house. I was certain of that. While Owethu was too smart to blow the plan.

Genevieve popped around the corner, still dressed as a noblewoman, but now carried her saber and a large bag. "There you are." She dropped the bag beside me and leaned on my shoulder. "My father, your father, and the chieftain have all departed for the docks, but I got a look at the letter, and I know where the Sparrowhawk is docked."

"Did you go home? Get your … clothes? From before?" I kept himself from blushing at the thought of seeing Genevieve dressed in pants again.

"No." She bit her lip. "I brought them with me. I was hoping we'd do something impulsive and all together very American, like

running off." Genevieve scrunched her shoulders and cocked her head to the side.

I chuckled. "What can I say? We've learned from the best."

She laughed, but fell silent as someone approached. Owethu poked his head around the corner. He emerged dressed in a tailcoat and ascot.

"Why, look at you," Genevieve said as walked over to Owethu. "You look quite dashing. Doesn't he, Alexander?"

For a moment I wondered why he didn't dress like a Zulu, but I stopped myself. Owethu could wear whatever he wanted. He was an honor to his people no matter his clothes. "So, are we ready?" I said, but Owethu shushed me.

"There are people nearby," Owethu whispered. "I had to avoid them. We must be careful."

We were all suddenly very aware of our surroundings. Every creak in the night intensified with my nervousness. I took a deep breath and gathered up my bag. "I'm set."

"Finn is nearby ready to take us."

"Wait, won't he get us in trouble?" I asked.

Genevieve smiled. "No, I paid him."

"I can see that being effective with Finn," I said with a laugh. "So, why bring your things?"

"In case you already had transportation. You weren't very specific on how we'd get to the London airdocks. Maybe you had already formulated a plan."

"I had a plan," I said as we started down the corridor. "Finn is just a better plan." I turned and walked backward, looking at the two of them, and pointed to myself. "But I did have a plan."

Owethu shook his head and Genevieve stifled her laughter. We slipped out to the main street where the steam carriage waited. Owethu and I sat across from Genevieve, but he spent the whole ride staring out the window, while I tried to keep from staring at Genevieve. All too quickly the carriage stopped.

My mind had run over the *how* of our plan, and although I still didn't have a solid plan, I knew what was at stake. I knew the why. Finn opened the carriage door. I stepped down and stared up at the airdocks as Owethu joined me. Finn helped Genevieve to the ground.

"Thank you," Genevieve said. "And remember …"

"Ner a word, Miss." Finn ran his fingers across his mouth as if it were a zipper.

Airships from around the world hovered above the river. As we walked toward the docks, I searched for the familiar aero-dirigible.

"There!" I pointed. "Third one over."

Owethu's eyes grew large.

"The Sparrowhawk." Genevieve said, her voice barely concealing her excitement.

Perched on the airdocks, the aero-dirigible tugged against her moorings. She might only be treated-canvas over a metal ribbing, but to me, she rose above the rest. To me, the Sparrowhawk was splendid freedom and adventure, with iron cannons running along her sides.

With her wingsails retracted, she looked like a bird about to spring into the air. The captain had refurbished her, or at least repainted her. The brilliant blue ribbed-canvas humpbacks of the airship looked like waves, while brass fixtures and wooden yardarms, trimmed the ship along with thick ropes running forward and aft. The dull grey belly hid in the clouds with ease, and the wooden frame held secret hatches which hid its true nature as a raider of sea ships and zeppelins.

"Now what?" Owethu said.

"We sneak aboard." Although I said this with confidence, I wasn't quite sure just how we were going to do it.

"That may not be the smartest plan. Last time we were nearly electrocuted," Genevieve reminded me.

"But they won't let us come unless we're already there."

Both looked at me with scrunched brows. Genevieve shook her head. "That's not really a plan."

"Sure it is."

Owethu's eyes went from the airship to me several times and then he rubbed his head.

I pushed back my hair. "We hide out in our old room until we are far enough away that they can't come back. That's a good plan."

"It's a plan," Genevieve said. "I'm just not certain it's a very good one."

Undeterred, I said, "It'll work; you'll see. First things first though, we have to get on board." I stood there trying to think of a plan, when Genevieve grabbed my arm and pulled me along the metal grating. "Come on," she said. "And keep an eye out for our fathers."

Owethu followed.

We walked up the docks to the Sparrowhawk. No one stood guard at the open cargo doors, but the faint echo of people within the ship spilled out.

"Come on," I said, taking the lead. But at the opening, I stopped. I wanted to step aboard. I tried to step aboard. But my feet wouldn't move. Visions of Captain Baldarich loomed before me. I feared that once I was on board, he would know. He'd just sense it and blast me with his lightning cannon.

Summoning all my courage, I stepped on the gangplank of the Sparrowhawk and stepped inside. Tranquility settled over me. These decks felt more real than Eton, like coming home. I took a deep breath, tasting all the familiar smells—the metal, the treated canvas, oil, with just a sprinkle of gunpowder.

Before I could take another breath, a man stepped in front of me, startling me, and cutting off all my warm fuzzy feelings. The blue turban identified him immediately, but I hardly recognized Mr. Singh.

"Indihar!" I clasped his hand and shook it fiercely, gripping his arm with my other. His arm rippled as his muscles bulged from beneath his vest. Having to look up at his face, I realized he'd grown taller than me. I'd grown, too, but the last time I'd seen him, we were the same height. Plus, he had a full beard now. I could barely grow stubble.

A bright smile let me know he wasn't angry. In fact, he didn't look surprised to see us. He released my hand, threw open his arms, and hugged me. "Alexander! Genevieve! It is so good to see you. I feared I would miss you yet again."

"Hello Indihar. I hope life has been good on the ship." Genevieve bowed and Mr. Singh returned the gesture.

I motioned and said, "This is Owethu, our new friend."

Owethu bowed, but Mr. Singh reached out, and shook his hand. "So," Mr. Singh said, "come to say farewell to your fathers?" Then he saw our bags and crossed his arms. My old friend Indihar vanished, and only the airship's boatswain, Mr. Singh, remained.

Genevieve and I both nodded, although she leaned toward me and smirked, "I told you it wasn't a very good plan."

Mr. Singh's scowl deepened, so I piped up. "Mr. Singh, you of all people should understand that we have to help. The KGC are back. We're chasing Hendrix. The battle the three of us fought last year isn't over."

The gears of his mind twitched in his eyes as he listened to my words. Now I just needed them to find his heart, or at least his sense of justice. He eyed me for several moments more before speaking. "Your parents will not like this." Both Genevieve and I nodded in agreement. "The only reason the three of us fought a year ago was because the chosen warrior—the baron—couldn't. This is their fight." I could see through the relaxation in his posture, that he wasn't convinced at his words.

"Mr. Singh," I said, "They're going to need us. All of us. You know as well as I—this tyranny has to be stood up to. All I'm asking is that you not tell anyone until we're over the channel … please."

"You want to stowaway on my ship?"

I leaned toward him. "Yes," I said. No sense lying. He knew Genevieve and I too well.

Mr. Singh raised an eyebrow. "Take the forward storage compartment. You'll have to stay there. If the crew spots you, we'll all get in trouble."

I pumped my fist. "You got it."

"Thank you, Indihar." Genevieve touched his arm and bowed her head. "We'll do whatever you say, and when everyone does find out, please assure the captain we will pay for our passage."

"Good. That will help. A little." Mr. Singh turned to escort us to the gun deck. He acted like he was none too happy about being put on the spot, but at least he wasn't going to give us away. "Wait till you see her," he said as we descended to the belly of the airship. Chain railings led down to an open deck lined with two cannons and a Gatling gun on each side. Everything had been repaired and repainted. Any signs of the chaos from the battle with the Sky Witch were gone.

"I see you fixed the place up," I said. "She's looks beautiful."

"Of course. Can't be prowling the skies in a piece of junk like the Storm Vulture, can we now?"

We laughed as he led us into the storage room. The large canvas tarp still hung down the center between our bunks. Seeing the odd expression on Owethu's face, I said, "Mr. Singh hung it last time we flew on the Sparrowhawk for Genevieve's privacy."

Genevieve pushed the tarp aside and let it drop back into place as she inspected her old quarters. I pulled two hammocks from the wall, and showed Owethu how to hook it to the support beam. "We'll stay in here. This is the gun deck, the lowest deck of the dirigible. Above us are the crew quarters, and above that is the bridge. The engine room sits in back, but Gears doesn't like visitors."

"I like these airships very much." Owethu jumped into his hammock, pushing against the floor to make it swing.

"Me too." I climbed into mine, sitting with my legs hanging off one side.

"Then we are in agreement." Genevieve's voice slipped over the tarp.

The engines whirled to life as the boilers whistled.

The sound silenced us.

Slowly, the bow of the Sparrowhawk rose into the air. My stomach dropped as the hammocks swung with the tilting ship, staying level as we climbed ever higher.

Throughout the ship, the crew moved in syncopated motion. They released the wingsails by unfolding the wooden yardarms on the sides of the airship. They stoked the engines to build the pressure for the propellers, and inspected the helium bags ensuring we stayed aloft. The groan of cannons straining against the ropes that held them in place mixed with the creaking of the metal struts. Music to my ears. As we climbed skyward and leveled out, the wind buffeted against the outer treated-canvas skin of the hull. I closed my eyes and felt the turbulence ripple through me. I was flying again. I was home.

After we'd leveled out, I jumped down from my hammock. Owethu was sitting upright in his hammock, gripping the edge of the material, causing red whelps on his knuckles. Still, he smiled.

I looked around at our quarters. 'Nothing's really changed."

Genevieve slid the tarp aside and said, "A few more crates, but they even left Rodin's bed." She pointed to the mass of cloth and coiled rope tucked up along the curve of the wall.

"What is a Rodin?" Owethu asked.

As I opened my mouth, the sound of beating dragon wings filled the deck.

A flurry of bronze wings whipped in through the open door. Genevieve sat up in her hammock, and Rodin landed on her shoulder. She nuzzled her forehead against his horned nubs. "Hey Rodin. It's good to see you, too."

"Buddy," I said, "good to see you." I waved, but he looked too happy tucked up against Genevieve. I didn't stand chance. They'd been born on the same day and shared a bond deeper than any other I'd seen.

"Is that a lizard?" Owethu stood up out of his hammock.

Rodin popped his head up and flared out his wings, which made him look much bigger, thicker. He flicked his forked tongue in and out of his mouth and eyed Owethu.

"Uh oh, you've done it now."

"What have I said?"

Genevieve smiled, "You called him the "L" word." She scritched under Rodin's chin. "It's okay. Owethu doesn't know your greatness yet."

I held out my hand toward Rodin. "Owethu, meet Rodin, a Draconis arcanus gigantigus," I said proudly. "He's the Kensington family dragon. A bronze dragon, as you can see by the coloring, which makes him one of the desert dragons, right?" I turned to Genevieve to see if I'd gotten it all correct, and she gave me a slight nod.

Rodin bowed and curled back into Genevieve.

"Do you have dragons in Zululand?" I asked.

"Never have I seen one. The dangerous serpents tend to slither not fly."

"He was my first dragon, too."

We all laughed and then remembering that we were stowaways on the ship, fell silent.

Just then I felt a small pang in my stomach. It wasn't the intense danger I'd felt during earlier episodes. But something was up. Owethu was facing the door. He stiffened and before I could turn around, a sharp gasp erupted behind me. I whipped around. The baron stood with his arms crossed, staring at the three of us.

Although I was shocked, I didn't move or say a word. I had hoped we'd be further away from London before they found us, and then I was hoping for one of the bribable crew members.

"Father!" Genevieve popped up and fell out of her hammock. Rodin growled and soared in a circle around her. She quickly stood and composed herself.

"Baron," I said as I stepped forward, "I can explain."

"Silence! I need not an explanation to understand this." He pointed to the three of us, but stared at his daughter. "We talked about this. You were supposed to remain behind."

"I will not be pushed aside because I am a *girl*."

"That is not the issue, Genevieve, and I will not have this discussion in front of others."

She huffed and spun around, turning her back to him.

Rodin landed back on her shoulder turned his back to the baron and fluffed his wings as he folded them back. The baron pursed his lips, but did not chastise his daughter further.

I held up my hand, but the baron stopped me.

"Do not start with me, Alexander. Might I say, your father will be incensed when he sees you. He's already against this journey, and now, *I'll* never hear the end of it." He spun back to Genevieve. "How … how could you bring Owethu? Do you know what you've done? This could cause an international incident."

She refused to turn around but said, "He has every right to be here, Father. The Knights of the Golden Circle are trying to frame his people for murder."

The baron sighed but did not respond to this truth. He tried. He raised his finger and opened his mouth to speak, but he stopped. "All three of you, on the bridge. Now." He stood aside and pointed to the door.

"We're only here to help," I said, knowing the

baron, and especially my father, would insist on returning to London. "Besides, we're a year older and wiser."

"Wiser?" the baron said. "A knight would have done as he was ordered."

His words pierced like a dagger that found its mark. I was worthy. Wiser—and a better warrior. So was Genevieve. But every time I tried to prove this to one of the Templar, all they wanted was for me to stay behind. "With respect, Baron Kensington, if we'd done that last year, it would have ended in disaster."

Seeing the baron and Genevieve's eyes pop open, as did Owethu's, I wish I'd held my tongue. But the words just slipped out. Would I never learn? The baron pointed toward the stairs, and in a clipped voice said, "March."

Genevieve turned so the baron couldn't see and winked at me, but it faded as she brushed past her father. Owethu and I followed, neither of us saying a word as we approached the door. Rodin flew around the gun deck and then soared back and slapped the baron in the back with his tail. I tried not to laugh as Rodin landed on my shoulder. I rubbed his head, but didn't look back to see the baron's reaction.

As we walked to the bridge, I stared at the Sparrowhawk's interior. This saved me from the endless scenarios forming in my mind of the scolding I'd have to endure between my father and the captain. She looked the same, but with a few improvements, upgrades, and new embellishments. "Hey they fixed that," I said pointing to the brass fixture holding the railing to the wall.

Mr. Singh stepped off the bridge and shut the hatch. Seeing us, he stopped. His mouth slightly agape. Immediately, he spun around, opened the door, and walked right back onto the bridge. I guess he wanted to watch our thrashing.

We stepped through the open hatch onto the bridge. My father stopped mid-sentence, and along with Chief Zwelethu turned to us. Both their faces dropped. My father removed his glasses and rubbed the bridge of his nose like he did when he'd been peering over his books too long. Chief Zwelethu narrowed his eyes on his son, but did not speak, either. We we're in trouble with a capital 'T'. This must be what stepping in front of a firing squad felt like.

Captain Baldarich, sat on his chair upon the raised platform in the center of the bridge. He stared at us, and a large smile spread across his face as he stroked his mustache, which ran along his cheek and joined to his sideburns. He hadn't changed at all. I grinned, openmouthed. I couldn't help it.

"Well, well, well. Master Alexander, it seems you have a bad habit of stowing away on my ship." He leaned forward putting the worn elbows of his red leather jacket against his knees. "And you know what I do to stowaways." He clapped his hands together and stood. "Mr. Singh, prepare the gangplank. We've got three thirsty crew members."

Mr. Singh nodded. He looked at me and shrugged.

My father spun around to the captain. "Surely, sir, we can discuss this. Let us take the kids back, and then we can continue."

The captain propped his hands on his hips. After a moment of tenseness, he sat back down. He raised his hand. "Mr. Singh, delay that order." He winked at me.

"Aye Captain."

Did he really just wink? He had a plan.

The baron stepped forward. "Captain. We will need

to return to London immediately. My apologies for this inconvenience. I assure you, there *will* be consequences for their actions."

The captain flew out of his chair as if it had exploded behind him. "That's going to be difficult baron." He walked over to the table. "We're already past the coast. You paid me to take you to Cairo via northern France and that is exactly what I will do. Nothing will divert us from that path."

"Captain, may I remind you who is in charge of this operation?"

"You may, though it is not you. I spoke to Grand Master Sinclair before our departure."

I pushed into the center of the group and said, "You did?"

"Yep. We even talked about this possibility." He swung his finger about, indicating the three of us. Then leaned in and nudged my shoulder. "He knows you better than you think."

"Wait," the baron barked, "Archibald Sinclair told you my daughter might stowaway on your ship and if she did, to *bring* her along?"

The captain ran his fingers along his mustache. "He did."

The baron stepped away. "I'll kill him."

"O-o-o-h, please sell tickets. I would definitely want to see that duel." The baron snapped the captain a look of malcontent, but Baldarich just laughed. The captain grabbed my shoulder. "They're better warriors than you give them credit for, and trust me, you're going to need them." He walked over to his chair and flipped open the four copper tubes rising up from the floor. "Attention! This is the captain. The son of our esteemed Zulu guest, Chief Zwelethu has come aboard, along with two returning members of the crew. Alexander and Genevieve are back! So, pay up. All of you!"

Ignatius Peacemaker stood up and dug a dollar out of his pocket. He pulled his Stetson off and tossed the bill in. He walked around to the other members of the crew on the bridge and each one added a dollar.

"Did you bet on my son?" my father asked.

"Of course. The crew thought you'd lock him up or something, but I know these two. Can't keep them from an adventure." He pointed to the young man in the blue turban. "Mr. Singh held firm, too. He knew they'd be coming." Ignatius stepped around Mr. Singh, and the captain said, "You'll get your cut, too, Mr. Singh, after Ignatius collects all our winnings."

Mr. Singh nodded. No wonder he wasn't surprised to see us.

Ignatius pulled the money out of his hat and handed it to the captain. "I'll go and round up the rest for yah, Cap," he said, his mix of western and continental accents slurring together. He slapped me on the back as he passed and grunted, "Welcome aboard, kid."

A few tense minutes passed before my father and the baron accepted, we weren't going anywhere. I don't think they knew what else to do. Besides, nothing bad had happened. At least not yet.

The captain leaned into me and Genevieve, "I got a new pilot. Say hello, Hienz."

I peered over at the small-framed man at the controls and wondered if he was a good pilot. Baldarich grabbed my shoulder, "My sister's kid, this one. She wants me to turn him into a man." He leaned over toward Genevieve and chuckled, "He's not bad, listens to orders, so I haven't tossed him overboard. Yet."

Heinz had my job. I'd hoped I'd get to try out for pilot, but I'd never get to now, not with family flying the ship.

Hienz shifted in pilot's seat and saluted, "Hallo."

With a quick wave, I said, "Hi." I pointed my thumb at myself and looked at Baldarich. "Well, if you need another, I'm pretty good."

"I'll remember that, lad." He winked at Genevieve. "But I'm staring at the lady of the clouds. I

still remember your skill at the controls, milady."

Genevieve smiled and tried to hide her excitement.

I fumed. I could have flown just as well as she, but I was down on the gun deck during the battle against the armada. I can fly. I just have to find a way to prove it.

The captain nudged me right out of my funk. "Good to have you two back on board."

"Thanks, Captain Baldarich. Me, too. I see you fixed her up a bit."

"Yes, the Sparrowhawk looks quite refreshed, doesn't she?" Baldarich tucked his thumbs under his lapel and leaned back. "I made sure she was worthy of serving as a privateer in the queen's service." He wrapped his arms around us and pulled us in. "But I left a few things, like that loose rivet above the engine room." I nodded and Genevieve smiled. The captain laughed. "Well, sit back and enjoy the ride."

He released us and walked over to the map table. I heard the rushing wind in the distance. I motioned for Genevieve and Owethu to follow. When we stepped out of the hatch, the deafening wind whipped Genevieve's long auburn hair around her face, and Rodin flew off. We walked past the cabins toward the door and saw that Mr. Singh had the main cargo door open. With the wail of the wind, they'd never hear me, so I waved my arms to grab his attention.

Stepping to the edge, he and two crewmen pulled hand over hand on a rope, retrieving a small pod, like a mini-Sparrowhawk, dragging below the airship. When I motioned for Owethu to come and have a look see, he shook his head emphatically and hung back by the cabin door.

Mr. Singh set the pod on the deck. He leaned

toward the device and checked the gauges mounted on its side. I recognized the temperature and wind speed dials, but not the others he studied. Recording the numbers on a slip of paper, he handed it off to one of the men who rushed them to the bridge.

Mr. Singh looked up at me and nodded, his blue turban slightly misshapen by the wind. He pointed toward the ground, and turned my attention to outside. We'd crossed back over land. France, I guessed. Below me lay fields covered in snow. Even though the bitter wind chilled me to the core, I could have stood here all day.

The aero-dirigible slowed and began to descend, pitching slightly forward. Owethu, still plastered against the wall, gripped the wooden railing with straining fingers, but kept stretching to see out the cargo door.

The baron stepped off the bridge as the wind settled. He walked up to the open cargo door, standing beside Genevieve and looked down. He motioned for us to come over and pointed to the ground below. Gently rolling hills and farmland spread as far as the eye could see.

The baron pointed. "Agincourt."

"Really?" I asked.

"Who is Agincourt?" Owethu asked as he stepped to the edge.

"Not who, but where," the baron answered. "The battle of Agincourt was fought in 1415 during the Hundred Years' War."

Genevieve continued. "The French knights were defeated by the English longbow."

"How?" I asked

"Mud," my father said as he pushed his glasses back up on his nose and joined us. "Weighed down by heavy armor and horses, the French knights became bogged down in the mud."

The baron pointed to a small rise. From here, I could see the terrain perfectly. "The English bowmen set up there, on the high ground between the forests," he added. "It had been raining for days."

The field squeezed between two dense woods was higher on one end. In front of the raised ground lay a depression. What now was a farmer's field, had once been an open expanse of deep muck, churned up by horses' hooves.

Studying every inch of the land below, I noted, "Alexander the Great ran into the same problem in India."

The baron nodded but stared at the scene as if the battle were raging right now. "Unable to maneuver, the knights found themselves cut down by the English bowmen, whose armor-piercing arrows went far beyond the range of the French archers."

"What happened?" Owethu asked.

"Many knights were killed. Around six thousand. King Henry V lost only a few hundred."

"Go England!" I said with a raised fist, but no one else cheered.

"Alexander," my father scolded, "now, is not the time."

"My ancestor fought in this battle." Genevieve reached up and held her locket.

"General Kensington, I bet."

"They were my wife's ancestors," the baron said. "Her line was almost wiped out at Agincourt." He put his arm around Genevieve's shoulder.

"Oh." I leaned toward the baron. "Where is your

wife now?"

The baron seemed surprised by my question, but answered. "She stayed in London."

Genevieve toyed with the locket on the silver chain around her neck but stared out to some distant point in the sky. I'd seen that look before.

The loss of our mothers was something we had bonded over last year. I wanted to comfort her, but she refused her father's gesture and stepped away. Rodin soared through the open cargo door and landed on her shoulder; he rubbed his head against hers.

I wanted to tell her everything would be all right. But even I knew that wasn't true. The pain of losing a loved one never healed. It only faded over time, and the wound would occasionally get ripped open again. Like now.

As the Sparrowhawk turned, the baron's expression changed. He reached in his jacket and pullout a collapsible telescope. Extending the segments, he raised it to his eye and adjusted the lenses. "We have a problem."

Owethu followed the baron's sightline. Genevieve dropped her locket and returned to her father's side. I looked up at the baron and my father, who put his hand over his brow and squinted. Off in the distance, I saw a castle surrounded by roses, but nothing looked out of place.

"What do you see Maximilian?" my father asked.

"The airskiff we have been following has landed." He handed the telescope to my father. "Look to the trees in behind the castle. See the red and black? It's the airskiff."

"I see it." My father adjusted the lenses. "Some of those trees aren't in the ground. They were moved in front of the airskiff to hide it."

The baron walked past us toward the bridge.

"Where are you going?" my father asked.

"To tell the captain we're stopping."

I followed the baron onto the bridge and saw him whispering in the captain's ear. Baldarich looked concerned but smiled as the baron finished.

"Bring us around, Hienz," the captain ordered. "I want guns on that castle."

"Aye, aye, Uncle."

The captain looked at the pilot, shook his head, but remained focused on the castle. He flipped open the brass tubes in front of him. "Battle stations. Prepare for ground assault." The Sparrowhawk erupted into activity. Crewmen hustled around the ship to prepare for battle. The captain sat in his chair but spun around to face Owethu, Genevieve, and me. "You two get to the gun deck and help Mr. Singh. Milady, if you would make certain Heinz doesn't drop my baby out of the sky, I would appreciate it." Genevieve nodded; a gesture repeated by Rodin. I nudged Owethu's shoulder and we jogged off to the gun deck. No time to lament that Genevieve got to pilot the ship.

As we were leaving the bridge, the captain's barrel voice echoed with confidence. "Ignatius, you're with

the baron and me."

Owethu and I slid down the ladder to the gun deck. Two cannons and a Gatling gun lined each side of the long room. The gun ports, already opened for ventilation, allowed the sunlight to fill the deck. The cold wind whipped through like a cannon ball as crewman prepared the starboard guns.

"This is going to be astounding." With a big smile, I nudged Owethu and pointed to the large guns. "Have you ever seen a Gatling gun fire?"

His answer was nearly lost in the wind, but I knew he'd said, "No."

I nodded. "You're in for a treat." I pointed to Mr. Singh who directed the chaos like an orchestra conductor. "We should see what he needs us to do."

He nodded.

We stepped over and Mr. Singh turned to face me. His stern expression softened and a smile replaced his warrior façade. He grabbed me by the shoulders. "Alexander, I am glad to have you at my side again."

"Glad to be here," I yelled. "What can we do? Captain sent us to help you." I gestured toward Owethu. "Put us to work."

Mr. Singh pointed to stacks of crates toward the back of the gun deck. "I need someone to secure that cargo."

I stuck up my thumb. "Done."

Owethu and I ran over to the crates and barrels stacked up in the center of the hold. I grabbed some rope for the crates and told Owethu to get the thick netting. We wrapped up the cargo and tied it down, securing it to the posts and structure of the ship.

"What about this?"

"About what?"

I followed Owethu's finger to a tightly wrapped canvas bundle behind the crates. I peered through the mass of wooden struts and saw an ornate brass burner in the shape of a bird. "It's an airship." I walked around to the other side. "But I've never seen one so small." On one of the struts, I saw painted lettering—Kite Skipper.

"We should secure it," Owethu said.

"You're right. Here take this end and tie it off. I'll loop the rope around the post over here."

Moments later Owethu looked up and said, "Done."

"Excellent."

"What is this word?"

"Oh, it means we did really well."

"We would say, *kuhle kakhulu* (very good) or *kahle ngempela* (really well)."

"Fascinating."

Owethu got a strange look on his face, and I quickly stuttered, "It means—"

"I know that word. I am very fascinated by your culture." Owethu chuckled and poked me.

I shook my head and laughed. "Me too. About your culture, that is. I hope to visit your land someday."

He nodded.

Mr. Singh rushed by and the serious look on his face deflated our laughter. He ran over to a copper tube sticking out of the ceiling. He flipped it open and yelled, "Ready to fire, Captain."

"Announce us, Mr. Singh," the captain returned, his voice reverberating out from the pipe.

Mr. Singh turned to the crewmen. I hit Owethu's arm and covered my ears. He did the same. Mr. Singh yelled, "Fire!"

The cannon exploded as smoke enveloped the gun deck. The artillery punched back straining against the thick ropes. A crewman cranked the handle on the side of the Gatling gun and bullets rained down on the castle. More smoke billowed across the deck only to be whipped up by the wind coming in from the other side.

The cannons and guns roared continually, and I felt the hot breath of each blast against my skin. The explosions hurt my ears even through my clenched hands. The crewmen pulled the guns back into position, swabbed them out, and reloaded. Their actions were choreographed like a well-oiled machine.

The baron, the captain, Ignatius, and Hunter walked down to the gun deck. The men walked over to one of the grapplers and a crewman opened a hatch on the starboard side of the floor. Hunter and Ignatius turned two wheels aiming the grappler at the castle and fired. The thick cable spiraled down, catching onto the stone battlement. All four men hooked straps to the cable and slid down toward the castle as enemy fire erupted.

I watched them tumble onto the battlement, pop up, and rush the guards. I wanted to slide down the cable and fight by their side. A wave of frustration washed over me, but orders were orders. Even though I'd saved London—and the entire world—they still saw me as a kid.

The guns beside me continued to roar. The next cannon shot slammed into the tower of the castle, destroying the artillery perched on top. Captain Baldarich zapped two men with his lightning cannon, the pistol he kept tethered to a box on his belt. They fell to the stones twitching uncontrollably as Baldarich stepped over them.

Ignatius ran alongside him, using every pistol he had tucked away to shelter the baron from incoming fire as he cut down several men with his sword. Hunter remained by the grappler line, set up behind some crumbled stones, and picked men off as they stormed the stairs of the forebuilding to the castle. Gatling gun lead rained down on them as well, shattering the stone like fine china, and filling the air with putrid smoke

It was beautiful, exciting, like the scene of a novel playing out before me. Yet scary. Deadly.

Owethu tapped my shoulder. I pulled back, and he pointed to Mr. Singh standing beside him.

"Get to the bridge and tell Heinz to keep me on target. He's drifting."

"Got it." I pulled back from the hatch. "Concentrate your fire on the courtyard, Mr. Singh. The wall is won."

He nodded. Owethu and I ran off for the bridge.

When we arrived, my father stood by the window, but it was Genevieve who looked in charge. She stood in front of the copper tubes with her hands on her hips, and Rodin wrapped around her shoulders. Before I could even take another step, she shouted, "Three degrees starboard with a one-degree downturn."

"Aye, aye captain." Heinz paused but turned and pushed on the wheel.

Genevieve looked out the window and nodded. "That should give Mr. Singh the view he needs." She spun around. "Alexander."

Rodin, jolted by her movement, popped off her shoulder and flew over to me. He landed on my chest, gripping the leather strap, and rubbed his head on my chin. Then he climbed up and sat on my shoulder.

"Hi, Rodin." I ran my fingers along the leathery skin of his neck as it stretched out. I stepped up to Genevieve as my father came over. "Captain," I said with a smile, "I have—had—a message from Mr. Singh, but you just fulfilled the order."

She shrugged her shoulders. "I only noticed that we drifted on the wind."

I nodded but couldn't stop grinning. She was so calm and collected. She looked as if she belonged here. With her long blue coat trimmed in gold, the pants and shiny black-buttoned boots, she looked like an officer in the Royal Flying Corps. "The wall is won, but this isn't over yet," I said.

"Too true."

"Too bad I don't have the Black Knight. I could smash through those walls and take the courtyard with ease."

She nodded and I saw her eyes dart to the side. She saw it, too. Cut through the hole in the eastern wall and smash through the main doors. That's what I was thinking.

"We should have brought the Iron Knights."

My father's eyes popped out of his head and he raised his finger. "Those infernal machines are not toys. Mechanized armor is not for teenagers."

"All I'm saying is they would be really helpful."

"Alexander," my father groaned.

Genevieve nodded, and so did Rodin.

The ship shuddered and we wobbled, but I didn't fall over. I ran to the window as Genevieve turned back to Heinz. My father and Owethu joined me.

Our allies had taken the courtyard, but the Knights of the Golden Circle still had cannons and guns in the keep's ruins. In the thick smoke smothering the castle, I searched for evidence that the baron and others had remained unscathed. An arc of blue lightning from the captain's cannon provided the response.

BOOK II: IRON ZULU

14
The Little Ship

Through the smoke enveloping the castle, I saw several figures slipping out the back toward the airship. "Look! Someone is making a run for it."

"Who?" Genevieve asked, scanning the scene below.

I squinted, hoping to peer through the carnage. "There," I pointed. "Three people." All were dark figures, but one turned, and through the haze, a flash of light glinted across shiny bronze plates. "Colonel Hendrix," I spit through clench teeth.

My father pulled back from the window and slid into his thoughts, pacing back and forth for a moment. He was putting something together. He had the same look when he translated ancient texts. He raised a finger and blurted out, "I think I know what's this is about." He rushed off the bridge. I watched him depart and said, "We should stop them. Let's drop the Sparrowhawk right on top of them and force that ship to stay on the ground."

Genevieve shook her head.
"I can't order that."

"Why not?"
Genevieve pointed

toward the castle. "This ship is the only reason my father and the captain are still alive."

I turned and saw the captain and baron fighting in the keep. The Gatling gun rained lead around the artillery and two were aimed inward. The gun crews scattered in the hail of fire but if they regrouped, our friends and her father would be killed. I nodded quickly wanting with everything to take back my request.

Genevieve smoothed out her jacket and pulled it down. She turned to Heinz. "Keep the Sparrowhawk steady, so Indihar can rain lead on our enemies." She patted her shoulder. "Come, Rodin, we have to think of something." Rodin jumped off me, glided to her, and landed.

As Genevieve turned away, Owethu hit my arm. "We use the craft to follow the assassin."

I jumped and grabbed his shoulders. "Brilliant!" I ran after Genevieve. "Wait! Owethu has the answer." She stopped and waited for me to continue. "The Kite Skipper."

Her brow peaked. I could tell she was intrigued, but she had a question.

"It's in the cargo hold. We just secured it."

She nodded. "Our parents are going to kill us for this, but we've got to do something to prevent them from firing on the Sparrowhawk, or my father and the others."

"First things first, though … we have to put it together."

The three of us and Rodin, rushed down to the gun deck and pushed through the thunder and smoke to the back where the Kite Skipper sat. Genevieve didn't look impressed. Owethu and I unbundled the canvas and wooden slats. I held two pieces up trying to see how they fit together.

Mr. Singh rushed over, "What is going on here?"

I looked up. His hard brow covered inquisitive eyes. He locked his hands firmly on his waist.

"Hendrix and the lady assassin are fleeing. They might even take a parting shot at the Sparrowhawk…"

"Or worse, the captain, and her father." His expression softened. "What is your plan, Alexander?"

"As they lift off, we charge, force them to head away from the castle. They're fleeing, not staying around for a fight. Once they've gone, we hang back in the clouds and follow them. Mr. Singh nodded in agreement. "The captain will surely want to search the castle for spoils…, I mean he and the baron will surely want to make sure none of our enemy remain."

Genevieve smiled. "My father will insist on searching for clues to their plan."

I pleaded with both of them, "Then we have to pursue these murderers. We can't let escape."

Mr. Singh stroked his beard. "What do we do when they land?"

I paused. "We'll contact the Templers and the Sparrowhawk."

"How?"

"I don't know; I haven't gotten that far yet." I shrugged.

"Well then we should get moving," Mr. Singh said with a large smile. "We'll never catch them if you keep screwing around."

Genevieve touched Mr. Singh's shoulder. "We're going to get in a lot of trouble for this; you might want to stay here."

"Kind words milady, but I would never leave my

friends in trouble. Besides, if I go, then you aren't stealing the Kite Skipper."

Genevieve hugged him and said, "Welcome aboard."

Mr. Singh explained how the Kite Skipper fit together, which was a blessing, otherwise we might never have figured it out. Within moments, we had the main struts fixed in place and the burner set. I started to light the small brass stove, but Mr. Singh stopped me and grinned. He pulled a ribbed canvas hose from the ceiling, took the seal off the end and secured the fitting to the balloon. He flipped the valve, and gas filled the balloon halfway in a matter of moments.

"Hook the struts to the balloon, Alexander. Its belly holds helium, not air."

"Fascinating. So, what's the burner for?" I asked.

Owethu held up a propeller. "This."

Mr. Singh nodded and leaned back to check on his gun crews. They continued to rain lead shot on the castle below. "Now, fix the wing sails to back of the balloon. They connect to the crew seats."

"Wait … that's what we are sitting on?" Genevieve gawked at the contraption with a worried gaze. Most airships suspended a ship's hull beneath the balloon, but the Kite Skipper didn't, it remained opened to the sky. Genevieve buried her concerns and jested. "Good thing I've changed into pants."

I looked at the wooden rods with leather straps woven between and knew this was going to be fun. There was nothing surrounding us. Only thick leather belts kept passengers tied to the Kite Skipper. Owethu and I secured all the connections.

Once the Kite Skipper sat assembled on the gun

deck, I don't think any of us eyed it with a sense of security. Brass, bamboo, leather, and canvas sounded good, but this contraption looked as if it might fly apart in a stiff breeze.

Mr. Singh, unconcerned, said, "Everyone aboard." As we boarded, he handed us each a pair of thick goggles and four heavy coats. "Put these on. You're going to need them in the winter sky." Then he sat down, picked up one of the belts and wrapped it around his waist. "Strap in, hold tight, and don't forget to lock your feet into the straps. They're all that keep you connected to the Kite Skipper and from certain death." I could have done without the final part.

I strapped in next to Mr. Singh, who taken the pilot's seat, while Genevieve and Owethu secured themselves behind us. "How do we get out of the ship?"

Behind us a crewmen yelled, "Enemy airship is lifting off." The joy slipped from Mr. Singh's face. "Hold tight." He pointed to a crewman, who pulled a lever on the wall. The floor beneath us opened up and we dropped out of the Sparrowhawk. We didn't fall like a stone, more like a feather.

Once clear of the areo-dirigible, with the wind whipping all around us, Mr. Singh ignited the burner between us, which spun the crankshaft running down the center of the craft. In response, the propeller whirred to life. He pulled a lever and a pair of winglets extended on each side of us. Turning the yoke starboard, we pitched left, and descended. I looked back and watched as we soared away from the Sparrowhawk.

"Look!" I pointed at Rodin as he zipped out of the Sparrowhawk and soared after us. He landed atop the balloon and hooked his claws onto one of the struts, a fitting masthead for our little craft.

The red and black airship, The Black Freighter, charged through rising smoke, and buffeted by the hot blasts of the cannons, pushed faster. A strong gust from the north pushed our tiny craft toward the battle. As Mr. Singh predicted, the coats were a necessity. The wind was cold, like an arctic blast. Snow still covered the surrounding fields and reflected the glare of the sun overhead.

"We're nothing more than a mosquito to an elephant," I yelled over the wind and whirring propeller. "What are we going to do?"

"We charge them." Mr. Singh forced the yoke forward aiming right for the airship's hanging bridge.

Mr. Singh couldn't be serious, but the determination glowing in his eyes told me otherwise. I tried to think of something, and turned to consult Genevieve. She'd freed herself from her belt, and stood up, hooking her boot under one of the struts.

She drew her saber and snagged one of the ropes of the balloon with her other hand. "No need for a suicide mission, Mr. Singh," she yelled. "Why don't we

poke a few holes in their backside and they'll never make altitude."

"You're the bravest person I've ever known." The wind whipped my words away, and she didn't hear them.

We soared past the Black Freighter's portholes. I waved. Although I couldn't see inside because of the sun's glare, I was really hoping they saw me. Mr. Singh pulled up on the yoke, and we brushed the underside of the airship, dodging several ropes dangling in their wake. We skimmed up the starboard side. As soon as Genevieve saw taut canvas, she plunged her sword inside the blimp. Three deep cuts later, we broke away and soared off. I spun around and saw puffs of smoke shooting from the airship's portholes.

"They're firing on us," I shouted. Fortunately, we were far enough away that nothing hit us. Even so, Mr. Singh changed course and dropped the Kite Skipper's nose to gain speed. When he thought we were out of range, he rounded our craft and faced the airship. Torn canvas flapped in the wind. The airship continued to climb, but it turned from the Sparrowhawk and headed south.

I threw up my hands. "They're running. We did it!"

In the distance, we saw the Sparrowhawk continuing to fire on the castle, and the castle returning a shot that fell under the aero-dirigible.

Genevieve dropped back onto the seat and strapped herself in. The four of us looked at one another. None of us spoke and our silence shouted volumes. Our true enemies were getting away, and we had the only means of following them. We each knew what our parents would say, but our minds had been made, solidified, like Roman concrete. I turned to Genevieve and Owethu. They both nodded, and I gave Mr. Singh the thumbs up.

He turned southward toward the fleeing Black Freighter and yelled, "We're off!" I looked back and saw Owethu had closed his eyes and tilted his head to the sky.

Even though the black airship dragged canvas like a whipping lure, they still managed to gain distance between us. "We have to fly faster," I said.

A devious smirk formed on Mr. Singh's lips. "You've yet to see why they call it a Kite Skipper." He handed me a scrap of cloth and said, "Find the wind."

Find the wind? It was currently smacking me in the face. My eyes would be sealed shut if it weren't for the goggles. I studied the torn piece of cloth in my hand. This made no sense.

Owethu leaned forward and pointed off to the southeast. "Watch the clouds."

I looked at him and my brow rose. "What?"

I shrugged. Genevieve shook her head and laughed.

Owethu grabbed the cloth from my hand and tossed it off the side.

"Hey, why did you do that?" I glanced over the side. The scrap shot back in our wake, but after tumbling for a moment it whipped back toward us heading southeast. "Oh," I said. "The wind."

They all laughed and I sank a little deeper into my seat.

Mr. Singh throttled back and right before we fell out of the sky; he pulled a cord and released the kite sail. The huge canvas sail flapped for a moment, but suddenly billowed out in front of us as it caught the wind. We lurched forward and began flying much faster. He then increased power to the engine and used the propeller to help him steer. Stretched out in a wide arc, the kite sail, bound to the craft by four ropes, pulled us ever closer to the wounded airship.

For the next few hours, we bobbed alongside the clouds. I couldn't stop staring at the world around me. From up here everything seemed possible. Snow covered the fields below, looking like a layer of clouds lying on the ground. Needles of cold wind pierced my cheeks below my goggles. I would need to remember to thank Mr. Singh for providing on our gear.

Every so often we would spot the enemy airship through the billowing, white mountains towering above us in the sky. The clouds kept us from sight, allowing us to trail silently behind them.

The clouds below us cleared and giving us a view of the land below. In the distance, I saw a city divided by a river. From its size alone, I knew the city that spread beneath us like a jewel set upon the land. "Paris," I said, pointing.

Everyone nodded, and I felt Genevieve's hand on my shoulder. She lightly squeezed my coat. The pressure alone sent a chill through me. I turned, from the smile crossing her lips, I knew she, too, was remembering. Paris faded into the distance, but I couldn't stop thinking about that night—the dress, the theater, the wonderful cheese, the romance languages, and my first kiss. Still the best day of my life.

Soon the snow-covered landscape greened until we were cruising over the vineyards and fields of southern France. The skies cleared, leaving a ceiling of blue above us. The patchy clouds that remained left us nowhere to hide.

We soared above and behind the Black Freighter, a good place to avoid being seen. The airship listed. They were in trouble, crippled, flitting back and forth like a drunken firefly.

"What's wrong? Do they have a leak?" I asked.

Mr. Singh pointed to the rippling canvas and exposed frame. "The aft section deflated over the flight."

Genevieve leaned forward. "They'll have to land soon. I can't imagine that is a comfortable flight."

As the airship suddenly rose higher in the sky, we all laughed. The Black Freighter continued to climb, and the fun abruptly ended as we were no longer above them, but behind them. A rear gun port flipped open on the airship. I pointed as Mr. Singh turned the yoke hard to starboard. Too late. A puff of smoke exploded from the airship. The cannonball exploded from the airship, leaving a black cloud in the sky. Lead shards cut through the front of the Kite Skipper.

One of the ropes holding the kitesail was severed, causing the canvas to whip wildly. Then the shattered cannon ball ripped through the helium-filled balloon, and it withered as the gas escaped. We plummeted downward out of the sky. Mr. Singh used what little remained of the kite sail and the remaining small winglets to control our descent, but we were clearly about to crash into the side of a ruined cathedral.

As Mr. Singh struggled to keep us on a controlled path, Genevieve yelled, "Get ready to jump."

The ground rushed up before us and my heart pounded as my head screamed "*Jump!*" But I knew I had to wait. If we were too high, we ensure a certain leg shattering. Too low, though, and we might get tangled in the sails of the airship and be part of the crash. I didn't want to let go, but everything inside me yelled, "Get out!"

Moments before we crashed, Mr. Singh yelled,

"Now!" I willed my grip to loosen and leapt away from the ship and into the grass. I tumbled to a stop and flipped up on my elbow, searching for my comrades as the craft smashed into the grass beside the ruined cathedral.

Stunned, I sat there for a few minutes, then patted myself to make sure I still had all my parts. Beyond some bumps and bruises, I was fine. A rush of relief washed over me as Genevieve stood up and brushed herself off. Owethu and Mr. Singh, too. They all hobbled toward me. I pushed myself up out of the grass. "Unbroken?" I asked each of them.

They all nodded, and Rodin growled as he landed on Genevieve's shoulder. Mr. Singh and I checked over to the shattered remains of the Kite Skipper.

"Now what?" I asked.

"We walk," said Mr. Singh.

Great. The long walk to some town in the distance, only to wait for my father, the baron, the captain, and probably the queen, chew me up and spit me out for ruining everything.

I turned to see where Genevieve had gone. She was looking away from us. "I see them," she called. "They're landing at that castle on the hill."

16
Cathar Castle

We trudged our way to the castle perched on the ridge at the end of the valley. The impressive fortification rose from a natural outcrop of rock and dominated the surrounding landscape. In the long shadows of the afternoon, we approached the stone fortress. I'd never felt more like a knight storming a real castle.

A symphony of sounds carried over the walls, but no one stood on the battlements. "Why are there no guards on the walls?"

"They don't expect an attack," Genevieve answered. "They shot us down."

Mr. Singh nodded. "We should keep moving. See if there's a way in."

Owethu pointed further down the wall. "The sound is louder from this direction."

We slid along the base of the tall, massive stone fortifications and slowly worked our way to the back of the castle, staying near the walls to avoid the sheer hillsides. As we neared the back, the grounds narrowed

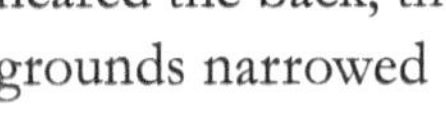

further. There, the fortress walls also were shorter, where we eventually had to crouch down in order to keep from being seen.

We each peaked over the edge of the abutment. On the other side of the wall, the grounds opened up to reveal what were once gardens, but the natural beauty had faded long ago, now transformed by steel and iron to create an air dock. One ship lay cradled in the moorings, and several men, slaves really, formed a line to load and unload the vessel.

The guards faced inward and kept a watchful eye on their every action. My blood roiled. They weren't here to keep people out. They were here to keep them *in*. This had to be the Knights of the Golden Circle, the only ones trying to resurrect that hated legacy.

Owethu tapped my shoulder and pulled me down as the three of them pulled back behind the larger fortified walls. I nodded and slowly followed, but the crack of a whip made every muscle inside me seize up. I continued on, but each command by the guards enraged me. I wanted to charge in. A knight was supposed to defend the helpless. It took everything for me to continue following the others, but if I did run in, I knew I'd get caught, and that wouldn't help anyone, including us.

Genevieve whispered, "We have to discover what they're doing."

Mr. Singh raked his fingers through his beard. "But the minute we step around the back wall, the guards will see us."

Owethu pointed up, suggesting we climb the outer wall. We all leaned back to see. A few stones appeared to have a broken ledge, or were sticking out, but most were flush to the wall. I didn't think I could make it, but I didn't doubt for a minute that Owethu might.

I sat down on a smooth rock at the edge of the hill as we discussed how to sneak through the air docks. I put my hand down behind me and leaned back to help me better think. I felt rough ridges along the backside of the rock. I turned and saw the outline of a Templar cross etched in the stone. The left arm of the cross came to a point, instead of the usual flared end like the others. Slightly turned on an angle, the pointed end aimed down the hill.

That's odd, I thought. Why would the Templar leave the cross outside the castle? And why was the cross different? Maybe an attacker mocked them, but no one would sit at the base of besieged wall to carve it. Something else was afoot. My mind flipped through a dozen possibilities, but all I knew for certain—the odd etching was a sign.

"What do you make of this?" They all came over and peered at the stone. I stood and followed the direction the arrow pointed. Down the hill, emerging from the grass lay a pile of rocks. A way in? Of course. The Templars thought of every possibility, even if everything went wrong and the castle were claimed by the enemy, they would have a way to get back in.

"Found it," I said as I slid over the edge and down the steep slope.

I heard a whispered but forceful, "Alexander," from Genevieve, but I had to focus on my feet or risk tumbling down. They did not follow me.

When I reached the stones, it was nothing but a pile of natural rock. Or so a Templar would want the enemy to think, I mused. I searched for another symbol on the mass of rocks and found one on a lone rock at the bottom of the pile, half buried by grass. This cross had the right shape, but had been turned slightly askew and looked like an 'X'. It couldn't be that easy.

I took a step back, and studied the cross, running my fingers through my hair, and pushing the two front locks back. The placement of the stones looked familiar. A large stone sat above two others like a naturally formed lintel. An oblong stone fit perfectly in the middle of the pile of stones and sat directly on top of the small rock with the cross. I would have sworn it was a toppled over Stonehenge, but one side was higher than the other, and the large stone blocked the center.

It was a door. It had to be. Kneeling down, I tried to push and pull the stone with the cross etched on it. At first it wouldn't budge, but then I turned the stone and the cross slowly rotated. When the Templar cross design had been set properly, the large, oblong stone slid back into the hill.

I popped up and motioned for the others to come down the hill.

"I found our way in."

"Very nice, Mr. Armitage." Mr. Singh slapped me on the back.

"You've done well," Owethu said, but Genevieve held a hard stare. As Owethu followed Mr. Singh inside, she leaned in close and whispered. "Please don't run off like that. I thought you'd fallen." As she descended into the opening, she turned back and said, "Most astounding; always trust an Armitage to find a way in."

I melted into a puddle of goo. She was worried about me, *and* I'd impressed her. I followed her inside unable to get the giant grin off my face.

Mr. Singh coaxed a flame in the mini-lantern on his

belt and unhooked it. Holding it up, he pushed back the inky darkness. The cut rock led deep into the hill. Dusty cobwebs filled the passage and the musty, stale smell stuffed my nostrils and made it hard to breathe, but we pushed on.

Once in the passage, we came upon a simple but beautifully constructed stone mechanism. By turning the stone above, I had unlatched the lock holding the main stone, allowing it to slide back into the hillside. It could easily be reset if needed. Genius.

We followed Mr. Singh down the passage and entered the dungeons. A metal sarcophagus, spiked chairs, and pear-shaped metal devices lay shattered or deteriorating in the corners. Torture devices, I assumed. This definitely looked like a place people were tortured. The air grew heavier and made it harder to breathe.

Genevieve stopped in front of me and asked, "What's our plan?" Owethu and Mr. Singh stopped. She looked each one of us in the eye and didn't look pleased with what she saw. "We don't have one, do we?"

I looked around and whispered, "We need to find out what they're doing."

"Obviously." She pinched the bridge of her nose. "However, we are in an enemy stronghold with the leaders of the Golden Circle."

"Exciting, isn't it?" I smiled, but no one else seemed to share my enthusiasm.

Mr. Singh lowered his lantern. "If we're careful, we can slip in and out of this place without alerting them."

I nodded. "The Templars will help us."

Genevieve shook her head. "They aren't here, Alexander."

"Maybe they are in spirit." I had seen the Order's

mystical nature last year. I knew we'd be okay. It was like a happy feeling in my gut.

Owethu turned to me. "Then what is the plan?"

They were right. We needed a plan, maybe even two, just in case one was compromised. "Well, we have to find Hendrix and see what he is planning. Once we learn when they are leaving, we can try to signal the Sparrowhawk, or fix the Kite Skipper."

No one protested or made another suggestion. They liked my plan. At least I think they did. But when Genevieve paused, I knew she pondered over another problem. "We don't know where they are."

I tried to think. "Well, the upper portions of this castle don't look the best, so let's hope they are closer to the ground."

Mr. Singh looked all four of us. "We should split up"

Genevieve shook her head. "No. Our only advantages are surprise and numbers."

Mr. Singh nodded. "Move silently, keep your head down, and if we get caught don't tell them we are the only ones. Maybe we can bluff them into thinking we have more people."

Owethu said, "Seek to be unseen."

"Exactly," I said, "but how do we do that?"

"Step slowly and carefully, breathe slowly, speak only with signs, and remain upwind."

"Excellent advice." Genevieve slinked over to the stairwell. "As I have the most experience lurking, I shall lead."

Owethu popped an eyebrow. "I have hunted since I could walk."

"Apologies if I offended you; that was not my

intention." Genevieve bowed. "However, I am better than these two."

"Hey," I said, which came out louder than I thought, and everyone spun around and stared at me. I covered my mouth with my hand.

Genevieve peered up the stairs and we silently stood here for a minute listening to the sounds above. The muffled sounds of the air docks mixed with the heavy footsteps above. Slowly, we inched our way up the stairs. Genevieve and I reached the top, two men walked nearby. We pressed ourselves against the wall and she held her finger to her lips, stopping us

We stood inside an alcove near the central room of the main keep. Soldiers and a few slaves milled about the chamber, packing equipment into crates. Whips cracked, and groans escaped from the men with each heave of the crates.

Raised voices drew us to the far side of the castle courtyard. A wooden door with thick iron hinges lay open and a flickering orange glow escaped. Twin copper pipes, bolted to the wall, ran into the room. One unmistakable voice rose above the others.

Hendrix.

"You yellow-belly!" he cried from inside the room.

My heart thumped. I wanted to turn back. Owethu stepped around me and squatted down in front of Genevieve. He pointed to a shattered doorway several feet along the same wall as the door we were watching. We all nodded and one by one, slipped from one crate to the next. I stopped behind a stack of oil barrels. Between them I could see the airdocks. Several workmen repaired the Black Freighter's tail section, but I could tell they still had a lot of work to do. That ship wouldn't be leaving for days.

Everyone slipped through the doorway, except for me. My stomach started to ache, the all too familiar feeling that danger was nearby. As I stepped out to follow the others, I heard boot steps on the stones. I ducked back behind the barrels as a guard passed by on the other side. My heart pounded so loud I thought he might hear. But I kept my wits and remained calm. Then he stopped. My first instinct was to run in another direction, to draw him away from my friends, but I'd be captured or shot for certain. From in between the barrels, I saw him shoulder his rifle. He rubbed the arms of his khaki jacket, and blew hot air into hands.

He looked annoyed, not curious. Then a slave dropped a crate creating a loud crash, and the soldier walked off in that direction. I dashed through the doorway undetected.

"We thought that was the end for you, my friend." Mr. Singh whispered.

"Me too." I motioned them closer. "They are dressed for the desert, and the airship will take at least a day to fix."

Owethu and Mr. Singh nodded, but I could tell from Genevieve's puzzled expression that she was wondering about that, too. Angry voices in the next room silenced me and drew us to an orange glow on the far side of the wall.

Several blocks had crumbled away from the wall, leaving a perfect window into the next room. Owethu and Mr. Singh were the first to reach the opening. They peered through and then pulled back. Mr. Singh raised his thumb, and I knew we'd found them.

They slid out of the way. Genevieve and I replaced

them and stared through the opening. A warm blast of air washed over us. Lanterns provided the light, and a Persian Rug and fine wooden furniture made the room look like a home. Hendrix paced back and forth in front of a seated Lord Kannard, who had more gray hair than when I'd seen him last. He still held that aristocratic smugness, however. Two soldiers stood in the far corners of the room, and the lady assassin stood with her back to us. Her hood was down around her shoulders, revealing short auburn hair.

Hendrix and Kannard argued in civilized tones, although I couldn't make out what they discussed. As the tension between them thickened, Hendrix threw up his arms. Then the lady assassin turned around and I froze. Genevieve's mouth dropped open. I had seen the assassin once before. In the locket around Genevieve's neck.

The faintest whisper escaped her. "Mother?"

17
A Gordian Knot

Afraid Genevieve was going to walk right out and give us away, I pulled her back. We worked our way to the stairs, and slipped out through the dungeon. Keeping low, we ran across the fields, returning to the remains of the Kite Skipper.

Genevieve hadn't said a word along the way. She stared beyond the horizon, as if looking directly into the past. I wanted to say something, to comfort her, but I didn't know how.

Owethu and Mr. Singh stared at the wreckage. I tried to focus on what could be salvaged, but couldn't turn away from Genevieve. I walked over and sat on a rock beside her. The fading sunlight caught her face and sent her shadow stretching out behind her. The burnished colors and mixed hues of the evening light radiated off her until she resembled an oil painting. Mesmerized, I could have sat there for eternity.

She turned and looked at me, her eyes sparkling in the golden rays reflecting off the silver locket around her neck. Her lips moved, but I did not hear her.

When I only smiled in return, her teary eyes switched to puzzlement, and suddenly,

the part of my brain that had been screaming for control for the last several moments took over. She'd spoken and I had no idea. She'd caught me staring and I had only a moment to think of a reason. Play dumb—it wasn't manly—or own up to it and get in trouble.

"Are you all right?" she asked in her sweet accent.

"Yes," I blurted out. "Fine, good, okay … how about you?" I kicked myself as she bristled at my comment. "What I meant to say was, are you okay? I know that couldn't have been easy."

"I … I don't know what to think." She clutched the locket tightly in her hand. So hard I was afraid it would bend.

"Is it really her?"

"No," she said quickly. "It can't be. She barely looks like her—my mother. She's an imposter who probably had surgery to look like her. I imagine she's after my family's fortune."

Owethu rubbed his arms as Mr. Singh pulled his coat closed and said, "We will need a fire, but we'll have to use the high-walled ruins of the cathedral to block the light from the castle."

"Good idea." I looked around. "Maybe there is some wood in the church we can use."

Genevieve stared at the castle as I gathered some wood. I made a place to rest in the cathedral ruins, in a section on the far side from the castle. Owethu and Mr. Singh brought up what they could salvage of the Kite Skipper.

A chilling wind howled from the north, but Owethu coaxed a small fire to push winter away. I reached into my bag and pulled out some bread I'd swiped from my lunch at Eton. I never knew when my father would be done and we'd get dinner, so at Princeton I'd started carrying food in my bag. It had saved my stomach on many an occasion. I tore it into fourths and passed them around. "Sorry I don't have more." No one argued. They took the bread and began to eat. Except Genevieve. She picked at the dough, but barely ate any. By the time night fell, we had filled our stomachs with my meager rations and rested around the fire.

I sat with my back against the marble base of a statue looted long ago. The fire heated the stone, and sent soothing heat through me. I exhaled. This should be the life. No studies to worry about. No one to tell me what to do—just a fire, good friends, and a centuries old cathedral. Except, Genevieve was in pain, we were cut off from our allies, and my greatest enemies had resurfaced. A dream life, no.

I sat back and pointed over my shoulder. "I wonder what they're up to over in the castle."

Genevieve unbound her hair from its braid and ran her fingers through the long locks. "What do we know to be true?"

Owethu poked the fire. "The metal man wants to kill the professors who aided the wars against my people."

"But then why my father? We weren't even at Eton yet." I thought about what he was doing right now, what he'd told me at dinner last week, but I hadn't been paying attention. It all sounded so boring. What was it? Then it hit me. I clapped my hands making them all jump. "I remember. Father was translating an Egyptian text of a far older tale: a pharaonic tablet detailing the sub-Saharan tribes."

They stared at me with puzzled faces. Genevieve asked, "How does that help us?"

I paused. My friends had the same look of confusion I did when I was listening to my father. I needed to explain the connections forming in my mind. "The soldiers, there in the castle, are wearing desert garb. My father is studying the ancient texts of southern Africa."

Mr. Singh tossed more branches and part of a broken pew on the fire, "So the first castle was a trap, to kill the Templers pursuing them, and now they are fleeing the second."

"Exactly." I wondered why the Golden Circle would want Africa, and then my heart sank. "What if they are searching for an even older source of the horsemen's power?"

Genevieve nodded. "Egypt is one of the oldest societies."

A hushed whisper escaped my lips, "According to the latest theories, the first humans come from Africa."

Owethu nodded.

Genevieve said, "If Kannard and Hendrix are here and heading south, then they are definitely up to something. We need to stop them or who knows what they'll do this time."

Mr. Singh tugged on his beard. "Is another comet coming?"

I shook my head. "Not that I know of."

"That's a relief."

Genevieve leaned closer to the fire. "Don't forget, they have had a year to plan."

"This is so complicated," I sat back. "It's just like a Gordian Knot."

Mr. Singh asked, "Whose knot?"

"Gordian's" I smiled. "But it's a place, not a person.

In the town of Gordium, King Midas tied an ox cart to the temple with a knot so complex no one could loosen it. It was said that whosoever could untie the knot would not only be king of Gordium, but all of Asia as well. In 333 B.C., Alexander the Great entered the capital of Phrygia. He saw the knot. He looked for the end but couldn't find it. So, he drew his sword and cut the knot in two. Thus, he freed the ox cart and became king of one of the largest empires in history."

Mr. Singh pointed. "I knew this was going to be an Alexander the Great story. I could tell by the light in your eyes."

"I have heard of the great king." Owethu's brow scrunched up. "Are you related?"

"Only named after him," I said, and Owethu nodded.

Genevieve's expression hardened. "The Knights of the Golden Circle are definitely complex."

"So, how do we cut through their knot?" Mr. Singh asked.

I sat up straight. "The Black Knight could do it."

We all laughed. Mr. Singh jerked up as if something just came to him. "Alexander, help me with the airship. Let's see what can be salvaged."

I shrugged. "Sure." We walked over to the pile of wood and canvas.

"The kite sail is in good shape," he said. "Here, help me." We lifted the canvas flap to reveal the bronze burner. "At least we still have a way of inflating the balloon."

"That is good news." I looked over the parts of the crippled ship.

"Gather the wing sails, ropes, and any wood that is not damaged."

"This might work, Mr. Singh."

"If anyone can make her fly, we can."

For the next few hours, by firelight, as we pieced together a jigsaw puzzle of parts, Mr. Singh and I tell Owethu about the battle in London last year. Genevieve didn't contribute; she only stared at the dancing flames. Not even the hint of a smile crossed her face when I mentioned her using the Bronze Knight to rip the heart out of the Iron Horseman last year.

Once we'd finished crafting our makeshift aircraft, with a grand arcing gesture, I said, "We christen this vessel the Kite Flinger." One of the winglets dropped to the ground. "It will be a miracle if we don't plummet from the sky."

"That does not inspire confidence, Alexander," Owethu stated.

"I can fling us into the sky. How long we stay there …" Mr. Singh shrugged.

Genevieve opened her locket and stared at the image inside. I knew she was thinking about her mother. I'd seen the look before when the baron's life was in danger. She stood and slipped off through the ruins. With Mr. Singh re-checking every connection, I went to find her. I wandered over to a crumbled wall. She sat on the base of a toppled column looking out at the castle across the valley.

"There has to be an explanation," I said as I dropped on one of the column drums.

"This must be some sinister plot, but for how long? My parents fought the Knights of the Golden Circle for years. Was my mother part of this … all along?" She looked at me as if I could give her the answer.

"From what you've said about her, I can't believe

that."

She shook her head as if trying to make sense of it. "My mother mysteriously returns … and is an assassin for the Golden Circle?"

"We'll figure out what's really going on."

"I will make her tell me when next we meet …" She swiped her eyes to whisk away any tears before they fell. "My heart can't survive losing her again."

We sat in silence. I wanted to tell her it would be okay, but in truth I had no idea what the future held. Every time I tried to wrap my mind around the diabolical plans of the Knights of the Golden Circle, I'd blow a steam pipe and it all jumbled back together.

I extended my hand. "Let's go back to the fire and get warm."

She nodded and slipped her fingers through mine. I sat by the fire with her beside me. A cool winter breeze whipped the flames about, and Genevieve curled up against me. I pulled her close, wrapping my arm around her. Rodin coiled up between us.

Mr. Singh stepped off. "I'll take watch."

I woke suddenly with two aches. One in my shoulder where Genevieve still lay against me. The other, my gut, twisting into knots. Danger. I stiffened.

Genevieve sat up and looked at me. "Trouble?"

Mr. Singh ran into the alcove. "Several men on horseback, riding out of the castle. Heading this way."

I got up and helped Genevieve to her feet. We peaked through one of the openings in the dilapidated cathedral. A line of horses charged toward us across the broad valley. I turned to her. "That is more than we can handle."

"Oh no. The Black Freighter is taking off." She pointed toward the castle as the airship rose above the stone.

We turned back to see Owethu and Mr. Singh prepping our creation.

"We don't have much time, Mr. Singh."

As Mr. Singh lit the burner and inflated the balloon, the craft started to take shape, and my confidence grew. Struts now secured the balloon above us,

and the kite sail was ready to unfurl.

Still, the ship looked rickety. "Do you think she'll hold together, Mr. Singh?"

"Of course," he shrugged and chuckled. "But the real question, is, for how long."

"They're getting away," Genevieve said, "and the...."

"Just a moment longer, milady." Mr. Singh tightened a rope as Owethu continued to stoke the fire in the burner with each exhale.

I turned back around to find the Knights of Golden Circle, halfway across the valley. I'd never felt more like a castle guard in my life. Pivoting to the Kite Flinger, I saw the balloon was almost taut, and Mr. Singh was testing his controls. Moments later, thick cables shot over the ruins. Soon a mesh of wires above prevented our escape.

Owethu joined me and Genevieve at the edge of the wall. The front ranks of KGC cavalry surrounded us, as the rest formed up in lines to the south. A soldier, his sword drawn, called out, "*Renoncer, Templar racaille.*"

"He wants us to surrender," I said.

Owethu asked, "What do we do now?"

"I don't know." My heart sank in my chest. "We can't fight that many soldiers, and now, we can't fly."

Genevieve reached over and grabbed her sword that rested against the wall. Pulling the belt through the buckle, she secured the sheath, and snarled, "He left off the part where they called us scum."

We laughed, but Mr. Singh, still filling the balloon, shouted, "Almost ready."

The soldier called out again, and I could hear them debating how best to strike.

Genevieve drew her saber. "We're out of time."

130

I heard the soldier yell, *"Charge de cathedrale!"* The order had been given. In moments, we would be surrounded, or worse, they'd charge in and cut us down. The thought of dying here on consecrated ground didn't appeal to me. Everything inside me screamed to run away, but there was nowhere to go, and if we fled, all of this would have been for nothing. I had to stop Kannard. I pulled the Thumper from my belt and we all retreated into the center of the cathedral, far from the doors, amongst the pews for protection. I steeled myself for the sound of hooves galloping toward us.

"Listen!" Genevieve gasped. The sound of hooves drummed against the crumbling walls around us, but in the distance, we heard thunder, and then a trumpet blared.

Genevieve laughed. Then she started pounding my shoulder with her fist. She rushed over to a crumbled wall. "Templars! … On metal steeds."

"What?" I darted to her side.

Cresting the ridge to the east, a long line of silver horses, with the rising sun behind them, swarmed down into the valley. They shook the ground as their dazzling hooves tossed clods of grass in their wake. Two knights, each in the white tunics and chain mail of the Templar Knights, rode atop one silver steed. Once they were within range, small cannons slid out the steed's chest and fired upon the soldiers. Explosions tore the ground around the cathedral, and disrupted the ranks of the KGC cavalry. At a full gallop, the Templar's silver steeds plowed through the enemy, knocking the enemy cavalry from their horses, crushing the men, their horses galloping back to the castle, leaving the soldiers surrounded and trapped within the Templers ranks.

"They've done it!" I cried.

As Mr. Singh and Owethu finished prepping the craft, Genevieve and I stepped out to face the only lone rider on a silver steed as he approached the cathedral. He appeared as nothing more than a shadow, with the morning sun behind him.

I shielded my eyes from the gleaming sleek silver steed as it continued to approach, hoping to see the knight who'd seized victory and rescued us. The darkness held and I only saw the outline of a figure with his hand raised. As horse and rider entered the ruins, the shadows disappeared, revealing Eustache de Moley.

My heart soared. "Eustache!" I knew a more formal greeting was the custom, but I couldn't believe my eyes. My friend was alive. I rushed forward. "You're alive!"

Eustache smiled and dismounted. "I'm a Templar, death is nothing more than a return to god, and my work is not yet done." He made a cross over his heart. "Surely, you didn't think that Four Thieves Potion was the only little treasure I had developed."

"But I saw Hendrix stab you."

"And it hurt a great deal."

"I'm just glad you are okay."

"Me as well." He turned to Genevieve, who stood with the grace of a noblewoman. "Milady, it is a pleasure to see you again."

She curtsied, and he bowed. "Thank you, but it is I who must express my joy at seeing you. We feared you had saved my father's life at the cost of your own. A price too high; but I owe you everything for returning him to me."

"It was nothing more than my duty, milady." Eustache nodded. "And it is a price I would have paid gladly. Thankfully, the fates have another plan for us."

"Thank you for saving us," I said, then pointed at the pieced-together airship. "We'd never have escaped the KGC without your intervention."

"What is that?" Eustache asked, pointing to the airship.

"The remains of our Kite Skipper." I smiled proud that she was still airworthy. At least I hoped she was.

"The remains?"

Genevieve smiled. "They shot us from the sky, but Mr. Singh here, can fly anything. Isn't that what Captain Baldarich's always saying?"

Mr. Singh chuckled, "Aye, 'tis true."

Eustache smiled and grabbed the reins of his steed. "Then you must get going. Follow them. My knights and I will storm the castle. I shall tell the baron you all are well, and where you have gone."

"But the ropes," Owethu pointed to the cables crisscrossing above. "We cannot fly from here."

"I'll deal with this web." Eustache jumped back on his horse. "God speed to you all."

"Wait. You should come with us." I reached out for him but quickly drew back. Pleading for his help seemed unbefitting a knight. Eustache was an important member of the Templar Order, and even in times like these, protocol must be maintained.

"Master Alexander, I have the utmost confidence in you. It is my duty to inform the others. Now go!" He pulled on the reins and the silver steed leapt atop a large cut block of stone, reared on his hind legs, and then sprang over a fallen wall, landing on top of a column no longer supporting the ceiling. When Eustache twisted the pommel, two spinning saw blades emerged from

the silver steed's shoulders. He pulled back the reins
and commanded the silver steed to leap upward, cutting
through the cables. When the horse landed, it felt as if
a monumental earthquake erupted. Eustache continued
toward the castle without looking back.

With open skies now above, we strapped ourselves
into the contraption, and with a strong gust of wind, the
aircraft soared out of the cathedral. Mr. Singh pulled a
strap releasing the kite sail, which pillowed in the stiff
breeze and drew us up into the clouds. Mr. Singh steadied
our vessel with the kitesail and winglets. It was good
to be in the sky again, and the warm winds from the
Mediterranean ended the stinging cold.

As the wind subsided, though, the craft began a
swift descent.

"What is happening?" I grabbed the struts as the pit
of my stomach suddenly pushed up against my lungs.

Mr. Singh pulled on the ropes. "There's not enough
hot air to keep us buoyant." Being the sailor he was, he
managed to scoop enough of the wind with the kitesail
and push us forward.

We cruised into a wind stream and it pulled us along
like a boat in a river. Mr. Singh kept us on the leading
edge at top speed and darted through cloudbanks. Ahead
of us, the Black Freighter chugged along, puffing black
smoke and leaving a perfect trail.

As the day continued, Mr. Singh used air currents
to soar high above the Black Freighter, and then
glide downward until we dipped below the airship. I
worried about being seen, but soon realized Mr. Singh's
navigational expertise prevented that. They'd need a really
good eye and perfect timing to see us.

We followed the Black Freighter to the coast and

then out over the Mediterranean Sea. My worries about the wind dying down exploded. Had trouble happened over land, Mr. Singh would have dropped us gently to the ground. But now, if the wind failed, we would plunge into sea, never to be found.

The Black Freighter pulled away, and as I feared, the wind changed direction over the water and we began to slow down. I prepared myself to get wet.

I pivoted to see how far from land we were, and saw a familiar dot in the sky. An airship soared far behind us, but even from here I could tell it was a dual-color, aero-dirigible. My heart soared. "I think the Sparrowhawk is behind us."

Everyone peered over their shoulders at the airship. Genevieve pulled Rodin close and whispered in his ear. He spread his wings and soared off toward the airship, quickly lost among the clouds and endless blue sky.

Moments later, as a current of wind rushed beneath us, Mr. Singh pulled back on the ropes of the kite sail to take us higher into the sky. As the Sparrowhawk soared up underneath the Kite Flinger, Mr. Singh pulled back hard on the ropes and we smashed down on the aero-dirigible. The broken wood struts of our makeshift craft slid along the taut canvas hull of the airship. He quickly let one rope slip through his hand and the kitesail lost its shape and waffled in the wind, finally falling flat. The balloon of our craft rippled as it deflated. We hurriedly untied ourselves and tumbled onto the Sparrowhawk. Mr. Singh grabbed a corner of the kitesail and quickly rolled it up.

I kissed the canvas of the Sparrowhawk as its top hatch flipped open. Hunter climbed out, followed by a couple of crewmen. They hooked lines onto our belts, and led us one by one back to the hatch. Three more men gathered the pieces of our craft to bring inside.

As I peered down into the open hatch, I saw my father's stern expression. Alongside him, the baron and the captain stared back at me, too. I pulled back, no longer wanting to climb inside. I wondered if a plunge into the ocean wouldn't have been easier.

Mr. Singh nudged me toward the ladder of the open hatch. Reluctantly, I descended, knowing that each rung plunged me deeper into trouble. I wanted to climb back up but Mr. Singh was already on the rung above me. I jumped off, the heel of my boot clanging the metal grating of the floor. The clatter sent a chill through my body.

My father's voice prickled my skin, "Alexander. Over here, please."

I stepped through the crowd of stern faces, until I caught a glimpse of the captain. He smiled and winked. My expression didn't change, but inside, my heart soared. The grounding I was certain to get would be worth it. We chased our enemies across all of France by ourselves, and even after being shot down, we'd persevered. We reconnected with the Sparrowhawk, and no one got hurt. No, this wasn't a time for scolding. This was a time of celebration.

Eustache stepped through the crowd and extended his hand to me. I shook it and he patted me on the back. He

stepped off toward Genevieve and her father.

My father stepped to far side of the ship, and I stepped confidently up to him. I stood straight and proud, refusing to allow his harsh stare to wither me. I resisted. I stood my ground.

"Alexander," My father began. He clasped his hands behind him. "Leaving the Sparrowhawk during a battle … without my permission … was foolhardy. Not to mention taking to the skies in that makeshift craft. You could have been …" My father snatched me close and his hot breath pushed through my hair. "I'm so glad you're alive." He pulled away from me, his eyes brimming with tears, and said, "Great work."

I froze. Obviously, I heard him in error. He'd never once in my life told me I'd done anything great. Even after arriving at Eton, when I'd aced one of the tests meant for his students. Instead of telling me I'd gotten them all right he said, 'I guess I need to rewrite it'.

Eventually, I managed a, "Glad to be back on board, sir."

I looked around and searched for Genevieve. She was on the arm of her father. Rodin clung to the baron's *aiguillette* atop his shoulder.

Mr. Singh was warmly greeted by Captain Baldarich and the crew. "That, Mr. Singh, was a right bit of flying there. I doubt that *craft* would have held up much longer."

"Long enough, Captain," Mr. Singh said with a smile.

"Yes." Baldarich slapped his back and pulled him off. "In celebration, we'll have Gustav fix something very sweet for dinner tonight."

My father pulled my attention back to him with a hand on my shoulder, "What did I just say?"

I stared at him, blank. I had no idea. I'd been focused on Genevieve, Mr. Singh, and Owethu. My newest friend was in the least amount of trouble. His father embraced him and that was it. They'd already headed off to the bridge with the rest of the crew. I was the one still under interrogation from my father. "Ummm."

"Try not to run off again."

"No, sir. I mean yessir. I will."

He ruffled my hair and we followed the others toward the bridge. As we entered, our allies stood around the map table. Captain Baldarich manipulated two bronze mechanical arms to separate positions over the sea.

"This is new," I said. "What is it?"

Baldarich pointed. "This arm keeps track of the Sparrowhawk's position on the map. The other I set to the Black Freighter's position. Then we just have to make a few adjustments along the way. The Tinkerer's gift for the help we rendered in London."

"Fascinating." I leaned in, starring at the intricate handiwork of the Templar's engineer.

"He called it the Arial Tracking Dial," Baldarich said as he set our position just off the coast of the Mediterranean. I thought we'd made it further, but then he adjusted the second arm in front of the other about an inch apart.

Confidence surged within me. Looking at the dot marked London, we'd tracked Hendrix and his goons across all of France. I wondered how far was the distance between where we were now and London? The key was written in German, but showed an inch was about ten kilometers. I smiled.

"Alexander, keep an eye on the Tracking Dial and

make sure this contraption follows their movements," the captain said. He ran his fingers through his distinctive bushy mustache that continued across his cheek to his sideburns.

I saluted, "Aye, aye captain."

Using a previous point marked on the map, Baldarich laid the tip of the ruler down, and drew two lines angled like a cone, including much of the Egyptian coast. One city dot sat in about the middle of the area. "They'll make landfall here."

My father studied the map. "That's a massive area, Captain. And it encompasses delta and desert. They could be going anywhere."

"They can't keep to the skies," the baron injected. "The Templar Air Corp would too easily spot them. I'd put my money on Alexandria. They could doubtless slip through the large crowds."

The captain leaned over the table, "Makes sense. They can escape by auto, train, camel, horse, or boat. We'll have to keep a close eye on them."

The baron ran his finger down the map. "We will hunt them through Egypt. I have enough contacts that they won't be able to slip by. Captain, please escort the children back to London."

Genevieve put her hands on her hips, "Father, I must protest."

"I'll not hear it. I thank you for all you've done, but this is not the place for the three of you. Mrs. Hinderman will—"

"I will not be sent back to my governess."

"Enough," the baron said as he turned his attention back to the captain. Baldarich just nodded and the three men continued discussing what to do once they reached the coast, as if the decision had been made. This time, I remained silent as a tense mood settled around us.

I pulled back from the table and stared around the baron to see Genevieve's reaction to his dismissive tone. She'd crossed her arms, her chin stuck out, and her eyes were fixed elsewhere, like an unconcerned, perfect aristocrat. Watching her, she periodically side-glanced back to the map, cocking her head to hear better. Yep. She was anything but disengaged.

Owethu, tapped my shoulder and gestured for me to follow him. I checked my father, who hovered over the map with the captain and baron, and slipped over with Owethu. He leaned in and whispered, "With all the equipment we saw, they will travel by boat or train."

"How do you know?"

"Camels and horses could never carry such heavy equipment, and the desert is no place for a car."

Everything he said made sense. I knew the Templars would have them all covered, but we could search those two places and continue tracking the lady assassin. Now, we just had to figure how to get *off* the airship.

Dinner smelled amazing and drew me to the galley. We were all invited to sit with the captain, so we all squeezed in around the table. My stomach growled wondering what feast Gustav would create. With my father on one side of me and Owethu on the other, I had enough room, but didn't see Genevieve. She and the baron were the last to enter.

Gustav burst in with platters in each hand. The rotund chef spun gracefully on his heel, "I have pretzel bread." He set down a plate stacked with long dark breadsticks. "And some of my finest spiced potatoes."

My mouth watered. Gustav disappeared and reappeared with a tray stacked high with sausages that smelled divine. He set it down with a large three-pronged fork, and quickly returned with a steaming bowl of cabbage. Gustav winked at me, "May I present the best sausages in the sky. Only the fatherland has better sauerkraut."

"It's true," the captain said with a playful smile. "The night I met him, he served his sauerkraut and sausage. The Kaiser said it was the best he'd ever tasted, so, of course, I knew I had to steal him away."

It had been ages since I had eaten so well. I couldn't stop shoveling the feast into my mouth, and Gustav kept bringing out more. I think my father said I should slow down, but I wasn't going to stop until I was so stuffed, they'd have to roll me out of there.

Soon the crew cleared out, leaving the captain and the rest of us talking around the table. Usually this would be the part I most wanted to escape from, but sitting here meant I could continue to pick from the platters. If nothing else, I could listen to conversation.

Eustache pivoted. "Baron, you spent the last year in Egypt. Surely you heard something about the Knights of the Golden Circle."

"Nothing, which I found unusual." The baron rubbed his hands together. "I spent a great deal of time investigating subversive groups and threats to the crown. Never once did I run into one of their agents."

My father pulled off his glasses to clean the lenses. "Odd; perhaps Egypt is not their final stop."

Chief Zwelethu added, "If it is the Zulu they are after, then southern Africa is what they seek."

The baron's hand went to his chin. "What could be

in Africa? An even older civilization?"

The captain pointed to the baron. "So, why were you in Egypt? Besides getting better."

"I must remain silent on that, but I can say we were tracking down several threats to Her Majesty's interests." The baron lifted his glass and finished the rest of his port.

"What about your crew, Captain? What prizes have you taken recently?"

The captain threw his head back and bellowed. "We've been raiding several nations' airships throughout the Mediterranean Sea."

"Has business been good?" My father asked.

"We might have made a few more enemies in the last year," the captain chuckled, "but our spoils have been good. Any news to share about our friends?"

The baron shook his head, "No, we've had no news on the Golden Circle, either."

My father pushed his glasses onto the bridge of his nose. "They were laying low until the attacks at Eton."

The captain slapped the table, waking those who'd grown lethargic from dinner. "So why have the vipers slithered out now?"

My father leaned back and stared at the table. "They were trying to stop those of us who were helping Her Majesty. McCafferty was a geologist; Cobblefield, an explorer and anthropologist."

"And you, Professor, a master of dead languages." The captain poured himself another glass of ale.

I shrugged. "Hendrix said they were cleaning up loose ends." All the adults turned to me, puzzled.

"There's something else." Genevieve searched my eyes, then dropped her head. "We learned who the assassin is. Well…," she lifted her gaze to the Chief and Owethu, "at least who it isn't."

The baron clasped her hand in both of his, "Genevieve? Who?"

"That woman who slithered out of the sands and joined you in Egypt."

The baron hadn't said a word as the Sparrowhawk descended toward the airdocks of Alexandria. Neither had Genevieve. They stepped into one of the cabins after dinner, and although their muffled voices could be heard, they hadn't said a word to anyone else.

Standing on the bridge, looking out the windows, I studied the city that Alexander the Great created, the place that bore our name. I had always wanted to visit; the great king had left after laying the foundation and only returned in death. Buried in a golden tomb within his city, the location lost to myth long ago. Now I was here. Only, I'd never imagined it would be in search of the Knights of the Golden Circle.

The city wrapped around the harbor, most of which appeared to be slipping into the sea. Not much of the original city remained. The treasures, like the great library of Alexandria and the temples where Cleopatra and Julius Caesar walked hand in hand, had been destroyed in antiquity. What remained was a city of minarets, a cosmopolitan of every culture in the world. I hadn't seen so

many different people in one place since we'd left New York.

My father came up behind me, "I wish we had more time. I'd love to show you some of the city."

"Me too," I said, "but don't worry, we're here for a more important reason than being a tourist."

"Too true."

The captain commanded, "Heinz, bring the ship in line with the airdocks and maintain a steady descent."

"Aye-Aye, Uncle," Heinz said, and the captain just shook his head.

Ignatius pivoted in his chair, turning from the wall of dials and meters in front of him. "Captain, pressure is building in engine three."

Baldarich flipped open one of the copper tubes in front of him. "Gears. What's going on down there?"

A voice echoed out of the tube, "Pressure's building, Captain."

"Are we going to make it to the ground?"

"I hope so."

"That's not the confidence I want to hear, Gears." The captain pinched his nose.

Baldarich pointed to the wall of dials. "Ignatius, if the engine redlines, shut it down. We'll just land a little hard." Ignatius nodded. The captain turned to the pilot. "Heinz, just get us down in one try. I don't think we'll get a second chance at this."

Heinz wiped his forehead and exhaled. "I'll try; Uncle, but we have some strong winds off the water."

The Sparrowhawk teetered toward one of the empty airship bays. Mooring arms reached out to grasp us as we settled into the embrace of iron girders. Everyone breathed a sigh of relief.

Captain Baldarich stood up. "Ignatius, shut everything down, and have Gears get in engine three, see what the trouble is, and sell off all the cargo we have onboard. I'm going to get some answers as the baron and professor head off to find metal man."

My father squeezed my shoulder and I looked up, "I will need to depart soon.

"I still want to come."

"I know, but it will be safer if you return to London with the captain. You've already done enough. A great job, really. Africa is a dangerous place, and I need to know you're safe."

Even though I had fought the German army and the Knights of the Golden Circle last year in London, for some reason that didn't matter anymore. I was seventeen; I would graduate soon and be a real man, but everyone kept treating me like a child. How was I supposed to become a knight if no one would let me near danger? I knew this fight was pointless, so I just nodded.

He squeezed my shoulder once more and departed. I stayed at the window gazing out at the city. The city didn't look dangerous. No more so than London. Yet, one thought kept cropping up: once my father and the baron were gone, Genevieve, myself, and Owethu could sneak away. If they wouldn't take us with them, we would go ourselves. Besides, we'd had better luck tracking the KGC than they had.

Gears' voice echoed out of the copper tube, "Captain, I got her shut down. She's all gunked up. I'm going to need some time for the engine to cool down and give her a good scrubbing."

Ignatius walked over and leaned into the tube. "Go ahead, Gears. I don't think the captain is leaving anytime soon."

Gears voice trailed off. "Dampen the fire boys, and someone get the water."

That gave me an idea. Without a word to the others on the bridge, I slipped off and rushed to find Genevieve. I knocked on the door of the cabin she shared with her father. The baron opened the door. Behind him, I found Genevieve sitting on her bed with her knees up and her arms wrapped around them. A scowl etched across her face. The baron nodded but returned to gathering the last of his things. I waved at Genevieve and she looked up. Her expression brightened, but I still saw the anguish in her eyes. I motioned for her to come out into the corridor.

"I wish you the best," Genevieve said to her father as she swung her legs over the edge of the bed.

The baron stopped and faced his daughter. "I will find her, Genevieve. I will stop this." He walked over to her, and as she stood, he clutched her tight.

She broke free from his grasp and ran out of the cabin.

I started to say something, but she ran past me to the ladder leading down to the gundeck. Rodin flew after her. Her father rushed out, releasing a soul crushing, "Genevieve…." He stopped when he saw me. He nodded, taking a moment to collect himself. "Keep an eye on her, will you? This bit about her mother has her understandably upset."

"Of course." I paused. I wanted to say more, but knew it wasn't the time. The baron patted his pockets and checked the blade within his cane. He gathered his belongings and walked off to the cargo doors and the gangplank.

I rushed downstairs to find Genevieve. My father expected me at the gangplank to say goodbye, but I needed to make certain she was all right. I checked the gundeck. The crew had already unloaded the cargo, so she didn't have many places to hide, but still, I couldn't find her. She could have already slipped off the ship, but a nagging in my gut said she was nearby. Our room.

I lightly knocked on the door and opened it slowly. "Genevieve, it's Alexander."

She sat on one of the crates with Rodin atop the pyramid of cannon balls beside her. Long bouncing locks of auburn hair covered her face. She reached up underneath her hair and wiped her eyes. I reached into my back pocket and pulled out a handkerchief. Extending my arm toward her, she reached out and took the cloth. I sat on the edge of my hammock, gripping the side, and wondering if she'd break the silence.

After a few minutes, I said, "I had a thought about getting off the ship."

"My father paid the crew to make sure I stayed on board. He's forbidden me from pursuing this any further."

"When has that ever stopped you—us—before?"

"He's thought of everything." Rodin jumped into her lap and stuck his head up through her locks. She rubbed the horned nubs on his head and sighed. "He's paid them to watch me while in port, and to ensure we depart immediately, so I can't escape."

I clapped both my hands on my knees. "Then I have some good news. We're not leaving right away. Gears has to scrub engine three before we can take off. Also, Captain Baldarich is already in the city."

She looked up at me. I could see the gears turning

in her mind.

"One day they'll understand we're ready, that we aren't children any longer. I mean, come on, we saved the earth last year." I kicked the deck with my boot. "I never did get to meet the queen."

"I'm sorry you couldn't attend the dinner at the palace."

"My dad said we shouldn't go." I ground my heel into the wooden floor.

She sighed and lowered her head. "I cannot defy my father. He made it very clear—I am not to go anywhere near that woman, or the Knights of the Golden Circle."

"He's just trying to protect your heart."

"*He* thinks that woman really is my mother. He's obsessed with her. When it comes to her, he can't think straight."

"This is tough on him, too."

She nodded. "I know." She sobbed, but choked back the tears, and turned her eyes to me. "Alexander, I know it's not her. It can't be."

My heart sank. Her pain was mine. I knew it all too well. I wanted nothing more than to see my mother one more time. But if it wasn't Genevieve's mother … the thought crushed me. A hot tear rushed down my cheek. "I'm so sorry. The Golden Circle can be so cruel."

"Alexander, you have … feelings. What does your gut tell you about her?"

I searched back when I'd encountered her outside my father's office. "I know she's the assassin who tried to kill my father—and us." I turned toward Genevieve, got up, and walked over to her. I took her hands in mine. "She may look like the picture in your locket, but she is nothing like the stories you've told me about your mother."

"Thank you, Alexander."

I patted my stomach. "My gut tells me we should go find them."

She laughed and her face lit up. Seeing her smile made my courage swell.

I stood up. Rodin took flight and landed on my shoulder. "Shall we, milady?" I bowed.

Genevieve pulled back her hair, and wrapped it in a bun. She stood up, smoothed out her coat, and curtsied. Genevieve took a deep breath. "Since I am being monitored by the crew, you'll need to tell Owethu, and gather the things we'll need."

"Get ready, but stay in your father's room. That will make them think you aren't leaving." I rubbed Rodin's head. "You're coming with me?"

The little dragon nodded. With regal grace, Genevieve walked out of the room. I waited several heartbeats and then stepped to the door. I poked my head out and looked her way. A crewman followed a few paces behind her. I waited until they climbed the ladder, and crossed the gundeck.

I stayed below as Owethu said goodbye to his father. I heard the chief, the baron, and my father on the deck above me. A sense of guilt washed over me as my father asked, "Where is Alexander?"

"Apologies, Professor, I asked him to look after Genevieve. She's not taking this well."

The baron's heavy boot steps echoed on the metal grating of the gangplank. "Come, we can waste no more time."

After hearing their footsteps subside, I rushed up and found Owethu coming toward the ladder. "Just the man I'm looking for." I pulled him close and whispered, "We're leaving." Without a word, he nodded. He followed me to our room on the gundeck. I gathered my things, which wasn't more than another set of clothes and the goggles I'd had around my neck since the Kite Flinger crashed. The dark lenses would be great for the dessert. I already wore my Thumper on my belt.

I needed a pair of pants, though, something thinner than my wool trousers. At least a pair that wasn't striped. I turned to Owethu who

stared down at his suit.

"My father only brought my English suits and Eton uniform." Owethu shook his head, "This will not be good in the desert."

"No, it won't. There has to be something around; this is the equipment room." I pulled back a tarp and found a pile of discarded clothes, helmets, and gear. "Maybe there is something in this stuff we can borrow."

We picked through and I saw a patched pair of pants. Putting them on, I used my belt to tighten the waist. I pulled the leather strap out of my bag and wound it around my leg, my waist and chest, all the way to one shoulder. No longer choked by starched collars, or bound in layered wool, I was free. With my Thumper strapped to me, I slipped on a leather jacket and wrapped the dark brass goggles around my forehead. I started to feel like myself again.

Owethu pulled out a pair of khakis overalls. It was easy to see they were two sizes too big for him, but after slipping into them, he tightened the straps and made it work by using a wide leather belt to gather everything together. He unsnapped his white button-down shirt and pulled at the neck. "Better," he said. Then we returned to digging in the pile.

I dug out two leather pouches. I fixed the smaller one in the strap and secured it to the holster I made last year for my Thumper, and hooked the biggest pouch on my other hip.

Owethu snapped up proudly holding a white pith helmet. He plopped it on his head. "Now, I am ready."

I chuckled.

"I have always wanted one," he said, adjusting the helmet and pulling the brass goggles down from the brim and centering them over his eyes. "My brother will be jealous."

"That it is one fine hat." I bowed like a gentleman. "I didn't know you had brothers, any sisters?"

"Yes, two of each, but my younger brother has been trying to get one of these." Owethu adjusted the pith helmet.

"Shall we call on the lady? I believe we have a boat or train to catch."

Owethu nodded. We walked out onto the gundeck and right into Mr. Singh.

The teenage Sikh stood with his hands on his hips, and a stern but upturned smirk on his face. Several *chakram* ringed the folds of his turban. Smaller ones adorned his wrists. His *shamshir* hung from his side, along with a double-barrel Katar dagger. A long, skinny bag was slung over one shoulder and lay diagonally across his back. "Not leaving without me, I hope."

"You're not here to stop us?" I cocked my head to the side. A big grin spread across my face. "The team is back together."

"I'm here because it is no secret what you're about to do."

"The baron hired you."

Indihar nodded with a bright smile.

"He doesn't trust us at all." I looked at Owethu, who shrugged. "Well, let's keep it between us. Don't tell Genevieve."

Genevieve' s voice hit me from behind. "Too late."

I scrunched my shoulders. We turned to see her step down the ladder wearing tight, white pants and a long, flowing tunic. She looked more like a desert raider than a British noblewoman. She looked stunning.

Her silver saber with the inlaid lapis-lazuli handle hung from one of several belts wrapped around her waist. "I expected as much. We don't have the best track record of doing what we're told."

"Wow, you look … I mean, that is really great … desert attire." My face burned red.

She curtsied and beamed. "Are we ready?"

"Wait, where is the crewman who was following you?" I peered around her to see if anyone else came down.

"Oh, him? I locked him in my quarters," she said, flipping her wrist as if it were nothing. "But we do need to leave quickly, in case someone discovers him."

Mr. Singh leaned in, "Then we should go before Ignatius finds us."

Owethu nodded and asked, "How do we get out of here when the gangplank is being watched?"

"This way." Mr. Singh led us to the aft section of the gundeck. He unhooked the pin of an unused hatch and propped it open with a scrap of wood. "It is only a short drop to the dock."

"Astounding." I didn't hesitate. I slid my legs through, held onto the edge of the opening, dangling for a moment before I dropped to the metal grating below.

Genevieve landed next to me and Owethu quickly followed. I looked around to see if anyone was paying attention, but most of the dockworkers and other crewman kept their focus on the crowd. Mr. Singh joined us and we slipped off into the city.

As we ran down an alley, I stopped abruptly and held up my hands, "Wait, what is our plan? Do we head to the boat docks or to the train yard?"

Owethu nodded. "Trains are the fastest way to

travel."

Mr. Singh said, "Heavy equipment usually travels by ship."

Genevieve pointed toward the setting sun, "The ships are that way, and the train yard is beyond them. I'd say geography has set our path."

"So, it has. Let's go." I motioned and everyone followed. "Remember, we're looking for Hendrix or Kannard."

Genevieve led us along the wide thoroughfare to the line of canvas-covered masts. Mr. Singh and Owethu scoured the vast jumble of small open vessels, while she and I slipped onto the large paddlewheel steamer. We checked all three decks before they chased us off, but I knew they weren't onboard. No heavy equipment.

When we regrouped, we each shook our head. No luck.

Next, Genevieve led us toward the train yard. Thick puffs of smoke floated above the crowd, marking our destination. Oil, coal, and incense assaulted my nose as we grew closer.

Through the flurry of goodbyes uttered in every language of the continent, and amidst the screech of grinding wheels on metal tracks, I wondered how we'd know which train to board.

"They could be on any one of these," I said.

Mr. Singh craned his neck to see over the people. "Look for the equipment."

"I have something that might help." Genevieve reached into her shoulder bag and pulled out a small round contraption, like a compass, but with two arms. "It's a divining compass. I brought it in case we need to find water."

"How is that going to help us?"

"Divining rods can find all kinds of things—water, metals, oil, buried objects, and maybe even horsemen hearts. If they have one, I think I can find it."

"Fascinating." I bent over her arm to get a better view of the device. "How does it work?"

"The divining rods come out like so." With her thumb, she slid a latch sideways. Two silver arms connected to the device at one end, rose upward out of the face. The arms pointed in opposite directions. "Now, I focus my mind on what I want to find." She perched the device on her fingertips and raised it in front of her as she walked forward. "When you discover what it is you're looking for, the arms cross over one another.

As I checked the first few trains and Genevieve studied the compass, nothing moved; the arms didn't even twitch. Then, as we crossed the next set of tracks to check more cars, the arms of the compass swung together.

Genevieve stopped and backed up until the arms uncrossed, and then walking toward the tracks again, she stopped when the divining rods crossed over one another again, marking her find.

She looked up at the three of us. "I think this is it."

I walked along the tracks, glancing into each car. On the other side of the train, I saw soldiers loading the last of the large crates into a car. Hendrix stepped out, and looked over the cargo. I waved all of them to me and pointed. "There they are."

Mr. Singh whispered, "We should find the baron and tell him about the train."

A whistle blew out a white jet of steam and the train screeched to life. Without a word, we all knew what to do. We hurried to the last car of the train. I checked to see where the conductor stood. He was securing the last of the doors and locking them in place. I motioned toward the train and we all jumped on board. Genevieve selected an unoccupied cabin near the back of the car for us to hide in.

The engine chugged to life as the wheels squealed and rolled forward. Slowly, as we pulled out of the station, I peered out the side window and saw my father, the baron, the chief, and Eustache. They were running up and down the platforms studying every train.

My father and I locked eyes. His mouth dropped as he reached out his hand. He ran after the train, but the station platform dropped off, ending his chase. The baron and the others rushed up to his side and stood staring as we departed.

I didn't know what to do. We were already moving.

My father pointed toward the train, saying something to the others. I waved.

I pulled away from the window. "We are in so much trouble." Mr. Singh and Owethu rushed forward and peered out of the glass. "So, now what do we do?" I asked.

Genevieve sat straight up. "We find them, follow them, and stop their evil plan."

"Cairo is only a few hours by train, so we cannot wait too long, but we should pause and let them get comfortable," Owethu said.

I sat down beside Genevieve. "Owethu is right. They will still be on alert as we pull away from the station, especially if they saw my father and the others."

"So, we wait." Mr. Singh said.

Owethu leaned against the wall as Mr. Singh sat cross-legged, meditating. Genevieve and Rodin curled up beside me. At first her shoulder barely touched mine, the gentle contact sending electricity through me. As if it were the most natural thing for her to do, she leaned firmly against me, her hair brushing against my cheek. She scratched Rodin's head, who squeezed into the warm spot between us. Her scent, even after

several days on the road, still retained a hint of roses. She reminded me of the tales of the Saints; the holiest of people were said to never be subject to the corruption of life. Never getting dirty, smelling foul, or possessing any of the other bedeviling curses of the body. She was perfect, an angel among we simple dirt dwellers.

After several joyous moments I hoped would never end, my stomach wretched. I tensed at the pain. Sensing my change, Genevieve sat up and looked at me, worry in her eyes. Mr. Singh snapped out of his meditation and Owethu twisted his head toward the corridor. We'd pulled the curtain closed on the cabin door, but I saw movement through the folds.

Genevieve put Rodin on her shoulder and slipped her hand to the silver hilt of her saber. I pulled the Thumper out of its holster. The weight of the metal baton eased the rapid beating of my heart. I slowly opened the breach to load a percussion cap. Sliding the top part of the baton back into place, I raised it toward the door.

Mr. Singh slid over and crouched under the window in the door. He gently slid a finger against the curtain to widen the gap, and then let it slip back. "Soldiers," he mouthed. We all stood at ready. Even Rodin, who wiggled his long tail and stretched out his neck, ready to attack.

"I'll check the last of the cabins," the soldier said. "You go check the top of the train," he directed another.

A soldier kicked the first cabin door open. The thwack of the wooden door against the wall resonated into our cabin shaking us all. People screamed. The soldier apologized and moved to the next door. The one next to ours. All five of us stood, ready to pounce. My heart raced. Fear gripped me, but I would *not* freeze like

I had a year ago. I was a knight. Maybe not yet in name, but that didn't matter. I had the heart of a knight—the courage of a knight. I tightened my hold on the Thumper and pointed it at the door. The cool metal had warmed from my hand.

Footsteps approached. The handle turned and the curtain flew up as it swung open. The soldier hesitated. His eyes darted from my Thumper, to Owethu's fists, and then to Genevieve's sword. They grew even bigger when he spotted the small dragon on her shoulder.

The soldier stumbled back, trying to ready his weapon. Mr. Singh stepped from behind the door and pointed his double-barrel Katar dagger at him, stopping the soldier, who dropped his rifle. With his focus now on Mr. Singh, I stepped up and whacked the soldier on top of his head with my Thumper. I'd thought about using the concussion blast, but was worried it would make too much noise and alert more soldiers.

The soldier crumpled to the ground. We quickly pulled him inside the cabin, Genevieve closed the door, and Mr. Singh grabbed some cord out of his bag and tied him up.

Genevieve leaned against the door. "We have to go now, before they discover our friend here is missing."

"Agreed; but if we stay together, we'll be caught for certain. Mr. Singh, Owethu, why don't the two of you climb on top of the train and make your way to the engine. Maybe find a way to stop. Genevieve and I will find Hendrix and Kannard."

Mr. Singh nodded. "Find them don't fight them." Mr. Singh shook my hand and grabbed my shoulder before he followed Owethu out of the window.

I opened the cabin door and cautiously stepped out

into the corridor. Genevieve followed with Rodin craning his neck, watching our backs. We snuck forward to the door leading to the next car. Opening the outer door whipped my clothes against me; my hair flew in every direction as the warm, dry wind enveloped us. I stepped onto the narrow gangway and look down at the large iron couplings holding the cars together. The ground rushed by in blur underneath us.

"Watch your step," Genevieve called with a playful smile as she stepped out from the cabin behind me.

"Funny," I said with a chuckle.

A shadow passed overhead, then another. Owethu and Mr. Singh leapt over us and continued on the train.

I turned back to the railing enclosed gangway that prevented us from easily jumping between cars. The short set of steps leading down on either side of the train was of little help, either. Nothing left to do but climb over the railing and jump over to the next landing. As the wheels clacked and screeched below, and the train jerked back and forth, my nerves rattled. I took a deep breath, climbed over the railing, and leapt across to the other gangway. Without any hesitation, Genevieve jumped right after me, and Rodin followed.

Cautiously, we entered the car. We slinked along the corridor, stopping before each cabin and quickly glancing in. So far, so good. Most were lost in their own world as we sped toward Cairo.

The next car held nothing but rows of seats filled with travelers of many different nationalities. There were even two goats. I shoved my Thumper back into its holster and Genevieve held her sword along her side. Trying to hide our nervousness and fear behind the mask of anonymity, we strode with confidence down the center aisle. As long as no one recognized us, we could move without worry. Fortunately, no one paid attention to us as we made our way through to the other end of the train car.

Beyond, the following car held many of the crates we'd seen being loaded into an airship in France. We slipped between the stacked boxes. I wondered what might be inside, but we didn't have time to search them. Besides, I already knew most held the equipment the Golden Circle was transporting deeper into southern Africa.

Stepping out of the car onto the platform, we jumped over the next coupling. I slowly approached the window and peered inside. Soldiers stood guard in the corridor of the cabin car. I spun around and pressed my body alongside the door, and pulled Genevieve beside me. "I think we found them."

Genevieve stepped in front of me, leaned over, and gave a quick glance through the window. "But how do we get in?"

I shook my head. "We'll never get through with those guards."

"Another way around then."

I grabbed the edge of the railing to my right and leaned out. The train curved around a bend in the track, but my attention turned to the car in front of me. A small ledge formed by the decorative molding on the outside of the car ran under all the windows. I pushed myself back against the train wall. "I've got it." I pointed my thumb to the outside of the car. "We shimmy along the molding."

Genevieve leaned over the side and snapped back against the train car. "Are you insane?"

"It'll be just like before, when we escaped your

house and climbed down the drain spout."

"That ledge was much wider, and not bouncing about."

"Think of it as fun," I said as I slung my foot up over the railing. As I slid my foot onto the molding, I grabbed hold of a small, metal pipe secured just beneath the roof by brass brackets. The toes of my shoes barely fit on the narrow ledge, but it was just enough to slide sideways. I scooted toward the first window as Genevieve leaned over the railing.

She climbed over the railing and followed me. "These pointy-toe boots aren't helping me."

"Just take it slow," I forced out through my grinding teeth. My heart and mind both screamed for me to go back, but I couldn't let the fear freeze me. We had a job to do.

Sliding one foot over, I reached my hand along the rail, and then forced the other side of my body to catch up. After only a few feet, I was starting to agree with Genevieve. This may not have been the best idea.

Still, I pushed on. At the first window, I leaned sideways and looked through the glass.

The cabin was empty.

I turned my head toward Genevieve. "No one is inside. Come on; I'll check the next one." When I reached the edge of the second window, I peered into the cabin. A woman stood with her back to the window, her hands waving wildly at two men in front of her. Kannard. I couldn't see his face, but I knew it was him by the signet ring on his hand. The other man, Hendrix, shoved past the woman waving his bronze-plated arm before sitting down in a huff. I popped back from the window and my foot slipped. Genevieve grabbed my sleeve.

I gripped the overhead bar and reaffirmed my footing, nodding at Genevieve that I was all right. I motioned toward the window, and mouthed, *"In there."*

She gestured toward the previous cabin and moved back the way we came. Once at the first window, Genevieve released her grip on the pipe, and tried to pry the window open with one hand. No luck. As she awkwardly lifted her leg and wedged her foot to open the window, the train lurched, and both her feet slipped off the molding. She dangled by one hand as the train rocked back and forth. Rodin grabbed her other hand and pulled, flapping his wings as hard as he could. I reached out to grab her, but she heaved herself up, grabbed the bar, and set her feet back on the molding. As if nothing had happened, she inched her way to the window and swung into the cabin.

I tumbled in after her and slid the window shut. Breathing a deep sigh of relief and flopping onto the seat next to her, I said, "I hope nobody heard that."

Genevieve reached into her bag and pulled out a small brass cone. Placing the larger end against the wall, she put her ear to the smaller end to listen to the conversation in the next cabin.

Rodin, on the luggage rack, his wings tucked behind him, watched Genevieve with a cocked head. As I slipped by her and moved toward the door, he focused on me.

I crept up to the cabin door and nudged the curtains aside, only to see the butt end of a rifle not more than a foot away from my face. I froze. Fortunately, the guard's back was to me and he was looking toward the other side of the train. When my heart beat again, I focused on the corridor. The soldier covered his mouth as he yawned. He shifted back and forth, and although I knew there was another soldier standing at the opposite end of the car, they didn't speak to each other. I closed the curtains, careful not to ruffle them, and slipped over by Genevieve.

She pointed to the wall. "Hendrix and Kannard are arguing."

"Your mom is in there, too."

Her face hardened,

"She is *not* my mother."

I kicked myself. "What are they arguing about?"

"I'm not certain," she whispered, "but I think it may be about Zerelda." She put her ear back against the cone.

I cupped my ear and leaned against the wall. The soft mumblings I heard in the next cabin became much clearer.

Lord Kannard's vile voice echoed against the wood. "Once we get this equipment in the south, we can get back on schedule."

Colonel Hendrix's gears squeaked as he stepped across the room. "Good, because we're getting too far behind."

"Don't worry, the horsemen will ride again."

"That ain't in doubt," Hendrix snarled, "but those Templers are meddling again. You didn't finish the job, and now they're more determined than ever to stop us."

A sultry voice spoke. "Ah, but *monsieur*, you're the one who changed the plan. If you'd have let me do it my way, they'd all be dead by now."

Hendrix huffed. "We kill the dad, and the kid will never join us."

I pulled back from the wall. That kid could only be me. Hendrix still wanted me to be horseman. I looked over at Genevieve, but she held her ear to the cone and faced the other way. I pressed back against the wooden panel.

"Enough of your chatter," Kannard said. "Anyone who follows us now is a fool. A dead fool."

"We need gold to complete the circle—and to seek revenge for my country." Hendrix smacked the wall, causing Genevieve and I to jump back.

"We need power," Kannard sneered.

"Gold is power," Hendrix said.

"The Hearts are true power. Once the digging is done, we will have everything we need."

"Still, the Zulu remain a thorn in our side."

"Those savages will be dealt with when we arrive, and the British certainly won't help them after the wars." Kannard chuckled, "Plus, the only man who knew our plan is dead."

"No," Hendrix snapped, "the professor and his brat."

Me?

"Maybe they'll figure it out, but it will be too late when they do, and the horsemen will destroy them."

"I still think we need the boy, Alexander. He *must* accept his place at our side."

"Choose another," Kannard said.

"Never," Hendrix yelled.

Kannard shook his head. "He fought against us; he'll never ride with us."

"He is the *key*. If Alexander rides, our victory is assured."

I pulled back and dropped down onto the bench. My heart ached from their words. I'd assumed they wanted me last year because I was some kind of pawn to play against the Templars. But now it sounded like destiny. Whichever side I choose would be the winner. I exhaled heavily, trying to force the pressure out of my body, but the tension in my muscles only strengthened. They wanted to kill my father. Everyone I cared about. My shoulders slumped, but then I thought, if I was that much of a threat to their plans, I must be doing something right.

"I shouldn't have come … what if that is what they

have been planning all along?"

Genevieve turned and sat down beside me. "You've already faced that demon, and you said no. You will have the strength to do so again."

"But why me?"

"You're a man of talent, Alexander. You are not cast into a noble class. Your actions define you, not your birthright."

She was right. She, on the other hand, was defined by her birthright. A destiny decided. A gilded cage she could never escape.

Genevieve and I sat in silence while I ran my fingers through my hair, and my mind raced over Hendrix's words. He still wanted me to be a horseman.

She whispered, "Do you think Mr. Singh and Owethu have made it to the engine yet?" Before I could answer, a distinctive *thunk* reverberated across the top of the train. The entire train lurched. Genevieve gripped one of the armrests. "I don't think that's Mr. Singh and Owethu."

Stomping feet thundered in the hall as someone ran past our car and pounded on the door to Kannard and Hendrix's cabin. I jumped up and ran toward the door and lifted the curtain. Kannard stepped out of his cabin and snarled at the solider. "What is this disruption?"

"Sir, an aero-dirigible has latched onto the train with grappler cables."

"What?" Kannard gasped.

I motioned to the roof, and formed my hands to resemble an airship. Genevieve smiled.

Hendrix stormed

into the corridor. "Damn them Templars! Battle stations. Prepare to repel our boarders." He and several soldiers rushed down the corridor to the front of the train.

Kannard boomed orders to the other soldiers. "The rest of you stay here. Shoot anyone you don't know." Kannard turned toward the inside of his cabin and said, "You stay here as well, my dear. You're my insurance."

"Insurance?" I repeated.

Genevieve shrugged. "We should get out of here."

"Agreed." I rushed to the window and scanned the sky, but no Sparrowhawk. From inside the cabin, though much of the sky couldn't be seen.

As I opened the window, a soldier pounded on our cabin door. Genevieve scampered past me through the opening and I quickly followed. As we slid our way along the molding to the end of the car, the sky above us darkened. I looked up. The Sparrowhawk! Two ropes dangled below the vessel and connected to the top of a train car.

"Alexander, look out!" Genevieve yelled.

A soldier reached around from the end of the car. His fingertips brushed my shirt, but I scurried along the edge toward Genevieve. Beyond her, another soldier hung outside the cabin window. We were trapped.

Genevieve nudged me and pointed up. "Climb," she shouted.

The lady assassin stuck her head out the window of her cabin and locked eyes on us. Surprise lit up her face, but her expression quickly hardened and she climbed out onto the side of the train as well.

As Genevieve pulled herself up, I slid closer to her. She planted her foot on my shoulder and heaved up onto the top of the roof. She leaned down, grabbed the back of my shirt, and pulled me up.

Once on top, I pulled my goggles down, to keep the wind from burning my eyeballs. I followed the grappling lines up and saw Eustache and the baron zipline down the cable, landing on the car behind us. Surprise registered on their faces as we waved. Eustache shook his head and pointed behind us. I spun around as the lady assassin leapt up onto the roof.

I got to my feet, grabbed Genevieve by the arm, pulled her up, and we ran toward Eustache. Reaching the gap between the two cars, Genevieve screamed, "Jump!" She landed safely on top of the next car. I followed but as I flew through across the opening, a hand reached up and snagged my leg. I slammed forward onto the roof and rolled on my back. The lady assassin stood over me with her sword drawn, but her eyes remained fixed on Eustache and the baron. Lord Kannard climbed up and grabbed me by the collar. I struggled to get away, but he pressed a revolver against my head. I froze.

Yanking me to my feet, Kannard turned and backed up behind the lady assassin. Genevieve drew her saber, screaming in defiance. Her father rushed up behind her, with Eustache at his side. Seeing the Templar filled me with courage. I struggled trying to pull free. Lord Kannard wrapped his arm around me, pulling me against his chest. The metal breastplate under his clothes jammed hard against my back. "Hello *old friends*," he screamed over the wind. "That's far enough, else I shoot this kid." He pressed the gun into my temple and cocked the hammer.

Eustache stepped toward Kannard and yelled, "I can't say it's good to see you again, my *old friend.*"

"I'm surprised you left the estate."

Eustache's expression hardened, "Let Alexander go.

This isn't about him."

"You don't know what this is about," Kannard yelled. "You never did."

Eustache took another step. "I preserve the old ways, just as you once tried to do."

Kannard waved his gun and screamed, "The old ways … Ha. We are beings of power. Peace and freedom are fleeting; the universe is ours to command." Kannard extended his arm and fired at Eustache. The jarring train made aiming impossible, and, thankfully, he missed. "I guess you didn't get my message."

Eustache didn't flinch. "I got your message, right in the heart." He tore open his shirt and jacket revealing a gold plate over the left side of his chest with the symbols of the Templar Order. "My will is too strong; my purpose divine."

Genevieve jumped back over and swung her sword at the lady assassin, "Let him go," she sneered at the woman.

Kannard backed up, not taking his eyes off the baron, Genevieve, or Eustache. As the lady assassin dodged Genevieve's every strike, the baron yelled at his daughter, "Genevieve, get back over here."

Baron Kensington raised his hands, trying to calm everyone down.

Lord Kannard tightened his grip on my shirt, nearly pulling me down as he backed away. His grunting and breathing so quick, I thought he might burst like a steam pipe.

"Kannard, you can't get away!" the baron shouted. "More Templar forces are on the way. Soon you'll be outnumbered, and the train will be ours."

No sooner had the baron said this, a bronze-plated

arm smashed through the roof behind him. Colonel Hendrix pulled himself up, the sprockets and gears of his mechanical arms shifting and turning as the three-finger claw retracted into his sleeve, only to be replaced with a gleaming blade of sharpened steel. He raised his arm at the baron, who countered by drawing the blade from his cane.

Genevieve, still on the attack, thrust he saber forward at the lady assassin, her hair swirling like a whip in the wind. The lady assassin parried Genevieve's attack with a long thin dagger while circling around her and pushing Genevieve further away from her father. Eustache eyed the side of the train, and from the twitch in his step, I could tell he was about to act. Beside Eustache, the baron pivoted his head between Kannard, Hendrix, and the lady assassin, but his blade remained fixed on the colonel.

Everything around me, from the sound of the engine, to the whipping fabric of the baron's coat slowed down until the universe ticked by in seconds that lasted minutes. This was the moment, the moment Alexander the Great always looked for. I was the key to this standoff. Without me as hostage, Kannard would be vulnerable. Without me as hostage, they might surrender. I had to act.

I waited for Kannard to re-grip my shirt as he had been doing for the last several minutes. As his fingers opened, I reached down and yanked my Thumper from its holster. Pushing away from him I swung the Thumper and struck his gun hand. Kannard's face morphed from surprise to anger. His eyes burned with rage and he raised the gun at me. I aimed my Thumper at the gun and pushed the button. The percussion cap fired, sending the thick top end out like a piston as it slid back the blast of concussive force slammed into the gun and his hand.

Kannard screamed out and released his gun as the bones in his hand and wrist broke. The gun skittered off the side of the train.

Immediately, I ran toward the lady assassin and Genevieve. Eustache drew a palm pistol from his vest and fired at her. Genevieve continued thrusting her sword at the woman. The lady assassin flipped backward over me, landing several feet away. The baron, still fighting Hendrix, turned to see why Kannard screamed. Hendrix slammed his bronze-plated shoulder into the baron, knocking him off the side of the train. Hendrix continued on, shoving Eustache to the top of the train and jumping over to our car and sacking Genevieve and I like a bunch of potatoes.

Genevieve tried to scream her father's name, but the sound was crushed by Hendrix's weight as we slammed into the roof. We both landed at Kannard's feet, and with the bulk of the colonel on top of me, I couldn't move. I managed to twist my head enough to see the lady assassin hurling knives which Eustache parried with his sword.

An explosive crack split the air, and bolts of blue electricity slammed into train. Hendrix yanked Genevieve and I up, hooked his arms around us, and walked backward. Captain Baldarich slid down the zipline from The Sparrowhawk and landed on the roof behind Eustache.

Kannard, down on his knees and nursing his broken hand, peered over his shoulder at Hendrix and us. He erupted into a maniacal laugh. I turned my head and saw only a dark horizon. Dense brown clouds, churning like a thick soup enveloped all the land in front of us. Like

death on the wind.
"Sandstorm," I yelled.

25
Sandstorm Pyramids

Lord Kannard cackled "Destiny is my friend, not yours."

"Let them go!" Eustache cried. The dark brown wall of churning grit and sand swallowed the train's engine. Captain Baldarich, grabbed Eustache by the arm and pointed toward the sky. "We leave now," he yelled, "or the Sparrowhawk will be ripped from the sky." Baldarich grabbed the grappling line. Eustache hesitated. He stepped away, as if in defeat. His shoulders slumped. He snagged one of the lines with his hand and cut it free from the train. Baldarich did the same and the two men flew off as the Sparrowhawk soared away.

Colonel Hendrix dragged us down into the train car as the sandstorm overtook everything. Through the windows, I could see the whipping winds stirred up walls of sand like a giant tornado. The thunderous howling drowned out the chugging noises of the train. It scoured and scratched at the glass, like demons tearing their way in, until all I saw was a blanket of black.

I hoped, the sand would clog the train's gears and we'd stop. However, we kept pushing onward, and despair seeped in. Our survival was up to us now. I knew the Sparrowhawk would never stop looking for us, but would destiny favor the Golden Circle as it had today?

Hendrix locked us in a cabin, oddly the same one we'd hidden in before. As he left, he turned to the soldiers in the corridor and held out his mechanical hand. "If one of them escapes, I'm punishing the lot of you."

Thoughts of Owethu and Mr. Singh quickened my heart, but I could only assume they had been pitched overboard by the raging sandstorm. On the other hand, if they hadn't been discovered, they might be hiding somewhere on the train. Not wanting to think the worst, I shifted my attention to Genevieve, who sat next to me and seemed to be lost in her world.

"Rodin? Where's Rodin?" I asked.

"He flew after my father when he fell off the …"

"I'm sure your father will be okay, and it's probably best Rodin isn't here." I stared back at the guard as he peered through the window. "Why didn't they take our weapons?"

"They don't consider us a threat." She sat back, almost slouching against the couch. "We just showed them they can take us down with ease."

"That's not true, we were—"

"Useless."

"But you fought the assassin."

"She bested me with ease. I was too emotional."

I couldn't argue with her, but I'd just stood there, a captive in Kannard's arms. I watched the raging sandstorm engulfing the train, the swirling chaos mirroring how I felt inside. This was a Gordian Knot, so complex and confusing that it hurt my mind just to think about. All I really knew was that Alexander the Great was never captured by his enemies.

"So, where do you think they are taking us?"

Genevieve toyed with her locket. "Cairo for starters." She let the locket fall against her chest. "After that, I don't know."

When the train slowed at the Cairo station, the lady assassin opened the door, soldiers on either side of her. Genevieve jumped up and drew her saber. I sprang to my feet and drew my bowie knife from the leather straps wrapped around me. I didn't think attacking was the best plan, but I wasn't going to let her stand alone.

The soldiers raised their rifles and the woman laughed. "A good show, but I'm afraid quite pointless," she laughed. "Let's go. I'd prefer you walk, but we will drag you, if you insist."

"Why should we cooperate?" Genevieve asked.

"*Genevieve*, come with me," the woman said, using the French pronunciation.

"Don't call me that. You are *not* my mother."

"Words do not change what I am."

"*My* mother died in a boating accident."

The woman's face hardened, but she did not respond. She merely turned and walked away. Then I recognized the telltale gears and squeaks of Hendrix. He stepped into the doorway and laughed. "You got two choices. Put your toothpicks down, or I shoot you and patch you up later. Either of which suits me."

I didn't doubt for one minute that he'd take great joy in wounding us. Genevieve glanced over at me as I lowered my knife. Slowly, she lowered her sword.

After a moment, she sheathed her sword. I put my knife away, too.

"Excellent. Besides Alexander, you are an honored guest." He tipped his Stetson. "Only the best for a future horseman."

The soldiers motioned with their weapons. We stepped out the cabin and off the train.

We were escorted out of the city by a camel caravan. In the distance, like mountains in a sea of sand, stood three immense pyramids. The only remaining of the Seven Wonders. They led us down a causeway, past a giant half-buried head.

I step closer to Genevieve. "I always wanted to see the pyramids and ask the sphinx my questions, but this isn't exactly what I had in mind. Well… I am here with you."

Genevieve hardened exterior held no cracks, but I saw her lips part slightly. "They are spectacular, and the interiors are breathtaking. Perhaps one day we can visit them together."

"The last time you were here was with Richard?" My stomach tightens and his name leaves a bitter taste on my tongue.

Genevieve nodded. "Yes, but we didn't visit the interior, we only stood at the base." She added, "I saw the inner chambers on my first trip to Egypt. My mother insisted." She paused giving herself a moment to exhale. She smiled and leaned toward me, "The Duke would not let Richard climb, despite his repeated pleas."

I couldn't help but laugh, thinking of tiny Richard throwing a temper-tantrum at the base of the giant pyramid. However, the head snap and grunt from one of the soldiers silenced me.

The caravan stopped when it reached long lines of tents and tarps.

I turned to Genevieve and she nodded.

My heart raced as I watched the guards. All I needed was for him to look off into the dessert, toward the blazing sun. As he turned, Genevieve and I sprinted off through the sand. Running around the dunes allowed us to get quickly out of sight, but our tracks were easy to follow. Genevieve debated where to run, but I ran past her, toward the ruined stone blocks rising out of the dune.

As we reached the other side of the stones, I saw a platform, and steps leading down to the great beast guarding the Giza plateau – the Sphinx.

We bolted up onto one of the paws, half buried in the sand. Shouts from the soldiers echoed behind us. Genevieve and I were moments from being seen. I point toward the head. "This way."

"They'll see us if we run."

"We're not running. Come on."

We climb up the sand to the back of the head, the face stared out to the east, and I don't want to run. How many people had these eyes seen? How long had it gazed over these sands? I wanted to know more but… the tips of the soldiers' rifles were cresting the dune.

A gust of wind whipped the sand up around us and we hid behind the headdress of the sphinx. Rock extended back from the head with a depression in the center. The sculpture was enrobed in sand, but the guardian had paws… and a body. "The sphinx is a real sphinx."

"Shhh. They'll hear you."

I whispered, "The sphinx is buried in the sand, and we're on top of it."

Genevieve whispered. "This isn't the time for a

history lesson."

"Stay here, I have an idea."

I darted to the depression, and stepped in a hole about three feet wide. My feet sank into the loose sand which meant it must go deeper. Pushing the sand out was easy, the wind did most of the work, carrying the grains away as it scoured passed.

I motioned to Genevieve and she rushed over, joining me in the hole. We had to squat and it was tight, but we squished in enough to not be seen.

Her soft body pressed against my arm, my leg, my side. Together, we radiated heat, which the warm desert wind made even hotter. This was the perfect day, except for the soldiers.

The soldiers were still in front of the Sphinx and heading toward the causeway. As they glanced toward the head of the Sphinx, we ducked. One soldier called out, "Check out the feet."

We don't have but a moment until they see us.

I turned to the pyramids, they weren't that far, a few hundred yards, and if we could reach them… I remembered reading about the rock cut tombs around the ancient structures. We could hide in one of those, or even inside the pyramids if needed. "Run for the pyramid."

"Which one?"

"Kafre's." She eyed me and I could tell the first son of Khufu meant nothing to her. I pointed to the one that still had its polished casing stones at the top, "the middle one."

She nodded and we sprinted through the sand which kicked up around our feet. We were running up hill which slowed us down, but we darted between the dunes so the soldiers wouldn't see us.

As we ran, I saw the large stones of a causeway sticking out of the sand beside them. When we reached a large depression in the sand, we paused and lowered down. The ground shifted beneath our feet. Before either of us could react, the sand drained below us, and we slid down on a wave of rocky grains. We fell down onto a floor of sand. My back ached. I flexed, checking for broken bones. Next, I turn to Genevieve, "Are you injured?"

"I do not believe so."

Looking up, I saw a square shaft rising to the blue sky far above. Darkness surrounded us, not beige shaft walls as tunnels stretched out in several directions.

"Where are we?" Genevieve asked.

"We must be in one of the underground tombs."

"You said the rock-cut tombs were over there," Genevieve pointed toward the pyramid. Her finger aimed down one of the tunnels.

The sand underneath us drained like water. Genevieve grabbed my hand and we ran toward the tunnel. The sand dropped out from under each step, and I started to fear we wouldn't make it, but my boot gripped firm ground and we ran into the tunnel.

Looking back, a huge square hole replaced the sand we'd landed on. I peeked over the edge but the passage descended into darkness.

Genevieve looked up, "We eluded our pursuers, but are we ever getting out of here?"

"Of course. That shaft is how the sarcophagus got down here. The guys who dug this place came down another way. We just have to find it." I flipped through everything I had with me, but the one thing I hadn't thought to bring was light, no fire either. After all, we had a dragon for that.

"If only Rodin were here," Genevieve said.

"I was thinking the same thing."

Genevieve reached under her jacket and retrieved a small rectangular tin. She shook it until the chemicals inside started to glow. She opened the tin with a hinge on one side and the white linen which encased the opening diffused the light. The soft yellow glow illuminated the tunnel.

The walls were unadorned but, in places, toolmarks textured the walls, remnants of the people who carved this place. My fingers slipped over the chiseled grooves. I wanted to study everything. Maybe that would be an effective way of eluding the soldiers? "If we spent months down here investigating the place, they'd probably leave without us."

Genevieve spun around and shined the light on me. Even covered in shadows I saw the sharpness of her glare, her slightly tilted head letting me know of her disproval.

"Yeah, I know, we don't have that kind of time."

"Exactly. Now can we please get out of here before we set off one of the Pharaoh's boobytraps." Genevieve passed the light over the floor and ceiling.

We walked down the passage toward a dot of bright sunlight in the distance. The light grew brighter forcing the darkness to the edge of the walls. As we reached another hole in the desert floor, we walked up a ramp to get out easily, the last few feet even had steps cut into the rock. We emerged cautiously into the sun and I looked around. The pyramids loomed above, and the soldiers were still over by the sphinx. Genevieve tugged my shirt and I heard the familiar whirring and clicking of gears.

"It's rude to leave without saying goodbye." The southern drawl ended with an eerie chuckle that sent shivers up my spine.

I spun around and found Hendrix eyeing me from under his hat. His three-clawed grappler arm slid out of his sleeve. I smiled. "We only wanted to see one of the seven wonders of the world."

Additional soldiers joined the dozen already behind Hendrix. With their weapons ready, I raised my arms. Genevieve shook her head. She pulled one my hands down and stepped toward the confederate. "Let us return, I believe you wanted to depart shortly."

"Now you see, them gentiles know how to be proper-like." Hendrix tipped his Stetson and motioned to the tents.

"It was worth it to get up close with antiquity." I stared up at the timeless giants rising out of the sand at the giant pyramid rising out of the sand.

We were escorted back to the tents, each step angered me more. *Captured again.* One of the soldier's assigned to Genevieve and I, shoved me forward and I tumbled on the uneven sand. He then reached toward Genevieve, but she spun around to face the brute.

"I am not someone to be man-handled." The fierceness in her eyes brought a harsh tone to her sweet accent.

"Sit." He grabbed his rifle and raised the butt above her head.

Steel flashed in the sunlight as she drew her saber, and in one swift, powerful downstroke, she sliced the straps holding the weapon on his shoulder and sent the rifle into the sand. The man raised his fist to punch her, but Genevieve pressed her sword under his chin.

He froze. All the soldiers surrounding us raised their weapons. Still, Genevieve held her sword firm against the man's neck.

She glared at Hendrix, as he strolled over, "I have *agreed* to be your prisoner, but I *will* be treated in accordance with my station."

Everyone, including me, stared at Hendrix. "There you go using that "P" word. Guest. You're my *guests*." With a wave of his hand, the soldiers lowered their weapons.

Hendrix' gears ticked and clicked as he bowed to Genevieve. She kept the blade against the soldier's chin for a moment before slowly pulling her saber away. The soldier retreated.

Hendrix cackled. "Be thankful the lady didn't take your fingers off with that little display."

Genevieve slid the blade back into its sheath. Lowering herself onto the sand beside me, she tucked her legs beneath her. Her stoic expression revealed nothing but contempt. Hendrix spun around, annoyed that everyone still stood immobile. "Get this train loaded, and be quick about it!"

What train? Beyond the tents in front of us, only sand and rolling dunes stretched across the great Saharan Desert as far as my eyes could see. And on the horizon, the setting sun ignited the rolling dunes causing the whole desert to shimmer with a bright orange glow as if on fire. No train, and nowhere did I see the twin iron tracks.

Slaves in tattered rags and soldiers in desert uniforms once again moved in and out of the long row of tarps and tents. I wanted to know what could possibly be inside, but feared I'd find out all too soon.

So much history had crossed these sands. Alexander

the Great had gone east into Persia to avoid this desert. I tried to take it in, but I didn't know what would happen. Hendrix was evil, and Zerelda tortured the crew of the Sparrowhawk in the short time she had them. They threw my father in a dungeon. What lay ahead for Genevieve and me?

I wouldn't let them hurt her. I owed it to the baron, and to me. However, at the moment, she didn't need me. In fact, I think I needed her.

Hendrix waved at the soldiers guarding us. One pointed. "Get up," he said in a southern accent.

I did what he said, but as Genevieve stood, the soldiers stepped back. We walked toward Hendrix. When we arrived at the tent, a slave pulled back the large flap and we followed the half-bronze colonel inside.

Two steps in and I'm stopped by a wall of riveted iron plates perched atop thousands of armored posts connected to the undercarriage by immense pistons, like the articulated legs of a mechanical insect. As we walked along the colossal monstrosity, I realized I was looking at train cars, if you could call them that. Each stretched fifty feet long with five legs attached to the undercarriage on each side. Every third train car boasted cannons mounted in turrets on the roof, and gun ports running along the side. An iron castle transformed into a monstrous millipede.

"This train has legs," I whispered to Genevieve as we moved along. "I've never seen anything like it."

"Neither have I," Genevieve said, but her attention was on the coming and going of people. She studied everyone who passed us, and tapped her leg as she counted the number of soldiers.

Hendrix stopped at the stairs for the second car.

The engine loomed in front of us and bore a huge boiler twice the size of any I'd seen before.

Hendrix stretched out his hands, "Magnificent, wouldn't you say?" We boarded the second car, a converted passenger car decorated like a Victorian parlor. Fine wooden furniture accented the long narrow room, and gas-lit sconces hung on the wall. Fed by brass tubes attached to the elaborate molding. A scarred soldier nudged me to the back of the car. Genevieve sat down and he pushed me into the chair next to her.

Hendrix stepped onboard, followed by the lady assassin and Kannard, whose eyes rolled around in an overly medicated haze. A soldier helped him into a chair at the front end of the car.

He looked old and frail, not the robust man I'd fought last year. Granted, right now he was barely coherent, but he'd been menacing enough at the French castle. I stared at his bandaged hand, which he clutched to his chest. A twinge of guilt washed over me, knowing I had injured him. Almost. However, thoughts of what this man stood for and the actions he'd taken to hurt my friends anchored me to my decision. Kannard wanted to enslave the world. He'd kidnapped my father,

poisoned the baron, and tried to kill us on several occasions. A little pain was karma as Mr. Singh would say.

Hendrix stopped, spun around in the middle of the car, and removed his hat in a grand gesture. "Welcome to the Milli-train, an invention of my own design. If I'd had this in the war, Sherman never would have made it to Atlanta, or the sea."

I'd never thought of Colonel Hendrix as the inventor type. I assumed half his brain was gone, too, and that was the reason he'd become a diabolical, madman who couldn't leave the war behind.

"The finest of American engineering," he continued. "She'll traverse any terrain, ford a river with ease, but she ain't for the sea." Hendrix motioned to train car. "Let your Templars come, boy. As you can see, we're ready for 'em."

I let my silence speak for me. Genevieve probably had some witty and perfect insult that would cut to his core, but all I wanted to do was yell at him for everything he'd done.

Hendrix turned to a soldier standing by a small telegraph machine bolted to the wall. "Tell the engineer to get underway." The soldier quickly tapped out a message on a large, black button on its mechanical arm. Within a moment, a second small metal arm tapped out a response, which spit out a ticker-tape message. The soldier passed it on to Col. Hendrix. He looked it over and read the message aloud. "The last of drilling equipment is loaded. Stop. All property and personnel are aboard. Stop."

Kannard coughed and moaned in agony, which snapped him back to reality. He focused on Hendrix. "Then let's go. We must find the next horsemen's heart."

Hendrix shook his head. "We are underway. Just get

some rest."

"I'll rest when the circle is complete," Kannard snarled, but his eyes instantly rolled back in his head and he drifted off.

"Baroness, keep an eye on our guests." He pointed at Kannard. "And make sure this one doesn't wander off."

"Where are you going?" she asked.

"The engine car, to make sure we're heading in the right direction."

The Milli-train chugged to life, belching smoke into the sky. The legs on one side cascaded forward, falling behind the one in front of it, and then the legs on the other side of the train followed, causing the train to undulate back and forth like a slithering millipede. Hendrix had named the train appropriately.

So many questions filled my mind, but I sat at the window lost in the movement of the mechanical legs as they moved in rapid succession. In the glass, the lady assassin's reflection watched me. Our eyes met, but I glanced back at the dunes. I stood with Genevieve in not trusting this woman.

The lady assassin stopped at a cart with crystal decanters, picked one up, and poured herself a drink. She swallowed the amber liquid in a single gulp, then glanced over at the two of us, the woman paused and turned back to the window. With a deep sigh, she adjusted her cloak over her shoulders and smoothed out her sleeves.

"Can I get you anything?" The lady assassin tried to keep her tone harsh, but a sweet French accent slipped through. "Water? Something to eat?"

"I need nothing from you," Genevieve spit through clenched teeth, her eyes never leaving the window.

Unlike her, I couldn't stop staring at this woman.

Maybe if I studied her long enough, I'd find the clues to prove she wasn't the baroness. As my father had taught me to do with ancient languages and documents, I searched for similarities between Genevieve and the woman—like mannerisms, speech, or maybe jewelry—but there was nothing. Until, that is, the lady assassin lifted her glass and I saw she had the same cute little thumb as Genevieve. Their whole hands were even alike. In fact, they were almost identical.

"I could use some water," I said. Genevieve snapped her head toward me, but I shrugged. "I'm parched."

"Water it is." The lady assassin motioned, and a slave poured the crystal-clear liquid from a large pitcher into an alabaster cup.

As the slave girl presented the cup to me and bowed, Genevieve groaned. "You're not going to drink that are you? It's poisoned."

I peered into the clear water and the cup's swirling pattern.

The lady assassin turned to me and groaned. "I'm not trying to kill you."

Genevieve huffed, "You already tried to kill Alexander's father."

"His father is a Templar … a threat. Neither of you are." She turned away from me, toward Genevieve. "I would never kill you."

Genevieve locked eyes with the woman. "You can drop the act. You're not my mother."

As I set the drink down, the two stared at each other for a long moment, as if in a mental sword fight. The lady assassin turned and stormed off, slamming the door behind her as she headed into the next car.

Genevieve twisted in her seat, and jammed her arms across one another.

I opened my mouth to say something, but caught her reflection in the window. Tears streamed down her cheeks. I paused. What could I say? *I'm sorry your mom is an assassin.*

The Milli-train continued over the sea of dunes. I rested my head against the chair and stared out toward the dark horizon. The moonlight shimmered over the desolate landscape. The sand sparkled in the night, mirroring the stars above.

BOOK II: IRON ZULU

We sat in silence, both lost in our own thoughts. The rhythmic rocking of the train became as monotonous as the thoughts in my mind. What could we do to stop the Golden Circle? Uncertain, I turned to Genevieve. She stared at the silver locket around her neck, rubbing the metal oval with her fingers. Slowly she opened the locket and stared at the picture inside. She didn't have to tell me what ran through her mind. She might not think the lady assassin was her mother, but enough doubt had been forged. The baron was certain, but I wasn't. Not yet.

I didn't want to believe that the woman who killed the professors at Eton, who tried to kill my father, could be Genevieve's mother.

Lifting her chin, she saw me, and snapped the locket shut and let it drop to her chest.

"Now what?" I asked, looking around the train car.

"Now nothing," she said. "We've bought ourselves time to be rescued."

"So, we sit here and wait," I said, as she locked eyes with me and cocked her head to the side. "That doesn't

sound very knightly. They're up to something, and we should find out what it is."

She leaned closer. "Watch what you say. Kannard might be out of it, but the soldiers at the end of the car might hear us."

The guards turned and stared at us until she sat back and pretended to look out the window. Then they returned to their conversation.

I knew Genevieve was right, and my father would agree: sit here and wait for the Sparrowhawk. Captain Baldarich would team up with the rest of the Templar Air Corp and come rescue us. It would take them a couple of days. But without a set of tracks to follow, would they be able to find us?

Kannard stirred and sat up, gripping his wrist. He kicked a table and sent it sliding across the floor, and into a chair. When he saw us staring at him, he snarled, "What are you looking at?"

"My friend, Owethu, says the Zulu have an elixir that can heal broken bones."

"And you believe this tale?"

"I do." I sat forward on my seat. "He knows about all kinds of things."

"You are a fool to believe these savages."

I bristled at that word and glared at him.

Annoyed, Kannard got up and walked over to the cart and tried to pour himself a glass of scotch. With his left hand, he struggled to remove the stopper from the decanter. Unable to open the carafe, Kannard kicked the table. "You," he bellowed, pointing to a soldier, "come over here and pour me a double."

"But I'm not a—" Kannard glowered at the soldier. A look so evil, I no longer cared how he suffered. "Yes,

Lord Kannard. Right away, sir." The soldier hurried over, filled the glass, bowed, and returned to his post.

Kannard stared at the glass, took a big slug, and exhaled sharply. Then he glanced down at his hand and turned to me. "You did this." He snaked his way over to me. I pushed back against my seat. Genevieve tensed up beside me. "I suppose I should be proud. You've become a warrior."

Normally, I would have been ecstatic about someone finally recognizing me as a warrior, but somehow, coming from Kannard, it left a bad taste—like bile—in my mouth. Why was it only men like Kannard who acknowledged my talent? The way the baron and my father talked; one would have thought I was nothing more than a child.

Kannard leaned down and shoved his bandaged hand in my face. "This will heal. The horsemen will ride again, and the world will tremble beneath our hooves." There it was again, that wild look, with eyes so wide his pupils looked like pin pricks. Kannard reared back up and smoothed his coat. "Is Hendrix right, boy? Are you the true fourth horsemen?" He stared at me—almost through me—and I couldn't tell what he saw, or if he liked it.

A chill ran up my spine as he spoke. Instantly, I was pulled back to Eustache's garden. The night he'd fought Hendrix and lost, allowing Genevieve and I to escape with the Four Thieves Potion. Hendrix offered power, wealth, and dominion over the nobility who saw me as nothing more than a commoner, or colonist. That day, he'd offered me Genevieve. Promised to spare her, and make her mine forever. I shuddered at his words. I could never be a horseman. I had the honor of a knight and the code of a defender.

Hendrix walked in and ordered Kannard, "Leave the kids be."

Kannard sneered and stormed over to Hendrix, staring at the man with the same dreadful expression he'd focused on me. The colonel held his stare, and his eye encircled in bronze, sparked with electricity. "*Lord* Kannard, please sit down. Soon we will be in the hidden city of the sky pirates. Zerelda is there, and she has the third heart."

Kannard roared as he whipped around and charged Genevieve, "It was you who destroyed one of my beautiful hearts."

Hendrix was quicker. His bronze, segmented hand slid deep into his sleeve, the gears whirling and clinking as his three-clawed appendage locked into place. Hendrix snagged Kannard's shoulder, preventing him from moving forward. Kannard winced and stopped.

"Private, please escort the lord to a room." Hendrix pulled Kannard close. "Rest, Lord Kannard. We will be in the south soon enough. Victory will be ours."

Kannard wrenched his shoulder free and stormed off. The soldier chased after him as Hendrix turned to his men. Another soldier stepped into the car and handed the colonel a note. With the casual stroll of a smug gunslinger, he stepped over to us. "The skies are clear. Word is the Sparrowhawk has docked in Cairo. Looks like we've given your Templars the slip."

Genevieve eyed Hendrix with dead certainty, and said, "My father will come."

Hendrix and his men spoke in hushed tones near the other end of the car. At first it was business, the stats of the train, and the status of their journey. It was good to know we were only a hundred and thirty-seven miles from Cairo, but none of that helped me decide what to do.

Genevieve pulsed with energy and shifted in her seat. Her eyes never left the sand. Was she counting every grain?

The desert, was beautiful, but every dune looked like the others, and I'd tired of the never-ending landscape. However, the rolling sea of dunes flattened out and the Milli-train entered a forested grassland. We went from being able to see to the horizon, to maybe a mile on the grasslands, and sometimes only hundreds of feet in the thick brush. We started to see more animals too, I wanted to see more, but the sun was setting. Besides, I wanted to stare at Genevieve for hours, watching every movement to determine her inner thoughts. I wanted to reach out and comfort her. Tell her everything would be okay, but I

couldn't. No one could. However, from the expression on her face, I didn't think she needed comfort, but I did.

Hendrix's dry cackle sent shivers through me and drew my attention away from Genevieve. He sat at the table, surrounded by his soldiers. "That's a good one," he said as he tipped his Stetson. "I ever tell you about Atlanta?"

Several of the younger soldiers leaned closer to the colonel.

"I was in charge of a gun battery outside Atlanta. It was almost Thanksgiving when General Sherman came to town. One company turned tail and ran. Said they were trying to lead Sherman away, but he didn't take the bait." Hendrix drank the last of his whiskey and slammed his glass on the table. "We tried to hold out, but he was fixing to roll over us." Then, with audible venom he added, "Sherman and his men had no supplies. They took what was needed. Scavengers, the lot of 'em, and they didn't leave nothing."

Hendrix's men nodded, enraptured by the story. "We fought tooth and nail for days. At one point, we were running low on black powder. I snuck off to procure some from a battery destroyed earlier that day. None survived, and since it weren't no good to them any longer, I brought it back. One of them pouches rips open as we're loading the cannon, spilling powder all down my side." Hendrix ran his hand down the bronze plates. "In our sights, Sherman marched on our position. Before I could command the attack, his artillery found its mark."

"An exploding shell hit the cannon and obliterated my crew. The powder ignited, along with my uniform, as shrapnel kissed every inch of me." Hendrix's words escaped through a low grumbling roar. "I'm on fire, flailing, my arm ripped to shreds, and those damn Yanks just rode on by, laughing."

The room was eerily silent. Finally, Hendrix whispered, his voice barely audible, "Sherman burned Atlanta, and spent every day to Christmas driving his army to the sea. We were those people's *only* defense and we failed 'em." Hendrix stood and shoved the table away from him, as his men scattered. "I vowed that day I *would* get my revenge. Never again would I lack the power to defeat my enemies."

His men cheered.

Hendrix rubbed the intact side of his face, and stood. "You want more stories, find a storyteller." He pointed toward us. "Keep an eye on those whippersnappers. Make sure they don't leave this car." Then he stepped out.

One of the soldiers dropped two pillows and blankets on a chair beside Genevieve and me. His hand ran back and forth over the fine linen, but with a snort, he spun on his heel and returned to the table with the other soldiers. They joked about the trip, and argued over the order of who would watch us. As we slipped deeper into night, they yawned and struggled with boredom.

I leaned into Genevieve and whispered, "We should go lurking."

She pulled away from the window. She nodded, but turned to see what the soldiers were doing.

"They keep dosing off."

"Except that one," she nodded.

"He won't be long."

"How do you know?" she whispered.

"Head bobbing."

She smiled, but stifled her laughter.

Genevieve grabbed her blanket and pillow, and we both lay down on couches across from one another. We moved slowly, quietly, so the soldier would think we were settling in for the night. Eventually, the soldier, too, nodded off, his snoring drowning out the drone of the engine.

It was time; we nodded to each other. She slid over to me and whispered, "We should leave pillows in our place, provide the illusion we are sleeping."

"Sounds like you've done this before."

"Mrs. Hinderman only opens the door to check on me."

I got up and piled the cushions and pillow along my couch and covered them with a blanket. Genevieve did the same, and we slipped quietly out of the door toward the car behind us.

A rush of icy wind stung my skin as I opened the car door and we stepped outside. We rushed into the next car to escape the crispness. Inside, we stood on a small landing. A couple of steps led down to the gun deck, which was filled with cannon, shot, and sleeping soldiers. They were crammed into the spaces all around the cannons. One even cradled the rounded iron like a pillow.

We climbed up another set of steps to the catwalk, spanning the length of the train car, and slowly made our way across the car. From there, a soldier could climb into the turret mounted on the roof, or shoot out of a number of arrow loops arranged in the armored walls. Thick armor plating covered every inch of the interior, too. This train had been built like one of the Iron Knights. Impenetrable. With a hundred times the firepower. "This isn't good," I said to Genevieve. "I don't know if the Black Knight could stand up to this behemoth."

"With the Bronze Knight and Iron Templar at your side, you might be surprised."

About halfway along the catwalk, we looked down and saw a table with maps and other papers arranged in proper order. Three different maps of Africa lay beside one another, along with a diagram of the different vehicles they might encounter, like cars and airships, and a diagram of the Sparrowhawk marked with a red 'X' indicating the most vulnerable spots. The third was a topographical map of the African continent. I leaned over the railing in an attempt to read the map and find our final destination, but the lines only showed where we'd been.

Genevieve tapped me on the shoulder and pointed to a fourth map labeled 'Mineral Deposits' that lay partially obscured by other papers. "That map shows gold deposits."

I nodded and pointed to an attaché case lying against one of the legs. It had the seal of Eton College on the front. I pulled Genevieve close and whispered, "They didn't just kill the professors, they confiscated what they were working on."

Reaching the end of the catwalk, we slipped out into the night air and into the first cargo car. Large doors ran along either side of the interior. Wooden crates were stacked to the ceiling with a maze of corridors winding between them. Although we didn't see any soldiers, I overhead a couple of the men discussing their farms back in the Carolinas. These were Hendrix's men, soldiers who had probably been following him since the war. A war that ended over a decade ago.

As the door clattered open on the other end of the train car, Genevieve and I jumped. My heart rocketed into my throat. Several soldiers entered, and we ducked behind some crates. Genevieve stepped back and pressed herself against me. I wrapped my arm around her waist and we squeezed into the shadow. Her energy mixed with mine, and thoughts of her kiss flashed in my mind.

"This way," one of them said, "the colonel wants that leather case from the gun car. But like I was saying … don't be asking too many questions. That'll be nothing but trouble for you."

As the soldiers passed, Genevieve pulled away from me and stood up. I reached out to pull her back in, but as she turned and could see me, I pressed my palm against the crate as if getting ready to pull myself up. We slipped into the third car, another passenger car, partitioned by a small entryway. I peeked through a small break in curtains that covered the window in the door. Unlike the Victorian parlor at the front of the train, three cabins lay at the front of this car, with seats arranged in rows at the back. Several soldiers slept curled up on the seats.

We slipped into the corridor and peered through the curtain of the first cabin. Hendrix sat in a chair with his legs crossed on a velvet-covered ottoman reading over some papers, a couple of candles burning nearby. The mechanics of his body never ceased to amaze me. Although I'd been close to Hendrix, I'd never just had a chance to watch how the mechanics of his arm worked. As he read, he stroked his chin, stopping at times to tap his metallic finger along his bronze-plated cheek. The gears connecting his fingers to his arm turned in clicks with each tap of his finger. The part of his scarred face that remained seemed to seamlessly wrap around the metal and make it a natural part of him. Even so, after hearing his story, I almost felt sorry for him.

A soft snore rumbled inside the second cabin, which was dark. Peering into the third room, I saw a woman in a silk robe brushing her short hair.

Genevieve slid up next to me to peer inside. As she stared intensely through the glass at the woman, I wondered what in the world we were doing, sneaking around on an overly-armored train traveling across Africa—and once again trying to save the world. We should be committed to an insane asylum.

My stomach tightened. The telltale ache, again, like someone reached inside me and twisted my guts. I glanced over at Hendrix. He hadn't move, so, he wasn't the cause. The soldiers who were sent to retrieve the attaché case, they would be coming back any minute. This minute.

I pulled on Genevieve's sleeve. "We need to get out of here. Now." She yanked away from me, keeping her focus on the lady assassin. I tapped her on the shoulder, grimaced, and pointed to my stomach. Understanding, she looked for a place to escape, but I pulled her backwards into the darkened cabin. I slowly shut the door so as not to awaken the person sleeping within. We hunkered down by the door and remained as quiet as we could, the rhythmic breathing continued to echo behind us. I turned and found Kannard on the fold down bunk. My heart pounded and I only hoped the soldiers wouldn't knock on this cabin door.

I held my breath as the soldiers knocked on Hendrix's cabin. Trapped between a sleeping rock and Hendrix's hard bronze, I thought we be captured for certain, but this was our only hope of hearing the soldiers.

A voice seeped through the door. "The leather case

as ordered, sir."

Hendrix sneered. "Set it down next to my desk and return to duty." His heavy steps walked past Kannard's door. Genevieve and I pulled back, even though the room was dark. Hendrix knocked on the third cabin.

"What?" The lady assassin fired off.

"Reports are in; more Templars are coming."

"Are you sure this is a good idea?" She asked with a harsh tone.

"You betcha," he said with a raspy chuckle. "Get 'em off their cobblestones and see what good they are? I've fought in the muck of swamps and the fine grasses of open fields, so let's see how they'll handle the savannah."

"Then we just have to find Captain Zerelda before the Templars find us."

"You mean, *when* the baron finally finds us. You're always so proper to say Templar, but I hear another word every time. We ain't going have issues once he catches up to us, are we?"

"That's not what I mean." Her voice lowered and sharpened. "Now, let's go over the plan for tomorrow before the old man gets up."

Hendrix stepped into the lady assassin's cabin and closed the door, because we couldn't hear anything but a low murmur. Behind us, Kannard rolled over and grumbled.

Genevieve dug her nails dug into my shoulder, which was good; it reminded me we weren't safe where we were and needed to move. I opened the door and we slipped down the corridor. Genevieve stopped in front of Hendrix's room. I motioned toward the exit, but she shook her head and darted into his cabin.

I rushed in behind her, my heart racing ever faster. Energy pulsed through my body. Every creak from Hendrix's footsteps echoed through the walls. I hadn't been this close to death since the Battle of the Thames.

Genevieve quickly searched the room, starting with the table. She picked up a notebook; one edge was stained red, and the writing was in German. She handed it to me and I skimmed the notebook.

"Whose notebook?" She asked.

"A guy named Schoenbruster. It's his field notes from his third African expedition." I checked the passage marked with a piece of cord, and quickly read it over. "It's his report of a strange find in Africa. A large chunk of jade buried thousands of miles from where it should have been found. Wait." I paused, at first unable to say the words I was reading. "The stone was in the shape of a heart; it was fractured like broken glass but remained intact."

Genevieve's voice trembled. "Another heart of the horsemen?"

"I'm afraid so. Come on, we'd better get back."

We raced back to the forward car, climbing over crates in the cargo car and crawling along the catwalk of the cannon cars. I peered through the window of the Victorian parlor car and saw the soldiers still slept. I turned the handle, and Genevieve grabbed my arm." Hurry! Hendrix just entered the cannon car."

I closed the door behind us quietly. We tossed the pillows from our seats, and dove under the blankets. The door opened and Hendrix entered. I stirred and sat up, squinting my eyes as if just waking up. Genevieve remained covered and still.

Hendrix eyed me, but kept moving toward his men. He smacked one soldier in the back, knocking him from his chair, and smashed his mechanical hand on the table to wake the rest. "Did I say sleep?"

"No sir," they all replied, scrambling. Some of the men stood up. Others rubbed their eyes.

He pointed toward the two of us. "If either of them leaves this car, I'll tie the lot of you to the back of the train and you'll hope to hell to keep up."

I lay back down as if I didn't care. Hendrix stormed off. Some of the men started playing cards, but soon fell asleep again.

Genevieve peeked from beneath her blanket, got up, and walked over to me. She picked a pillow from the floor and placed it on me. "I want to be close to someone, but decorum …"

"No need to explain." I scooted back against the cushions, and she lay down with the pillow between us. "I'd appreciate the company."

She fell asleep quickly, but I couldn't. Having her close was unnerving, wonderful. However, I hardly wanted my moments with her to be under guard in the Milli-train.

At some point I drifted off.

I found myself flying through jungles and a narrow fissure in the rock, which expanded to reveal the remains of a caldera, the remnants of long dead volcano. Inside lay the hidden city of the sky pirates. I flew as if I was an aero-dirigible. Below, steel clashed with steel. Looking down, I saw Genevieve in a sword fight with a mysterious figure in black. As she cut down her opponent, a second enemy slashed at her, and as she dispatched the foe, a third stepped forward to face her. I wanted to race down and help her, but I was being pulled away from the city until I could no longer see her. I landed in an open field with undulating grassy hills all around. The ground rumbled, and the horsemen pushed up through the soil around me, their iron hooves clawing to get out. Fire rose around them as the wind began to howl. I heard the call of a distant horn. A long note rang from a range of tall, jagged peaks. The biggest mountains I'd ever seen. Dark clouds gathered above and Colonel Hendrix reached through them to seize the Earth in his mechanical hand. He squeezed and the world began to crumble.

When I opened my eyes, I jerked up and flung my legs over, planting them on the floor. I leaned my sweat-soaked brow in my hands and rested my elbows on my knees, trying to regain my composure. After a minute, I realized Genevieve was back on her couch, covered and sleeping soundly. I sighed; thankful I hadn't disturbed her.

Genevieve popped up. "Are you okay?"

"I had a dream … a vision. Like last year."

"What did you see?"

"You, fighting three duels."

"Me?"

I nodded. "You defeated the first two."

She smiled. "And the third?"

"I don't know. But I think the horsemen are back." I gripped the edge of the couch and looked over at Genevieve, questioning. "What if the oldest source of the horsemen's power wasn't the most powerful?"

"What do you mean?"

"What if Schoenbruster found a horseman's heart more powerful than the urns on Malta?"

Terror filled her eyes. We'd barely defeated the horsemen last year. In truth, we'd only defeated one of the four when Genevieve thrust her Iron Knight's sword into the Iron Horseman of Plagues, destroying its cannon and exposing the urn within—the heart of the horseman. If they'd found a more powerful source of the horsemen's power, we were in even more trouble.

Genevieve let out a deep breath. "Terrifying."

All I managed was to nod in agreement.

Then, as if trying to lighten our mood, she said "Three duels, you say? I suppose I should start practicing."

I chuckled. Only Genevieve and the baron would look forward to duels.

The soldiers never brought breakfast, but shortly after midday, Hendrix came in and sat at the table on the other end of the car. The lady assassin joined him, and then slaves entered with trays of food and set them down. Every tray that passed by me smelled more delicious than the one before, and my stomach protested loudly.

Hendrix waved his hand. "You two come and join us."

I hesitated, despite my stomach growling.

"I know you're hungry," he said. "There ain't no strings attached. You're my guests; I'll not let you starve."

Genevieve stood and bowed. She walked over and sat down, choosing a seat opposite and as far away from the lady assassin as possible. I slowly approached the table and had to choose one of the last two remaining chairs. One next to the lady assassin. The other beside Colonel Hendrix. Not much of a choice. I either sat within easy poisoning distance of the woman, or next to the man who kept trying to kidnap me. I sat beside Hendrix.

A buffet of sliced meats, cheeses, and breads, along with dishes of chicken and beef lay before us. And pie. There were no less than five choices. I ate a piece of each.

In between bites, the colonel asked, "So, what do you think of my Milli-train, Mr. Armitage?"

"It is fearsome," I said, then quickly added, "at least what I've seen of it." Genevieve shot a wary glance in my direction. "I must commend your ingenuity."

"A train that can go anywhere. Soon, there'll be no need for tracks. My Milli-train will conquer the world."

"A train need not be a monster," Genevieve said, her chin raised. "Trains bring civility to the outer most reaches of our world." Hendrix turned away from Genevieve, tore off a piece of bread, and pointed it at me. "That kind of talk is why she'll never be in the Golden Circle." He laughed, shifting back toward Genevieve. "I guess you're more of a daddy's girl, hey?"

"Civilization can only be brought once the wilderness has been pacified." We all looked across the table as the lady assassin spoke.

Genevieve's gaze narrowed, but her expression remained stoic. Like stone. But then, for the first time, Genevieve's gaze darted away, downward. The first and only crack in her façade. Then regaining her demeanor, she said, "Pacifying … enslaving those in the Empire is not civilized. It is barbaric."

"Spoken like a true blueblood." Hendrix nudged me with his left elbow. "There's another reason she'll never be in the Golden Circle. A new world is coming, forged in a fiery crucible of the horsemen's heart. Hammered into a golden circle."

Kannard walked in and sat down beside the lady assassin, staring from me to Genevieve for a long moment before he said, "Must we dine with the prisoners?"

"Prisoners? We don't have any prisoners onboard," Hendrix said with a crooked smile. "These are our guests."

Kannard snarled in annoyance. "Fine, but maybe your *guests* should be locked up in more suitable accommodations."

Hendrix let loose an eerie chuckle, more like a punch to the gut than a laugh. "I'll take that into consideration, Lord Kannard."

"How is your hand, Lord Kannard?" the lady assassin asked.

Kannard narrowed his eyes and stared at the woman beside him, but did not answer.

Hendrix turned to me. "You really should reconsider our offer, you know. The Golden Circle is more of who you are than the Templar Order, who, by the way, still have not accepted you. Have they?"

The man knew where to strike.

"No … but one day they will."

"Ha! One day. You are worthy now," Hendrix said. "Just because a bunch of old men tell you can't, doesn't mean you aren't capable." Hendrix wrapped his mechanical arm around my shoulder, pulling me close. He slammed his remaining hand on my chest and pounded. "Everything that you will be, is already inside you." He released me and returned to eating.

Strong, encouraging words from my enemy. I took a deep breath, but tried not to let them seep inside me. I didn't want to tell him I agreed.

Kannard snagged a slice of sausage and said, "Soon the horsemen will ride again. Nothing your precious Templars do can stop us. Join us or don't. Either way, the world will tremble."

Hendrix nodded. "Let them come. This train will blast them from the sky and crush them into the ground."

"Speaking of this train, I slept horribly," Kannard

groused. "Too much moving around. You should have built a boat. Then we could just sail down the coast."

"A boat?"

"Yes, an elegant boat. Not this monstrosity of the modern age … this iron serpent."

"Careful, Milord." Hendrix wiped his mouth and stood up. "Baroness?" He held out his hand. "Shall we? We have much to discuss."

The woman stood to follow Hendrix. "And you."

"I'm not done," Kannard said, popping some cheese in his mouth.

"Yes, you are." Hendrix motioned toward the soldiers as he headed to the door. Kannard eyed the soldiers, stood, grabbed some grapes, and headed off with Hendrix, never giving us a second glance. The lady assassin followed, along with the guards. As Hendrix approached the door, he turned and called to the last soldier, "Lock the door behind you. We don't want our guests to think they can come and go as they please."

After the last of the soldiers left, Genevieve said, "They appear to be fracturing."

Psssst.

I glanced sidelong at Genevieve, and she raised her eyebrow.

Psssst.

The sound came from the back of the train car. I stood up, but before I could even move, Mr. Singh and Owethu popped up from behind a chaise lounge.

"Indihar! Owethu!" Genevieve and I yelled.

"We thought you might be …" Genevieve halted.

Mr. Singh laughed, "Fear not, Milady. We merely stowed away."

Owethu, jumped over the back of the lounge and

stood on the cushion. "We are here to rescue you."

Mr. Singh cocked an eyebrow and stared at the table full of food. "You do need rescuing, right?"

Mr. Singh and Owethu stared at the food and I motioned, "Please, dig in." They hurried over to the table and snatched up some fruit.

"Being a stowaway is horrible," Mr. Singh said as he shoved a strawberry into his mouth. "Not like being a guest of the Golden Circle."

"Yes," said Owethu. "We at least expected to untie you." He smiled and tore off a piece of meat.

"Where have you been?"

Mr. Singh motioned toward the back of the train. "Atop crates, on the roof, wherever we needed to hide until we could rescue you."

"Better yet, how did you get in here?"

"Easy," said Mr. Singh. "As you all slept, we snuck into the car and hid."

Genevieve put her hands on her hips. "We've got to get off this train."

We all looked at Genevieve, and I said, "But this is taking us to the hidden city of the sky pirates."

"Yes," she nodded, "but I don't think we want to be on this train when it arrives."

Mr. Singh grabbed some more food and said, "The captain knows where the hidden city is."

I held my hands. "Then what are we waiting for?"

The door swung open behind us and the lady assassin stepped in. We all spun around.

"Bonjour! Look at what we have here. Guests … *and* stowaways." She drew a rapier from the sheath at her side. "I'm afraid I'm going to have to insist you come with me."

Genevieve stepped into the middle of the train car, and drew her silver-hilted saber with lapis in the pommel. "Apologies for disappointing you, but we've decided to disembark." She raised the sword in salute.

The woman chuckled. "I guess this was impossible to avoid. Given our history. But my dear, can you fight your mother?"

"You are not my mother." Genevieve hardened her stance, and without looking back at us, said, "Get out of here. I'll catch up."

"But Genevieve," I appealed.

She smiled. "This is duel one. That should inspire confidence."

Mr. Singh did not hesitate. "To the roof."

He grabbed me by the arm and pulled me toward the door. Owethu followed, but before we were able to escape, the lady assassin spun and whipped a thin spike deep into the door frame. Mr. Singh yanked on the handle, but it wouldn't budge.

Genevieve charged and slashed with her sword, forcing the lady assassin to give ground or get cut. The blades clinked together as her opponent blocked every attack. Genevieve pressed harder, pushing her back to the couches. I smiled. Genevieve moved like an artist, as if I were watching one of the great masters in their studio.

Mr. Singh and Owethu pulled at the door to no avail. The lady assassin twisted and parried Genevieve's blade, but she countered with a thrust that held the woman away from us. Mr. Singh pulled his Katar dagger and dug the wide blade into the wood.

Failing to pry out the spike, Mr. Singh twisted his Katar free. "Alexander! Quick, your Thumper!"

Without taking my eyes from the battle before me, I reached in the pouch on my belt and pulled out a percussion cap. I slid the piston forward and loaded one into my Thumper. "Stand back."

As Owethu and Mr. Singh scattered, I aimed it at the door, pressed the trigger, and obliterated the door jam and spike.

"Get up on the roof." I said pointing toward the shattered door. They nodded and disappeared.

I turned back as the lady assassin flipped over one of the coffee tables, landed on the couch, and pushed off to attack. Genevieve parried with her saber.

Loading another percussion cap into my Thumper, I aimed at the lady assassin. Before I could fire, she twirled, plunged her hand into her cloak, and slung several spikes toward me. One lodged in my Thumper. Another cut through my shirt. The rest sank into the wall behind me.

As I pried the spike out of my Thumper, Genevieve thrust forward, and cut through the assassin's cloak.

The lady assassin stopped and reached under her clothes. "You drew first blood. I'm impressed."

"I was trained by the best. My father and my *real* mother."

Flashes of steel filled the parlor as the two women

fought like warriors of old. Genevieve advanced with a flurry of quick thrusts and cuts. Each time, the lady assassin retreated only to lunge in response. I aimed my Thumper, but did not shoot. I could not chance hitting Genevieve.

The lady assassin spun, tossing pillow after pillow at Genevieve. She batted them away, slicing open several, and sending feathers flying in every direction. Relentless, the rapier pierced the cloud of feathers and ripped into Genevieve's cloak. She paused, momentarily stunned. She looked down at herself, no blood, so she twisted, and swung her blade to parry the rapier away.

The lady assassin whipped her sword back and forth, pressing Genevieve back toward me. Their blades danced in the chaos stirred up by the wind. She lunged forward in an attempt to impale my friend. I raised my Thumper and fired, spinning the assassin to the floor.

Genevieve looked from the woman to me, and back again. There was no time to waste. Others would be upon us soon. I glanced back at the door. Hendrix and his soldiers were advancing through the cannon car.

Without a word, I looked up to the ceiling, hoping that armor plating there was not as thick as the plating on the sides. I raised the Thumper and pointed it above the table. The concussive blast ripped through the roof, tearing open a hole a few feet wide.

"Let's go," I yelled.

Genevieve sprang onto the table and jumped through. I climbed onto the table, glancing back at the lady assassin, who lay on a Persian rug, stunned, but not dead. I turned away, grabbed the edge of the opening, and pulled myself up.

Once on top of the undulating train, we ran toward

the rear, where Mr. Singh and Owethu stood waving their hands. As we jumped from one car to the next, I looked over my shoulder. The lady assassin sprang out of the hole and once again pursued us. Hendrix climbed out as well, he yelled something back into the car and pointed at us, the soldiers charging out beside him ran after us, too.

I turned, jumped the gap between two cars, and yelled, "Faster!" to Genevieve. I still didn't know how we were going to escape, and we were quickly running out of train cars.

Mr. Singh and Owethu had reached the end. Both nervously peered over the edge. I looked at Genevieve, then back toward our pursuers, who, too, were quickly bearing down on us.

"What's the next part of the plan?" I asked.

"I thought this was your plan." Genevieve said.

"Jump," Mr. Singh yelled. Then he and Owethu leapt off the back of the train.

Genevieve sprang over the next gap and said, "There has to be a better way."

"If we leap off the sides the legs will chew us up. The end is the only way."

With the lady assassin and Colonel Hendrix now only one car behind us, there was nothing else to do. As we passed under several trees Genevieve leapt off and grabbed hold of a vine. I had to go now. Jumping off I reached for a vine. It snapped and I plunged into a trampled bush below.

I rolled out of the tiny branches and green leaves. Pain pricked every part of me, but I had to keep moving. Hendrix reached the edge of the train. With his right arm raised, he fired a grappling line cable from his arm. The spiraling line arced toward me, moving faster than I could react. Genevieve dropped from the vine and knocked the grappler away with her sword. Hendrix, stared at the four of us and retracted the line.

"The Milli-train is circling back around." Mr. Singh pointed as the train turned back upon itself.

Mr. Singh and I followed Owethu and Genevieve through the trees and dense brush. We turned away from the sound of chugging legs and slipped behind a rise in the land. My heart pounded and every muscle in my body twitched as the Milli-train crested the hill to our right and continued on through the trees. They hadn't seen us. For the time being, we were safe.

The Milli-train turned wide, changed direction, and crisscrossed through the forests and grasslands as they searched for us, but all that doubling back allowed us to slip further away. We continued in a zigzag pattern for the next hour until we were certain they wouldn't find us. Thankfully, the underbrush covered our tracks which made them impossible to follow. To be certain, Mr. Singh climbed a tree and peeked over. The Milli-train marched southwest again, and had left us behind.

Great. We'd escaped a moving train, only to face certain death in the jungles of Africa.

I dreaded thinking about our fate and what horrors sat in the next tree or behind every bush. The heat of the waning day still beat down on us, as if we stood in an oven. Sweat poured from every inch of me, and swiping it away brought little relief as more rolled down to soak every fiber on my body. I'd always lived around water, and after today, I'd never leave it again.

We trudged along in silence before I finally said, "Anyone got a good plan?"

No one answered.

We all turned to Owethu, and I said, "Do you know which way to go?"

"No, I'm not from here."

Mr. Singh gestured, "But they said you're from Africa."

Owethu shook his head. "Africa is bigger than Europe and America combined."

Mr. Singh shrugged.

I nodded. "Then what do we do?"

Genevieve pointed at the Milli-train's tracks. "We follow our enemies."

"We know their headed for the coast." I looked around. "Which is…"

Mr. Singh pointed to the southeast. "About 250 leagues that way. Let's go."

"Leagues… that's like three times the miles." I stopped. "You do realize, we are stranded with no water, no food, and no hope of survival, right?"

Owethu whipped out a canteen. "I brought water."

We all broke out in laughter. The tension disappeared, and for the moment, so did our worries about this predicament. After taking sips from the canteen, we continued on through the grasslands. The late afternoon sun cast long shadows, but offered no relief from the heat.

Owethu walked beside me. "I hope when this is over, we can visit my homeland."

"Me too. It might actually be sooner than later if the Knights of the Golden Circle want to overthrow the Zulu and seize your land."

"I am worried." Owethu stared out over the dunes. "What if these people destroy Zululand?"

"Well, the good news is, you aren't alone. We've dealt with them before."

Owethu smiled. "I am very glad I went to Eton, Alexander."

"It's been good meeting you as well. Just think, if we hadn't discovered the connection back at Eton, no one would know your homeland was threatened."

Mr. Singh shook his head. "Leave it to Alexander to find himself in the middle of trouble."

"I don't mean to find the center of trouble."

Genevieve chuckled. "Of course, you do. Alexander the Great used to look for a moment to seize victory. You look for that same moment, but from the midst of chaos." She slipped around me and continued through the desert.

Owethu grinned and nodded.

I hid my joy from the others. We might be in the middle of nowhere, but we were together and that was all that mattered.

Once the sun dipped below the dunes, the temperature plummeted as a chilly wind enveloped us. The ground still radiated heat, but Mr. Singh and Owethu began to rub their arms. Still, we carried on.

Genevieve slid up alongside me and slipped her

arm through mine. She tucked in against me, stealing my warmth "You're so warm," she said, "as if you'd stored the heat from today."

I laughed. "More like an internal boiler fed by all the food I eat."

I pressed against her and shifted us so the wind hit me first.

A bellicose roar shattered the night.

"What was that?" I tried to remain calm, but trembled as the sound hit me.

Owethu looked off toward the east where the roar still reverberated through the land, now in short bursts. "That's a lion, the king talking to his subjects."

I looked off into the darkness. "We're going to get eaten, aren't we?"

We stepped into a clearing and the land stretched out in front of us. It dipped toward a huge body of water. Was it a sea? The water was so immense that I couldn't see the other shores. This had to be the source of the Nile.

As damp moist air replaced the dry desert winds, we found a small village on the shore of this immense lake. A dozen airships and sailing vessels were moored to a make-shift dock.

"Well, this isn't the Hidden City of the Sky Pirates, is it?"

Genevieve eyed me. "That's not even Zanzibar."

"Ever been to the Hidden City?" I asked Mr. Singh.

He gazed off toward the coast. "No. The captain tends not to fly this far south."

I turned to the others. "We can do this; we only need to get to pirates before the Milli-train."

Genevieve turned to me. Her eyes dazzling in the

moonlight. " …"

She was beautiful. So in command. So determined. She turned to me her eyes narrowing into slits before rolling back. Mr. Singh smacked his forehead and Owethu laughed.

I hadn't heard what she said. My brow must have wrinkled because a slight smile crossed her lips as she shook her head.

"We do not know where we are going." She said over the wind.

"We kind of know. The Hidden City of the Sky Pirates."

Everyone shook their heads.

My head bobbled with nerves. "Yeah, I know it's hidden, but we can find it."

"How?" Mr. Singh's face contorted. "No road or path leads into the hidden city. The only way in is by air."

"We find someone else who's going."

Genevieve turned to me, I started to wonder if she thought me mad, but she smiled and nodded. Mr. Singh held up his thumb.

All three of them turned to me, and suddenly I felt like the captain in front of sky raiders, but I didn't have the answers like he would. They wanted to know what to do next but what could I say. I had no idea. I took a deep breath.

Genevieve pointed at the air docks on the lake shore. "Your plan is to stowaway on an airship and sneak into the city?"

"Exactly." An excellent plan. I'm glad she thought of it and that I'd inspired it.

Genevieve eyed me. "How will we know which one is going to the pirate city?"

Owethu motioned toward the airdocks. "The one with most cargo. They might head for Zanzibar, where we can get another ship, but more likely its booty for the pirates."

I chuckled. "Owethu, I like the way you think. We're going to be friends for a long time."

Owethu nodded in agreement.

Genevieve looked at me. "We're good at getting onboard but once there, we have always been caught."

"We never had Mr. Singh."

Indihar put his hand on his turban and looked at me. He shook his head. "Maybe if we hide in the cargo… come on."

With stealth we slipped through the darkness toward the airdocks, which were nothing more than rusted metal beams braced to each other by other rusted beams some of which had buckled and been hammered back into place. The web of warped metal barely looked like it could hold one airship, much less the dozen moored here.

Mr. Singh pointed to a vessel so stuffed with cargo that they had lashed more goods to the hull with cargo nets. "We can hide on the outside and no one will see us."

Genevieve eyed the airship. "How do we know if it's heading to Zerelda?"

Mr. Singh pointed to the black flag on the ship's prow. "That's a pirate flag."

I hesitated. "The real question is what if we fall off?"

Genevieve walked past me and Mr. Singh. "We'll be in the rope nets."

Owethu continued after the other two leaving me the only one thinking that this might be a bad idea. Mr.

Singh and Genevieve climbed up the rickety iron frame and slipped into the thick rope cargo nets.

I pulled myself up through a hole in the net, and rested on a wooden crate too big to slip out. Once low enough that no one on the dock could see me, I grabbed hold and turned toward Genevieve. She had wrapped herself in the rope netting and looked more secure than I did. So, I wove my arm through the net and held tight.

The airship lifted off. The cold wind whipped across my face biting my skin. A familiar feeling. I started to enjoy the flight. The cargo didn't shift much and we were well secured. I took the moment to look around, to the land below covered in this immense body of water, to the starry sky above.

Genevieve kept her fierce gaze aimed forward, though her knuckles were white around the rope.

We glided under the sea of stars until a circle of lights ignited the grassland. We stayed far to the North. If it was a settlement, the airship seemed to avoid it, but as we drew closer, we saw metal walls studded with cannons. The Milli-train had stopped, circling the cars to form a fort.

In the darkness we slipped past the compound created by the Milli-train until we were far from their enemies. The lights nothing more than dots on the horizon behind us.

I wished for daylight, to be able to see what lay below us. I pushed over to the edge of the crate and glanced over the edge. In the moonlight I could see light and dark splotches on the land. What did the trees hold? What slept upon the plains? Questions flooded my mind, and after a while I started to wonder if we were headed the wrong way. I was certain we'd traveled in one direction, southeast, but after hours we were still over land.

"Africa is so big. Thank goodness we didn't have to walk." I knew no one could hear me but the words just popped out. Walking would have taken weeks.

I looked up and Genevieve was staring at me. She pointed at her ear and shook her head. Oh no, she thought I was talking to her. She pointed at her ear and shook her head.

S oon we soared over the water and I stared off at a small land surrounded by smaller islands. The city of Zanzibar perched on the edge of the largest island looked to be a buzzing maritime port, but we continued on toward a volcanic island off the coast.

The airship descended between the high rock walls of a ravine. Genevieve and Owethu looked around but I studied everything, fascinated by the entrance.

The waning sunlight disappeared, and eerie shadows enveloped the ravine. Every so often we would see cannons and other anti-aircraft guns lining the sheer walls. The caldera, the high walls of the ancient volcano created a circular depression that encased the city. The jagged rim of this ancient volcano was topped with fleets of pirate airships that lined the multi-level airdocks. Buildings perched on the stone and throughout the city were connected by a latticework of steel beam gangplanks and catwalks which crisscrossed the caldera creating a series of rings. All ways lead to a tall black tower at the center of this hidden city.

One thing I did know, it was a good thing the Sparrowhawk and the rest of the fleet weren't here. Only sky pirates were welcome in this city. No Duke's allowed.

The airship drifted toward the caldera, and I gripped the rope even tighter. The mooring clamps extended. We lurched as it caught us and my foot slipped on the crate. I held strong because of my grip on the rope, but of course, Genevieve scooted up onto her feet, but remain crouched under the netting – perfectly poised to spring off.

As the airship came to a complete stop, Genevieve climbed over the netting and dropped onto the airdocks. I shimmied down and slipped out the hole. Hidden behind the cargo and at the back of the airship, no one noticed us.

Genevieve pointed toward a building on the rim of the caldera that looked to be a hub for the walkways. Mr. Singh nodded, and motioned for us to follow. Owethu kept his eyes on the large cargo doors on the side of the airship, and I had to catch up.

Once we were away from the airship, I gripped the railing and studied the city with my father's eye.

"What are you doing?" Genevieve asked.

"Watching for anything out of the ordinary." I continued to scan the city, from the pirates that unloaded their loot along the airdocks, to the crowds gathered in the gaming pits. "From this vantage point I have a better chance of spotting Zerelda."

The web of iron surrounded a multi-level city of flimsy-looking wooden buildings and converted ships hulls. I pointed to the bow of a ship now serving of as the awning of a store. "This city wasn't built; it was pieced together."

"I don't see a single tree or bush," Owethu noted.

He was right, a few birds darted through the buildings or circled the rim, but no grass or any trace of nature remained. It was a city without an overall design, formed with whatever could be found, salvaged, or reinterpreted.

"What a strange and extraordinary place, but such darkness." Genevieve pulled her coat closed. "This place just feels evil."

Once away from the airship, Mr. Singh looked around. "We're really here, The hidden city of the sky pirates."

"Are we safe?" I asked.

Mr. Singh shook his head. "No. They prefer pirates to privateers like me, but a good sneer on the face should make most people leave you alone."

I tried to make my best mean face, but it made Genevieve smile.

She turned to scan the lower city. "Where do we start?"

Mr. Singh pointed to a tall black tower, the only building made of stone stood surrounded by high walls with jagged iron shards protruding to form battlements, it dominated the center of the city. "Tower Black."

I stared at the ominous structure. "How do we know Zerelda's there?"

Mr. Singh started walking along the catwalk and Owethu followed. "After fleeing London, the Sky Witch told every pirate and scoundrel where she was going. She swept in and seized the town. If I didn't know better, I'd say she was gunning for the title of 'Queen of the Pirates'."

Genevieve motioned for me to follow. "I thought the pirates liked their autonomy."

"The Sky Witch has a horseman's heart, and you know what they say about the golden rule – she which has the gold, rules." I pointed at the tower. "Sounds like a good place to start."

We walked along walkways made of wood, metal, and the occasional stone. As we entered the city below, we were assaulted by smells of grease, gunpowder, oil, sewage, and everything was coated in grime. I didn't want to touch anything. I tried holding my nose, but no one else did so I let go and tried not to breathe.

We slipped through the alleys and rushed through the streets. It's a wicked city, beggars sit in slop and fight over the occasional coin or scrap of food. We avoided the men doing deals, and ran as we spotted the flash of a steel blade.

Mr. Singh slipped behind some barrels to avoid a group of pirates. We jumped beside him and hunker down as they passed. My heart pounded in my chest. I spun to identify every sound around us.

Genevieve led us between two buildings made from wood still stained with packing crate logos. We stepped into a market, with bits of sail cloth stretched over wooden poles to form booths. The stinky smell of the outer city waned, replaced by the aroma of spices, food, and then the strong tannins in the dye vats brought back the foul air that burned my lungs.

My eyes went to every stall with food. I wanted to grab the fruit, the bread, but then I saw the flies on the meat and my appetite wavered. As we passed a pile of desert dates, black plums, and tamarinds, Genevieve stopped. She pulled out a few coins and set them down for the man, then picked up one of the bags of dates. We continued on.

She ate one of the dates and passed the bag to me. I took a few and handed it to Owethu, who ate a few and gave the dates to Mr. Singh. I said, "Thank you," as the fruit returned to Genevieve.

On the other side of the market, a wide road led to the center of the city and provided the best view of Tower Black we'd had since the rim. A shiver ran up my spine, Genevieve was right, this place did feel evil, and that tower was its heart.

Genevieve stopped. Mr. Singh scanned the area. Owethu perked up.

I stepped toward her. "What is it?"

"Where are the guards?" Her hands went to her hips. "I don't see a single person at Tower Black."

I look down the street and she's right. No one walks the battlements. One guard leaned on the large front door, but that's all I saw. In fact, the sun had left the caldera in darkness, and yet no light flickered in the tower's windows.

I shook my head. "I don't think anyone's home."

Genevieve turned to me. "Then where is Zerelda?"

I shrugged. Owethu and Mr. Singh did the same.

My stomach began to ache. Not the kind of pain that normally doubled me over when there was trouble, but still it hurt. As I steadied myself with my palm against a barrel of salted fish. I saw several swarthy men emerge onto a street a couple of blocks away. That wasn't unusual; this city was filled with pirates. What caught my attention was the woman with long, dark, curly hair and a sultry stride.

"Zerelda," I blurted out. Genevieve and Owethu followed my finger to the pirates. "With bodyguards."

Genevieve leaned closer to me. "That *is* her. Let's go."

The Sky Witch was easy to track. All we had to do was the follow the crowds. Around every bend, people attempted to rush up to Zerelda, blurting out their issues, only to be knocked away by the four burly men who cleared the streets ahead of her. She strolled along with a sultry stride, holding her head high, like a queen with a smug, aristocratic expression mocking the nobles I'd seen at Lord Marbury's manor.

I pushed through a crowd of men who smelled like gunpowder and oil, checking behind me every few steps to make certain the others kept up. I bumped into a man stumbling out of a bar. He spun around, but instead of yelling at me, he punched the guy beside me. In retaliation, the man bashed his fist into the bushy and beer-soaked beard of the drunk. The two then fell into the dusty road as four more men joined in the scuffle.

Genevieve grabbed my arm and pulled me through the gathering crowd. We'd lost sight of Zerelda. After a short distance, we stopped at a set of stairs leading down to the mid-level section of the city. From this

vantage point, we could see half the city. I scanned the area below in hopes of finding her again. Nothing.

"We've lost her." I kicked the metal grating and the sound echoed across the entire city.

"We didn't." Owethu pointed to a nearby building, better constructed than most on the outer levels of the city. The multi-story building, perched like a bird along the rim of the caldera, was connected to the airdocks with catwalks. "Look," Owethu said, "she rises up the side of the wall."

I turned. "A steam-powered elevator … here?"

Zerelda and her bodyguards stood on the wide platform wrapped in a metal railing, as it rose to the second floor of the structure.

I scratched my head. "How do we follow her without being seen?"

Mr. Singh put his hand on my shoulder and aimed me. "There. On the side of the building. A door."

Owethu leaned in. "But what about her guards?"

"We need a distraction," Genevieve added.

I looked around for anything that might draw her men away. Think like the captain, like a Templar, I told myself. Something, somewhere deep inside me screamed that it was foolish to fight all her bodyguards.

"Won't the fight suffice?" Mr. Singh pointed to the bar brawl still raging behind us.

"That's probably normal. We need something out of the ordinary." I nudged Mr. Singh. "Like that." Nearby, a man struggled to tie up a dozen camel, behind the dozen already secured to the building.

"What do you have in mind?" Genevieve asked, her coy smile growing.

"Free the camels. Herd them toward the building

to distract the guards, and then slip through the side door while they are busy."

"Then what?" Genevieve asked.

"Then we find the Sky Witch. Remember, Zerelda has a heart. That's why Kannard is here. We get to it first."

Mr. Singh and Owethu nodded in agreement. Genevieve nudged me with her arm as she walked past. "I like the way you think."

Although I knew we were probably walking into something we might not get out of, I couldn't wipe the grin from my face. Hearing Genevieve acknowledge and admire my plan gave me the courage to move forward.

One after another, we slipped along the raised street toward the camel dealer, careful to avoid his field of view. I paused between two buildings and scanned the area to be certain we weren't being followed or watched.

I stumbled toward the camels tied to the building and slipped in between the herd. I grabbed the rope that bound them together, struggling to untie the knot, when Mr. Singh joined me. He raised his Katar dagger and in one quick slice, cut through the rope.

"Gordian's knot," he whispered.

I stifled a laugh.

Slipping to the back of the camel herd, Mr. Singh slapped one on the rump. The camel bound forward, breaking free. When the other camels realized they were free, they broke loose in a panic and we rushed them toward Zerelda's soldiers. People along the walkways fled or tried to dodge them. As dromedaries dashed along the catwalks the soldiers ran in front of them, waving their arms. In all the chaos, we slipped in the side door undetected. Inside, I led the way up the stairwell to the second floor. Near the top, I stopped. I peeked my head up over the floor and saw a large room full of people: pirates, captains, well-dressed gentlemen, and servants.

Owethu tapped me on the shoulder. "Trouble."

I looked over to him. "You got that right." But he wasn't talking about what I saw. I followed the nod of his head to two men standing at the bottom of the stairs. "Oh … you meant that trouble."

"Follow my lead." Genevieve drew her saber and stormed up the steps past Owethu and me, her heels clattering on the wood.

I sprang up onto the floor and followed her. I knew exactly what she intended. Another duel. Her second. A finish to the duel they began on the Sparrowhawk a year ago. Genevieve pushed through the crowd and seized the center of the room, standing before Zerelda. I came up along next to her. Owethu and Mr. Singh followed.

The raven-haired sky pirate sat on a throne crafted from airship parts with two cannon barrels for armrests. Her corset was still adorned with silver skull buttons, but now, each donned a four-pointed gold crown. Zerelda merely smiled as her guards surrounded us. Fortunately, there were only five. The others still herded the camels.

34
The Duel

Genevieve pointed her saber at Zerelda. "I've come to finish our duel, Zerelda."

"That's Queen Zerelda, you blue-blooded brat." She motioned with her hand and her pirates moved in closer. I chanced a quick look and saw that two of the men drew revolvers, and one even whipped out a blunderbuss.

"Afraid to face a little girl? Afraid you'll lose?"

Queen Zerelda leaned forward on her throne, and, in a Dutch accent, spat, "I fear nothing. Especially the prattle of a little tart such as you."

"Is that why you fled when we faced each other last year on the Sparrowhawk?"

Zerelda gripped the cannons and glared at Genevieve, but she did not rise.

I had never been more impressed by Genevieve. She imparted such strength, yet retained her noble grace. Her eyes burned like fire, and never wavered from Zerelda.

"I demand an end to that duel."

"You demand," the witch cackled. "I don't take commands. I give them." She

doubled her fists and pounded on the cannons.

Zerelda glanced at the others in the room. So did I. I knew that the focus wasn't on Genevieve, but Zerelda. Her reaction to the command from Genevieve, would speak volumes to the room full of vipers.

To save face she would have to kill Genevieve. It was the only way she'd retain the throne. This plan didn't seem like such a good idea anymore.

Zerelda stood up and drew an old flintlock pistol that rested against her hip beneath her skirt. She raised the gun and aimed it at Genevieve, "Let me show you how a pirate duels."

Genevieve didn't flinch, but my heart jumped into my throat. Flintlock pistols were notoriously inaccurate which meant she could hit any one of us. One of Mr. Singh's steel ring chakrams whizzed by my ear, and the sharpened edge cut into the flintlock's barrel.

"Afraid to fight me with your sword, I see," Genevieve smiled. "I thought you were a queen, a horseman."

Zerelda looked at the steel ring embedded in her gun. "If you want die, then I shall be happy to send you to hell." When she stepped down from her throne, everyone, except Genevieve backed away. Never taking her eyes from Genevieve, the Pirate Queen, took a swordsman's stance, with her feet slightly wider than her shoulders. Her skirt was bound up in front by a pair of metal clasps. She drew the wicked cutlass from its shark skin sheath. As her blade caught the light, her heeled boot ground into the floor and she lunged at Genevieve.

Genevieve parried Zerelda's blade and slashed with her own silver saber. Everyone's attention was fixed on the two swordswomen, but remembering the reason we came, I scanned the room for the horsemen's heart. The small urn, earthenware bound in iron bands could be anywhere, but knowing Zerelda, she kept it close.

As Genevieve pressed her attacks and Zerelda twirled to avoid them, I slowly slipped over toward the sky pirate's throne, scanning the room to make sure no one noticed. At one point, I stopped when Zerelda thrust her cutlass at Genevieve, who dodged the attack. Zerelda followed through with a kick to her stomach, sending Genevieve tumbling across the floor. When she landed by one of the pirates, he kicked her in the back.

Mr. Singh stepped forward, pulled out his double-barrel Katar dagger, cocked the hammer, and aimed it at the pirate. Genevieve stood up, turned, and kicked the man in the knee, then attacked Zerelda again with a flurry of strikes.

The Sky Pirate Queen blocked Genevieve's saber, but the baron's daughter pulled back and quickly lunged forward, slicing Zerelda's shoulder. Zerelda roared and rubbed the blood between her fingers. Genevieve kept her blade aimed at her opponent, as a drop fell to the floor.

I rushed up to Zerelda's throne. Scanning over the chair, I saw a semi-circular cutout on the left side of the seat. The top of the urn poked out of the recess.

As I reached down to retrieve the urn, Zerelda screeched, "Get away from there!" She charged and thrust her cutlass at my hands.

I drew my hands back as the blade slammed down and dug into the seat. I stumbled back and grabbed my Thumper. Zerelda rushed at me. I sprawled back onto the throne, and the pirate queen aimed her wicked cutlass at me. "Guards surround them, and shoot them if they move!"

A shadow covered the sun and everyone looked up. The Sparrowhawk sailed in above us. "Yes!" My heart soared into the sky at the site. Not since the first day I'd seen her on the docks had that aero-dirigible looked so good.

Ziplines spiraled down anchoring to Zerelda's hideout. Several people slid down the lines landing on the balcony.

Circling the line, the familiar bronze wings of Rodin darted around the others and landed on Genevieve's shoulder. He rubbed his head under her chin and along her cheek. She scratched behind his ears and horns, but never took her eyes off Zerelda. Rodin hardened and lowered down; his eyes narrowed on the pirate queen.

"I'd stay right where you are." Captain Baldarich landed on the deck with his lightning cannon drawn. He strolled into the light in the center of the room.

One of Zerelda's pirates cringed and backed away as if seeing a ghost. "That's ... that's Captain Baldarich of the Sky Raiders."

Baldarich smiled. "Yes, and as you can see, we have you surrounded."

"Lies," Zerelda snarled. "They would have come in guns blazing and my men would have sounded the alarm."

"We're not done," Genevieve said as she stood in front of Zerelda.

"I'm done with all of you." Zerelda stepped over to throne and sat down. With a wild look in her eyes, she pulled cords on either side of her.

"Everyone down!" Baldarich grabbed Genevieve and hit the floor.

The throne's cannon armrests spit flames, smoke, and lead. Zerelda wickedly cackled. The air smacked my chest, knocking me back from the throne.

Rolling to my side, I saw Zerelda reach into the throne's recess and grab the urn. I raised my Thumper and fired, but it was difficult to focus and impossible to breathe through the smoke. The concussive blast ripped apart the back of the throne, but missed Zerelda entirely. She spun on her heel and locked eyes with me. My heart skips a beat, as I fear she'll come for me and I don't have another shot. She turns, her wicked laugh trailed off, and her curly hair whipping about in the debris and smoke. She bolted for the side of the building. Once there, she kicked a lever and the wall fell apart. Jumping into the air, she snagged a pole with her arm, and disappeared below.

"Genevieve!" the baron's voice broke through the groans of everyone in this room. "Genevieve!"

"Here I am." She still lay with Baldarich on the floor. She rolled over and slowly stood up. "The captain and I are okay."

"Speak for yourself. I can't hear a blasted thing." Baldarich sat up and drew in the cord to pick up his lightening cannon.

A ripple of pain in my stomach wrenched me into knots and kept me balled up on the floor. Danger. The most intense … since last year. I forced myself to stand and move beyond the pain. I ran to where Zerelda escaped. Looking over the edge at the ground below the airdocks, the Iron Horsemen rode toward us. Zerelda slid down the pole to the ground far below, where two Iron Horsemen awaited with black-cloaked riders. Hendrix and Kannard. Hendrix pulled back his hood and set his Stetson upon his brow. Zerelda jumped onto the iron steed behind him, and the colonel looked up and tipped his hat at me.

My father called out through the smoke, "Alexander, where are you?"

I didn't answer. I gripped the wall for support as the blood surged in my temples pounded with each beat of my heart. I was staring down the barrels of the Horseman of War's cannon, along with the Gatling gun in its chest.

Terror anchored me as I stared at the large ballista on the steed of the white Horseman of Disaster. I jumped back. "The Horsemen!"

The remains of the building around me exploded. Shards of wood and torn chunks of iron ripped through the room. We all hustled down the stairs and outside. The unrelenting bombardment from the Iron Horsemen brought the crumbling building down around us. The ground shook and tore apart, as the thunderous stomp of the Horsemen of War fractured the valley. What remained of the building exploded and I tumbled across the street.

I heard voices calling out, but they seemed so distant. I crawled slowly through the dusty street. Captain Baldarich burst through the smoke and rushed up to me. "The Iron Horsemen have disappeared." I nodded as two camels ran past.

We all climbed aboard the Sparrowhawk as the crew lowered a rope ladder. I'd hoped a warm welcome would be waiting for us, since we had managed to escape capture and avert certain death, but when I saw my father's face, I wanted to jump right back into pirate city.

The baron grabbed Genevieve and hugged her tight. Baldarich embraced Mr. Singh, as did Owethu's father to him.

"Welcome aboard," Captain Baldarich announced with wide-open arms. "My congratulations on surviving that mechanical monstrosity and this den of pirates."

"The Milli-train," I said. "At least that's what Colonel Hendrix called it."

They all looked at me. Their smiles faded. It was like I'd taken a giant pin and popped the only balloon in the room.

When my father grabbed me by the shoulders and squeezed, I seized up, thinking I might get one of his unending lectures again. He stared into my eyes. That's when I saw that his eyes were red and glossy, his

cheeks still wet from tears. He didn't hug me, just smiled, fixed his glasses, and patted my shoulder. I grabbed his arm and said, "I'm okay. They treated us really well."

In a voice muffled by the Iron Horsemen's blast and the competing with the non-stop ringing, I barely heard him as he said, "No more heroics, all right?"

I didn't reply. I couldn't. He wouldn't like it anyway.

The captain sat down in his chair and rubbed his temples. His voice sounded distant like a fading echo, but if I focused, he said, "Heinz, get us out of here and head south."

Within moments we were rising into the sky. Ignatius walked over to the captain, "Gears says all three engines are in working order and we'll have full power to take us to southern Africa."

"Wonderful news." The captain stretched. "I have Hunter keeping an eye out for our slithering desert friend."

Ignatius checked the Arial Tracking Dial. "Captain, the Templar Fleet is north of us. Should we reduce speed to allow them catch up?"

The captain spun in his chair and looked to the baron, who shook his head. Baldarich nodded and turned back to Ignatius. "No, stick with the Milli-train."

"We need to get to Zululand before the Golden Circle," the baron added, "Sinclair and the others know our destination."

Baldarich stroked his mustache. "We'll find the Milli-train and slow it down."

"Excellent. Thank you, Captain." The baron headed off the bridge.

Assuming he was leaving to find Genevieve, I waited a few moments and followed. I'd been wondering where Genevieve was and wanted to make sure she was unhurt. He led me to the gun deck, and entered the front room. I sat on one of the cannons and waited. I didn't want to intrude on their time, so I opened the gunport beside me to look out over the desert. Night had fallen, and the cool evening air whipped around me, chilling me. I didn't mind. The crispness let me know I was alive. I'd faced death, overwhelming odds, and all three Iron Horsemen riders. It felt good to just sit and breathe cool, clean air.

The door swung open and the baron stormed out of the room, startling me. He nodded, but headed up stairs.

The clatter of falling metal accompanied Genevieve's "Ow!" I stood up and rushed to the door.

"You okay?" I asked as she appeared in front of me, hobbling on one foot and grumbling beneath her breath. Rodin hovered behind her flapping his wings.

"I … yes. It's nothing, really." Genevieve limped ahead of me to one of the cannons and sat down. I knelt in front of her. Rodin landed on and curled up on her shoulder. "I kicked a cannonball with my boot, then the rest of the cannonballs got involved.

"Ouch, but they do tend to gang up."

She chuckled and let go of her foot. We slipped into an awkward silence. I stood up and sat beside her on the cannon. Rodin uncurled and crawled over to me.

I tapped my foot to force the nervous energy building inside me. I looked over at Genevieve but then turned away. Shifting back to her, I blurted out, "You were amazing today."

Genevieve looked down, her cheeks turning pink. "Thank you."

"You fought two duels… and won."

"We ran from the assassin, and Zerelda ran from the other," she said.

"Do you have any cuts on you?"

"No."

"Under the rule of first blood, you won both duels."

Genevieve leaned against me. "Thanks, but you and the captain are the only ones who think this."

"Is that why your father stormed out of here just now?"

"He doesn't want me to fight the assassin."

I wrapped my arm around Genevieve. She rested her head on my shoulder and Rodin curled up on both of us. "I've enjoyed this adventure with you, Genevieve."

"Taking me off on adventures," Genevieve said softly, "seems to be your modus operandi."

I smiled. "It takes a lot to get you alone."

"We did get to see the pyramids."

"And Alexandria."

The stairs rattled as someone walked down on the gun deck. I snatched my arm from around her and we slid to opposite ends of the cannon so fast we polished it. Ignatius poked his head down and said in his not-quite-western accent, "Gustav cooked up some grub for everyone."

"We'll be right up," I said.

"Ignatius, have we met up with the rest of the fleet?" Genevieve stood up with Rodin now clinging to her shoulder.

"The Imperial airship and its escort fleet will be here soon. The rest of the Templar Air Corp is still to the north."

Genevieve bowed her head, "Thank you."

I stood up as Ignatius disappeared up the stairs. Genevieve jumped off the cannon and spun on her heel and faced me. She took my hands in hers, her eyes piercing my soul. "You're the best for cheering me up." Then she wrapped her arms around me and hugged me. I wondered—hoped—that what I was feeling, she was feeling, too.

Once night had swept completely over the land, Mr. Singh motioned for me to follow. We climbed up the conning tower and out onto the top of the Sparrowhawk. He pulled out a flare gun. He looked to the stars, finding the directions he fired into the Northeast sky. A bright red, burning glow soared into the air and exploded like fireworks before slowly drifting back down to the sand.

"Will anyone see that?" I asked.

"Everyone in the desert will see that falling star." Mr. Singh said.

A short while later, I saw five stars, dots of light, drifting above the sand. They moved toward us. The soft sound of engines pulled my attention to the dark clear sky above, and then I saw two smaller airskiffs, two airfrigates, and the Duke's imperial airship approaching from the Northeast. Each had hung lanterns beneath their hulls to ignite the airship as well as the dunes below.

My joy deflated like a punctured balloon. The Templars were here… but so was the Duke. Worse yet, Genevieve's betrothed probably waited onboard. I kicked at the decking, but forced myself to calm down. More important matters lay ahead.

Mr. Singh raised his flare gun, and fired, a burning red orb soared into the sky, illuminating the Templar flag on the side of a couple of airships.

Spiraling down around the flare, the familiar bronze wings of Rodin darted in and out of the red light as if playing with the ember. He soared over and into the cargo doors. We rushed down and I found him perched on Genevieve's shoulder.

The next morning, I awoke with my belly still filled with Gustav's stew. Lying in my hammock, with Owethu swinging next me, I let one leg dangle over the side and stared up at the ceiling. I stared at Rodin's bed, the one Genevieve and I had made. He wasn't in it, which wasn't surprising. He was most likely up in the baron's cabin with Genevieve.

Although my father snored on the other side of the cloth wall that divided the room, it gave me courage to know he was so close. I wished he believed in me, the way I believed in me. The way Genevieve believed in me. But he was too focused on his work to notice anything about me except when I'm was in trouble. I wondered if Owethu had similar issues with his father.

I would find out what his world was like soon enough.

The day was filled with maintenance issues, checking the lines with Hunter, reinforcing the hull with Ignatius, and helping Gears clean some sprockets. It was good to be part of the crew again.

After finishing my duties, I retreated to the gundeck, staring out one of the ports.

The setting sun ignited the African savannah in a spectacular golden light. The magnificent landscape adorned with mountains of rolling grassland, was broken only by patches of shrubbery. We were flying too high for a clear view of the vast herds spread over the terrain, but they dotted the land in the millions.

Owethu, who'd taken a seat on the cannon across from me, had a big smile on his face. "We are almost to my home."

"I can't wait."

"There is much I want to show you; and many people I want you to meet."

Owethu not only wanted to show me his homeland, but he was excited about it. I didn't know how he felt about me, but I was happy to have him as a friend. "Our fathers and the baron have been going on about a big meeting when we land," I said, "but after that I want to see everything."

Owethu nodded. We sat in silence staring at the world below, until he saw a river he recognized. Then he became animated. "There. My village is atop the hill."

I hadn't known what to expect. I'd heard so many tales of the Dark Continent, but what lay before me was astounding. Clusters of circular huts, if one could call them that, adorned the hill. To use such a small and basic word seemed an insult. All of the elaborately constructed houses were topped with thick brown thatch. The entire village was surrounded with thickets of thorn bushes, like the different areas of London.

As we landed near Owethu's village, he rushed off to find his father. Not wanting to miss anything, I continued staring out the window as we descended. My father came up behind me and said, "Alexander, we'll be participating in a welcoming ceremony. Be ready to disembark. I can't stress enough that you should be on your best behavior."

I winced at his words. "I know, and I will. You didn't have to tell me."

He continued as if he hadn't heard my words. "I also want you to let the baron and the Templars deal with this. We are not warriors; we are scholars."

Again, I cringed, but just nodded, which must have been to his satisfaction, because he walked off.

I wrung my hands together trying to force my anger away. I am a warrior. I might be in training, but I've tasted victory and defeat. Obviously, my father didn't consider me a warrior, but he didn't realize that I wasn't a scholar either.

When Chief Zwelethu stepped off the airship, all the people of his village greeted him like a returning hero. They filled the air with their singing, and the women danced in jubilation. Several of the other chieftains traveled with the king to welcome him back to Zululand. They cheered Owethu with the same intensity. No one at Eton would even raise an eyebrow when I came back.

The other airships landed, and soon the Duke, Lord Sinclair, Eustache, the Tinkerer, and several other Templar airship captains joined us.

We entered through a gate made of wood and tusks, with an immense elephant skull seated at the top of the arch. In the center of the village, large bonfires blazed, lighting up the night and chasing back the cool breeze. Food was brought out and laid before us on earthenware trays and bowls, or on woven straw mats. Unlike the theatres back home, the dancers performed in the midst of us.

I wanted to ask Owethu a thousand questions, but I was trapped between my father and the baron. He sat next to his brother, who was jealous of Owethu's pith helmet, just as he said he'd be, and who kept asking him about every little detail of his adventure. Owethu's sisters and his mother sat with several women near Chief Zwelethu.

The Duke sat in the center of our delegation. He even brought a high-backed chair elaborately decorated with a velvet seat. The chair looked as oddly misplaced as did the Duke in his dress uniform.

Richard sat beside the baron and Genevieve. Before he sat down, he acknowledged my father; then, expecting him to have the decency to acknowledge me, I looked up. He looked right past me as if I wasn't there. He bowed and took Genevieve's hand and kissed it before sitting down and turning his back to me. Rodin who was sitting on her shoulder stared at Richard, but did not fly over to him like he did to me. The bile in my stomach churned. Normally, I'd be thrilled at his lack of attention, but I burned that I could be so easily dismissed. I tried to concentrate on the dancing, the food, and the conversation between my father and the Duke, but found myself miserably listening whenever Richard spoke to Genevieve.

After dinner, the talk turned to why we had come. Lord Sinclair, the Duke, the baron, Eustache, and Chief Zwelethu spoke with the other elders and airship captains. For once, we were allowed to stay and join in, but only to give our account of the past events.

"We must develop a plan." Grand Master Sinclair pounded his fist against his palm. "A strategy for dealing once and for all with the Knights of the Golden Circle."

"How do we even know they are coming here?" the Duke asked.

The baron shook his head at him as if he couldn't believe he asked the question. "We believe they are after the gold they learned about from the geological surveys conducted in the area by McCafferty."

I stood up. "Actually, they're after something far worse." I didn't mind being an insolent pup. "They're after a new heart, for the fourth horsemen … to replace the one Genevieve destroyed last year."

"Impossible," the Duke said as he glared at me. Richard let out an audible gasp, but this time I ignored him.

"No, it's true. I had a … we saw the horsemen in the Hidden City of the Sky Pirates." I didn't think mentioning this had only been in my dream would sway them.

Everyone looked back and forth at each other, but only I noticed the Zulu woman who sat at the back of the Chief Zwelethu's entourage. Richly decorated with beaded necklaces and bracelets. And wrapped in a blue cloth. She leaned on a walking stick, her skin dark and vibrant, but cracked into deep set wrinkles. Her gaze chilled me, but I couldn't look away.

"Do we have the Iron Knights?" the baron asked.

"They are en route," Sinclair said. "May be two or three days before they arrive with the rest of the aircorp."

The baron stepped forward. "We first need to learn what we don't know. So, I would suggest some of us go and find where Kannard and the others are hiding."

"An excellent idea." Sinclair pointed at the baron with his cane. "Once we know what they're up to, we can prepare our defense."

"I will go," the baron offered, "but, if possible, Chief Zwelethu, I would ask for a Zulu escort."

Chief Zwelethu nodded, "I will send five of my warriors with you."

The baron bowed. "You are most gracious, sir. Thank you."

It wasn't long before we left the gathering and headed back to the Sparrowhawk. My father indicated for me to go to bed, but I wasn't sleepy and didn't want to lie in my hammock staring at the bulkhead. I sat against the landing strut gazing between the stars hovering above, and the Zulu village below. A river of stars passed over the village, but since I wasn't used to the southern hemisphere, all the constellations were not where I ordinarily saw them. But that didn't diminish their beauty. Owethu walked up and I motioned for him to join me. He shook his head. "Please come with me. Someone would like to meet you."

"Who?" I asked.

"Our *Umthandazi.*"

"Your shaman?" Owethu had been teaching me some of his language

Owethu led me to a hut adorned with totems, charms, and the bones of spirit animals woven into the construction of the hut and arranged around the outside. He stopped me before we entered. "This is an *indumba*, a sacred healing hut. I do not know why the *Umthandazi* wants to see you, but it is a great honor."

I bowed my head. "I am fascinated, excited, and honored to be here."

When we stepped inside, I was reminded of the mud-daubed walls of Southwest American adobe houses. Four fire pits, each placed at the cardinal points of this circular hut, smoldered with a dark orange light as thin streams of smoke rose upward to fill the room. The Zulu woman who'd gazed at me earlier sat opposite the entry. I followed Owethu and knelt down across from her.

I started to speak, but Owethu touched my leg, so, like him, I bowed my head and remained quiet. When the woman spoke, her voice grumbled like an approaching summer storm. "Welcome, Dream Diviner."

My eyes popped open and I raised my head to meet her penetrating stare. I opened my mouth to ask, "How did you know?" but she waved her hand and I fell silent. She leaned in closer and said, "The winds have brought me visions of you." Then sitting back up, she said, "You have a question you want to ask."

I didn't know what she meant. I was here because Owethu said she wanted to meet me. Puzzled, I said, "I guess I'd like to know if we're going to be victorious against the Milli-train?"

The woman waved her hand. "That has not yet been determined. But... that is not the question you want to ask." She folded her hands in her lap and waited.

I looked over at Owethu, but he shook his head. I didn't have a clue what she expected me to ask. There was one, however, something I'd always been curious about. The one question I'd had for years.

"Why is it that whenever danger is around, I am doubled over in pain?"

"A-a-a-h, there it is." She smiled and rocked back and forth. "You are connected to the spirit world. The ancestors, they talk to you; they aid you on your journey." She pointed to my stomach. "It's how they warn you."

"But why?"

"Because it is *you* who must face the Horsemen."

"Me? Can't be, Genevieve is better with a sword. Mr. Singh is better with a gun. And the baron is better at everything."

"The lion is the greatest warrior, but can be brought down by a single thorn."

I've always been a thorn. "Why me?"

"Because the visions come to you."

The shaman stood and walked over to a small table along the back wall. There she gathered several herbs and oils, mixing them in into a bowl. A pungent aroma filled the hut. The shaman returned with the bowl in hand and knelt down before me. "Do you desire to see more?"

I'd only tried to induce a vision once before, but that was for my father. I nodded to the shaman. "I would."

She stuck her thumb into the thick, inky substance and smeared it on my forehead. Instantly, I felt a weird sensation running throughout my body. My heart pounded. As my stomach began to ache, she laid me back, and I faded away before my head touched the mat.

In the pitch-black dark, the pings of hammers striking chisels echoed like a haunting wail, the rumbling of dynamite washed over me like thunder, and an eerie sensation zapped me to the core—I was not alone. In this blackest night, the Zulu groaned in agony as the crack of a whip shattered souls. Fingers tore clumps of the darkness away like dirt. The sun sped across the sky, only to drop below the horizon and rise again on the other side. The streaking light revealed a large chunk of jade in the shape of a heart emerging from the earth. Inlaid gold wire gave the stone a regal appearance. Colonel Hendrix snatched the heart from the cracked dirt and yelled in triumph. I heard a monstrous roar, a mix of groaning metal and hisses of steam. A creature rose up above me and smashed down around me. It tore the Zulu village to pieces, and then turned back to me. Light shone out its eyes, and its gnarled metal teeth gaped open. An Iron Armor rushed between us and thrust an Iklwa into the beast. The armor didn't resemble the Black Knight, but rather held the Zulu spear and shield. The monster reared up, and crashed down on me. Everything went black.

BOOK II: IRON ZULU

Isnapped up, drenched in sweat and breathing hard. My heart raced so fast; my entire body thundered with each beat. Firelight seeped in casting beams through the dust. The shaman was gone, but a sweet voice filled my ears.

"Welcome back. You had us worried there for a minute." Genevieve knelt beside me and dabbed my forehead with a handkerchief.

Owethu sat on the other side of me. "What did you see?"

"Do we need to rush to the airships?" Mr. Singh asked as he stood at my feet.

"No, but the Iron Horsemen are coming and there's something worse. I ... I don't know." Fear gripped me and I held the words deep inside.

"Tell us everything." Genevieve said as she helped me sit up.

"The Knights of the Golden Circle are coming ... here. What they want is close, maybe even in the village, but the Zulu are in the way and must be ... eliminated."

"We must tell

the others." Genevieve said.

Owethu stood. "They are with my father." He stepped to the door of the *indambe* and motioned for us to follow. "This way."

We rushed through the village, to an immense archway, behind which lay the largest and most elaborately decorated dwelling. The walls and roof had been banded in different colors, like the brickwork of some London flats. My father, the elders of the Templars, as well as the Duke and Richard sat outside on a semi-circle of short stools, talking with Chief Zwelethu.

We walked up and everyone turned. With everyone facing me, my resolve started to waver, but the shaman's words rung in my ear. I mattered.

"Alexander," my father said, "I thought you were in the healing hut."

I stepped into the center of the group and said, "I had a vision."

The Duke rolled his eyes and said, "Come now," he laughed. "Now the pup admits he's mad?" Richard mirrored his father's expression.

Chief Zwelethu raised his hand and leaned in. "Go on."

"We have two days."

"Until what?" Richard asked sarcastically. I ignored him and looked toward Grand Master Sinclair.

"The Milli-train, the Knights of the Golden Circle, and two of the horsemen arrive in two days." I turned to Chief Zwelethu. "Your land ... your village is in their way."

Grand Master Sinclair smacked his cane against his palm. "Exactly! The gold. I knew it."

"We need to plan for our defense," Eustache said.

I shook my head. "Not gold." Everyone fell silent. The air grew heavy, thick, and the tension smothered us. "The gold is only a distraction, maybe a ruse for Kannard. They're after a heart. One of cracked jade trimmed with gold. I've seen it." My shoulders slumped. "What's worse, I know they'll find it."

"What are you talking about?" Sinclair asked. "All our spies say they're seeking gold."

"No. When we were on the Milli-train, we saw a journal that Lord Cobblefield had procured. It belonged to Schoenbruster, a German anthropologist. In it, he described a heart made of stone, which the natives worshipped. In battle with the Zulu, it was lost. I think they are going to try to invade the village, force the Zulu to leave … so they can find the heart."

Sinclair rapped his cane against the ground. "The Crusader's Heart!"

"Those were destroyed," the baron said as he pointed at the Grand Master, "at the end of the Crusades."

I looked to my father. From the look on his face, I could tell he knew exactly what they spoke about. "What are the Crusader Hearts?" I asked.

Eustache stepped toward me, "Do you remember our conversation in my study? I spoke of the times throughout history when the horsemen have ridden again."

I nodded. "Yes, the last time was the Spanish Armada."

"Excellent memory," the French nobleman said, "Well, during the Crusades, the Templar fought the Horsemen. They defeated them in the battle, but as such, they lost the war. All we really know is that in the final days of their occupation of the Holy Land, the four hearts were said to have been lost."

"So, how did one get here?" Genevieve asked.

"We don't know."

My father pushed his glasses back onto the bridge of his nose, "We know the hearts on Malta represented the oldest ever made, and I remember from the readings that the Crusader Hearts were said to have been the biggest and most elaborate of the demonic urns. He must think combining the two sets will give him the most power."

The baron slid his fingers along his chin. "And all this happens in two days?"

I took a deep breath. "If we can't defeat them … on the third day, the sun will set forever."

"*Tres bien*," the Frenchmen said. "You have done excellent."

"We do have one problem, however." Sinclair tugged at his beard. "The Iron Knights are on their way, but they are three days away at the earliest."

The Duke looked at all of us sitting here. "You mean to tell me we have a handful of airships, and these *savage* warriors to go up against the Milli-train, two Iron Horsemen, and Hendrix's seasoned troops?" He shook his head, "It cannot be done. I will call in Her Majesty's soldiers."

"Yes, that would be good, but they, too, are more than two days away. We will do what we can and hold the line until more help arrives." Chief Zwelethu leaned forward. "I will send word to the king of the Zulu to send all our warriors to fight these invaders. I pledge those in my service, and my sons."

I glanced over at Genevieve, who nodded. She'd

been sitting there, listening, taking in everything. She'd been eyeing me with an expression I'd never seen before. I didn't know what it meant, but right then I couldn't focus on her. I had one more thing to share.

"Actually, there is one last part of my vision." I wrung my hands together and avoided my father's eyes. "The Tinkerer and Owethu are the ones who are going to save us."

"I am?" the Tinkerer said in his thick Scottish accent.

"Yes, you're going to build another Iron Knight— for Owethu. An Iron Zulu."

Silence settled over everyone. Even the crackling fire seemed to hush. Owethu's eyes grew round as saucers. Genevieve smiled, her face glowing in the firelight.

The Tinkerer's eyes darted back and forth as his fingers pointed to an unseen list. He smiled, as solutions popped with each raised eyebrow. "If I can cannibalize one of the smaller airships, then I'll have her done in no time. No problem."

Suddenly, the Duke said, "Are we really going to listen to a boy?"

Before I could respond, Chief Zwelethu said, "Yes. We are." Looking at the Tinkerer, his soft voice pulling in the silent crowd, the chief said, "Build your Iron Zulu. My son is the right choice; he connects with your mechanical world."

"Thank you," I said to Owethu's father.

The chief nodded and motioned to a man standing beside him. "Send a runner immediately."

"There is one more thing we need to know," Eustache said. "Where is this *fer coeur*? The Knights of the

Golden Circle must know to focus on this village. If we found it first, we would have an advantage."

"Actually, it's not iron, it's jade," I said with a shrug.

Eustache laughed and bowed. "I stand corrected." He took me by the shoulders. "Did you see this place? Could you find it again?"

"No, but according to my dream, it must be in this village."

38
Train Hunting

Back on the Sparrowhawk and still buzzing from the vision and the Templar's planning session, I lay in my hammock replaying the remnants of my dream. When my father walked in, he stood at the end of my hammock, leaning against the ropes, and for a moment he just stared at me. "At some point, Alexandar, we're going to have to talk about these visions."

I sat up. "The Zulu shaman showed me their importance."

"From the sound of them, I would say she is right."

Surprised, I said, "You're not angry?"

"No." My father nudged my leg. "I care that you are safe. These visions warn of danger, so hopefully you'll avoid some of it."

I got up and hugged him. He held me tight. When he let go, I slid back into the hammock. He left without another word, but then I heard him say, "He's inside."

Genevieve walked in and I leapt out of the hammock. My foot got caught and I stumbled with one leg dangling behind me. Hopping on my one foot, I pulled myself free.

"Hi," I said as I

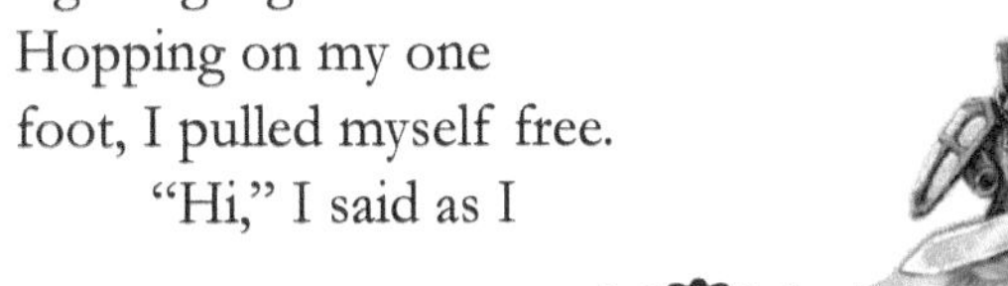

awkwardly leaned against the ropes of my hammock.

She threw her arms around my neck and leaned her head on my chest. At first, I was too shocked to move, but slowly I wrapped my arms around her waist. "You were incredibly brave tonight," she said as she pulled back to see me. "What did the shaman do to you?"

"She explained my visions. Apparently, the ancestors speak to me. Through my belly."

Genevieve giggled. "That is fascinating."

"Then she smeared this stuff on my forehead." I wiped my forehead and the black inky residue was still there. "She knew everything about me, even my visions."

"Astounding," Genevieve said, her arms still around my neck.

"I may not have the sword work of you or your father, and I might not be as rich as the Duke and Richard, but apparently I have weird, important visions."

"I think you're a leader," she said with a soft smile. "A leader needs vision. Besides, you have the swagger of a captain."

We laughed and I pulled her up against me. I never wanted to let her out of my arms. She nestled her head against my shoulder again.

From the gundeck, we heard a commotion as if someone had been knocked down, followed by "Ahhh, get away from me you overgrown bat."

Richard.

Immediately, Genevieve pulled away from me and took a few steps back. "I have to go," she said and headed for the door.

I followed her. As we walked out, I saw Rodin whip around Richard's head, diving at him and then soaring off as he swatted at the dragon.

"Rodin, come here," Genevieve said. Rodin flew back and landed on her shoulder. "Richard, what are you doing here?"

"Looking for you." He straightened his coat. Then seeing me, he glared and said, "My father extended an invitation to you and your father to stay with us. We have much finer accommodations than in this air latrine, or that savage village."

"They're not savages," I said.

Richard narrowed his eyes and clenched his jaw, but I stood my ground. Genevieve, perhaps sensing a confrontation, said, "Yes, Richard, let us go." She wrapped her arm through his and tugged him toward the gangplank. I looked at her, wanting her to stay, but she avoided my eyes.

As he started to step on the gangplank, he stopped. "Genevieve, go ahead. I'll catch up."

"Richard …"

"Go."

"I am not your property!"

Richard ignored Genevieve and leaned in close to my face, "You're as bad as these savages. You're not special. You're a commoner, nothing more than a—"

I punched him. A right hook to his jaw. He spun and fell against the cannon. I looked down on him and said, "They are *not* savages; they are Zulu."

"Alexander!" Genevieve put her hand on the hilt of her saber.

The intensity of her expression was usually reserved for her opponents. Was she going to draw her sword on Richard—or *me*?

Hate in his eyes, Richard jumped back up and drew a dagger from his belt. He pointed it at me. I drew my

Thumper and aimed it at his head.

"I will cut you, colonist."

"You try and I will obliterate half your face."

"Genevieve is *mine*, you unworthy ape."

"She isn't a prize; she's a lady. A woman who deserves more than the likes of you. Now get off this ship before I forget I'm a fellow Etonian and not a Sky Raider."

"Stop! Both of you … Neanderthals. I am not a prize to be fought over." Genevieve's voice was full of anger and frustration.

Richard turned and seemed surprised to see her. He backed away and replaced the dagger in its sheath, then sneered at me, "You're not worth dirtying my blade."

"You're the savage," I yelled as they walked away. I jammed my Thumper back in its holster and sunk down on one of the cannons.

Richard charged back toward me, but Genevieve rushed and stepped between us. "We need to go, Richard. We need to find our fathers and discuss the battle plans."

"No," Richard put his hands on his hips. "There is no way you are fighting in the coming battle. Let your father drive that infernal armor."

"Excuse me?" Genevieve stepped back and her expression hardened.

I shook my head. "Richard, you need to stop. Genevieve is an amazing warrior, and you won't ever diminish that."

Genevieve whipped around and faced me. "Alexander Armitage, I do not need you to fight my battles. I can stand up for myself."

My mouth dropped open, but I didn't respond. Richard didn't even listen, he stepped around Genevieve and said, "Quit trying to steal my betrothed, colonist." He took a step closer. "You need to step off, commoner. I don't care about you, or your little friends. These armors are going to *real* warriors, *real* knights. My betrothed is coming with me, and you can go fall off the end of the earth."

"Step off yourself, *your grace*; this isn't Eton." I stared him down. "If you continue, I will challenge you."

"Challenge *me, colonist?*" Richard's eyes burned wild. "If you want a fight, I will give you one." He drew the long sword from his scabbard and raised the blade toward me.

I didn't know how to react; I didn't even have a sword, only my Thumper and the knife the captain had given me. If I pulled a weapon, we would duel, an outcome as destructive as a war.

I had to resist. The Templars would never accept me if I attacked a member of the royal family, and the Duke would have his dog. Even if I won, I'd never actually win.

Richard extended his arm, and his legs slipped into a fighting stance. Genevieve released an exacerbated sigh, drew her saber, and parried Richard's blade toward the ground. "What are you doing? And you … I can stand up for myself."

Before I could respond, Richard pressed her shoulder, trying to force her aside "Out of my way, this is a matter of gentlemen. It will take just a moment to deal with this thorn."

Genevieve spun out of his grip and swung her saber at Richard. He backed up and brought his longsword up to block the blade. With the slight movement of her wrist, she hooked his blade with the end of her curved saber, twirled her wrist, and sent his sword flying from his hand. "I want you to understand something, Richard," she said, her voice sharp as her sword's razor edge. "I will always be able to defeat you with a sword. That will not change when we are married. No matter what, you will never raise your sword to this man."

His eyes narrowed and he turned toward me, but she pressed her blade to his chin. "I'm not done yet. The Bronze Knight is a part of me, and I will defend the crown as my father has done, as my family has done for generations."

He pushed her away. "You are as bad as your mother."

Her face transformed. The fire in her eye blazed, but still, I thought I saw a hint of doubt. How did she really feel about the lady assassin?

For a moment, they stared at each other, then the inferno in Richard's eyes subsided with her steel still against his chin. He backed off Genevieve's blade and walked off. She lowered her saber and slid it back into its sheath. She dropped her head and her long auburn hair covered her face, which muffled her soft sob. I wanted to comfort her, but didn't know what to say. Without a word, she slipped away.

The next morning, we prepared to leave the village and search for the Milli-train. Captain Baldarich boarded the Sparrowhawk, along with the baron, Eustache, Owethu, and me. Genevieve joined us as well, her stoic grace restored.

As we lifted up over the land of lions, elephants, giraffes, plus hundreds of other creatures I had only read about in books, I settled down beside the windows on the bridge. I was excited to be setting out on my first African safari, even if this one was from the air.

Zululand was extraordinary. Grassland stretched out in every direction, rolling hills rose upward into small mountains. Streams meandered between them and joined larger rivers that rushed to the sea. Gone were the cold days in London, the harsh bitter winds replaced by a warm breeze, and a sun that, by midday, drenched me in sweat.

The captain set the course of the Sparrowhawk to where Owethu and the Zulu thought the Milli-train might be. Nothing. Not even any signs of tracks. By mid-afternoon, we'd come no closer to finding them, and our spirits were faltering. When we returned to Owethu's village, Captain Baldarich had Heinz wiggle the Sparrowhawk's wings to let the others know we'd found nothing. Then we headed off in another direction.

That evening we returned to the village, disheartened. We'd searched a huge swatch of northern Zululand and not found anything. Tomorrow was another day, but we only had one more to find the Milli-train and stop the Iron Horsemen.

39
Iron Zulu

I walked up to the Chief Zwelethu's dwelling with Owethu and Captain Baldarich. The fire outside crackled, sending embers soaring into the night's sky. My father and the rest of the Templar Order sat in discussion.

"We have one unfinished Iron Knight hobbled together from bits and pieces." My father ran his fingers through his hair and pushed his glasses back to the bridge of his nose.

"Which won't matter if Hendrix, Kannard, and the lady assassin find the fourth horseman's heart before we do," Sinclair said. "We need to hold the line here. Until the Templar fleet arrives."

My father turned to Sinclair. "Hardened soldiers against villagers and a handful of your people? We have to find another way."

"No professor." The Grand Master put his hand on my father's shoulder. "If we don't engage, they could find the heart before our reinforcements come, which would mean our certain deaths. We are all that stands between the world and the horsemen."

"He's right," I said. "The Golden Circle is coming here because of Schoenbruster's journal. We have to stop them, but sir, my father is also correct. I don't know if we'll be victorious without reinforcements. Besides, they know our fleet is on the way, too, I doubt they will wait to attack."

My father looked at me and smiled. "You are getting too good at this. If only you'd put this much effort to your studies."

"I want the next language I learn to be Zulu."

Chief Zwelethu laughed. "I like your son. My shaman tells me I should heed his words. I will send the children off across the river with their mothers and the cattle."

Sinclair nodded. "An excellent idea." He pointed his cane at me and said, "You go with your father and help the Tinkerer finish the armor for Owethu."

"You got it. We'll get it moving before our enemies arrive."

Sinclair ruffled my hair with his large hand. "Damn fine work, lad. I thank you."

"My honor, sir."

He tipped his head before turning to Chief Zwelethu to leave. My father then led me to the Imperial Airship, which rested just outside the village. Twice the size of the Sparrowhawk, the royal airship had gold trimming and finely crafted wood covering the metal frames. We remained in the crew section, which consisted of rooms and hallways. However, to reach the other end of the airship, we had to go through the cavernous main section. Metal beams and support cabling ran the entire length of the airship. The large helium tanks above us looked like giant icebergs suspended from the ceiling. We walked along the catwalk toward the aft section. Amazed at the structure of the airship, I wanted to stop and continue to take it all in, but my father continued to the gangplank.

The Tinkerer, already in the workshop he'd set up right outside the cargo door, worked on an engine. All his tools, along with a pile of scrap iron and every spare part he could muster, surrounded him. Even a porcelain sink pulled from one of the ships of the fleet. I shook my head.

Sitting in the center of this metal maze was the fully-assembled engine and treads for an Iron Knight, along with the feet and legs. The Tinkerer was folded over inside the engine compartment, but spun around as we approached. He still wore his thick apron over an undershirt, and his trousers were drenched in sweat and smeared with grease. His enormous pupils filled the multi-layered lenses of his goggles.

"Good yer back," he said in a thick Scottish drawl.

My father pointed to the armor. "I finished that intake valve. So, we're here to do whatever you need."

"Installed. Thank you." He turned to me. "Glad to have an extra set of hands. Search through these piles of stuff for something the driver can sit on."

"Will do." I darted through the piles of stuff in search for something cushiony. Because the Black Knight, my armor, was a prototype, it had a hard metal seat that battered my entire body with every explosion or vibration on the cobblestone.

I found a twisted mess of metal bars with a bicycle seat attached. I also discovered the padded back of a broken chair and took both to the Tinkerer. "Best I could do."

"Perfect," he said, nodding with a welding torch that spit blue fire. "I've got your father working on the joints. I don't suppose you've ever had an interest in riveting?"

"I'll rivet whatever you need."

"Good, then load some rivets into the furnace there and we'll get started, but first put that apron on."

I did as he said, grabbing the rivets with a pair of tongs. Then dropping the iron rivets into the brick furnace that radiated so much heat it was hard to approach even with the apron on. The Tinkerer nudged me. "Use those tongs to place the rivet in the iron armor, and I'll do the rest."

"You got it."

Gears walked up to us. "What are you doing here?" I asked.

"Captain, thought I might be able to help, too."

The Tinkerer nodded. "Another set of hands is always appreciated."

So, the four of us worked throughout the night to complete the newest armor. The ping of a hammer striking iron never ceased. I thought I might lose my mind, but eventually, the sound became a drumbeat driving me onward. Amazingly, the Tinkerer worked from memory, not missing a single detail. As the night wore on, I'd done so many different jobs, that by first light I could have probably build an armor myself. My favorite task had been working on the shield, an *isihlangu*, the traditional Zulu *impi* shield, which maintained the elliptical or leaf-like shape of the smaller version. I'd reinforced it with iron bands on the back of the shield, and even painted a cowhide pattern to match the smaller version. Finally exhausted, I fell asleep in the armor.

My father opened the door and I popped awake. When he grinned at me, his white teeth shone, they were the only part of him not smeared with grease. He was almost as filthy as Gears.

Rubbing my eyes, I said, "We made the chest from an airship hatch. It even has a porthole that the Tinkerer reinforced."

"It looks great," he said. He turned toward me then and put his hand on my dirty white button down. "You've done really well."

"Thanks," I said.

He removed his hand, but the dark stain of his print remained on my shirt. "Sorry, son, we'll get you a new shirt back in London."

I nodded but shrugged. "I don't mind." In reality, I wouldn't have minded if I'd never had to wear another starched white shirt.

He stood there for a moment more before rushing off in answer to the Tinkerer calling for assistance. As I stood there admiring our handiwork, Rodin surprised me and flew up and landed on my shoulder. I rubbed behind his horns. "Why, good morning, Rodin, how are you? I looked up, expecting to see Genevieve, but she wasn't there. However, Owethu and his father walked up, followed by several women from his tribe, including the shaman.

"Owethu! It's so good to see you," I said. His father shifted and I bowed.

With delight in his eyes, Chief Zwelethu said, "We have come to see the progress of your machine."

"Excellent timing. We have to get Owethu ready for the Iron Zulu." I couldn't wait to show him, and motioned for them to follow.

We rounded a hunk of scrap metal and the iron armor came into view. The machine rose to twice my height, and appeared patched together with a mix of dark iron and brass. They stopped and stared in awe at the contraption. Chief Zwelethu kept nodding his head, but did not say anything. Owethu froze, and the tears in his eyes reminded me of the first time I set eyes on the Black Knight.

"Meet the Iron Zulu," I said. "Let's start with the shield, since I made it."

"You did this? Very nice work." Chief Zwelethu ran his hand along the shield. "It looks just like an *isihlangu*, only bigger."

"I tried to be as authentic as possible. This one is made of iron, though, not cattle skin."

Owethu finally approached, "Can I see inside?"

"Of course." I grabbed the *mgobo* that ran vertically just behind the shield to move it aside and then pulled the door open. Then I lifted the visor. Rodin craned his neck to see inside. "Make sure this is up when you get in so you don't hit your head."

I opened the hatch. Inside, the compartment was just big enough for one.

"By the ancestors," Owethu gasped, but didn't hesitate to climb inside.

"Put your arms in up here and you should feel the controls. Your legs go on either side of the small seat. Feel the pedals?" I turned to him and demonstrated with my hands, "Your hands control all the upper systems— the arms, hands, and weapons. Your feet control direction and speed."

"I see," Owethu gave me a thumbs up.

"Check this out," I said, "we used steam pipes

for the inner arm and then plated them with additional armor." I pointed to the back. "The boiler came from one of the airships."

"I am humbled," Owethu said.

"I felt the same way when I saw the Black Knight."

"All I see is the shield. Where are the weapons?" Chief Zwelethu asked.

I pointed to the shield. "Behind here is a grappling hook and a short barrel cannon. There is a longer barrel that flips forward on the sword arm, here on the right. The shield holds the club, a *knobkerrie*, and an *Assegai* spear. Both are Iron-Knight sized. But here is the best." I walked over and struggled to lift the short spear. "We made you an *iklwa*."

Owethu's face lit up.

"This is a Zulu," his father said. "There is no mistaking it." With a motion of his hand, Owethu stepped out of the armor and the women brought forward a white-haired ox hide with a few black markings and handed it to him. Chief Zwelethu placed the hide over the shield and tied it to the braces on the back with leather cord.

Chief Zwelethu stepped back and the shaman swept forward. She clutched a bundle of sacred herbs and flowers that she placed into a stone bowl and mashed them until nothing but powder remained. With her dusty hand, she smeared the mixture over the shield as she chanted.

I leaned in to Owethu, "What is she doing?"

"She is adding a spell on the shield, so I will be invulnerable in battle."

"Fascinating." I didn't want to tell Owethu how much he might need that protection. "I wish we had more time for training, but don't worry, last year we didn't have much time, either, and we're still here."

The Tinkerer popped his head out of the engine, approached the chief and Owethu, and shook their hands. He leaned in and pointed at Owethu's chest. "He's forgetting the most important part. These are great machines, but the soul of the machine is in the rider. If your will is strong, then the armor will never fail you."

"My will to protect this village knows no sunset." Owethu took a deep breath, bent down and scooped up a handful of dirt. He pressed it on the chest hatch and then rubbed the soil in his hands together. "

"Now, let's get you inside and light the fires." I helped Owethu get situated in the armor. As soon as I closed the chest hatch and flipped down the visor, my stomach twisted into knots. I doubled over, as the horns warning of danger echoed through the village.

The Tinkerer adjusted his goggles and pointed with his mallet. "You'd better find the captain or Lord Sinclair to make sure they know we're ready. I'll finish up with Owethu's orientation."

"Good luck, Owethu." I shook his hand. "When the rest of the fleet gets here, I'll roll out in the Black Knight, and together, we'll tear the Golden Circle apart."

"I look forward to it."

I rushed off to find the Grand Master, or the captain. I turned to Rodin. "Go find the baron or Genevieve. Make sure they know we are ready." As he flew off a wave of elation came over me.

Captain Baldarich walked up and wrapped his arm around me. "Alexander, with me."

"Captain, what is it?"

He pointed at the Sparrowhawk. "The Milli-train is

coming, and I am looking forward to raining lead down on that iron serpent with you alongside."

"Aye-aye, Captain." I saluted and followed him. "Do we know when the rest of the fleet will be showing up?"

He stroked his moustache. "They won't arrive until this evening, at the earliest."

"So close …"

"And yet this battle will probably be over by then."

"We just have to hold them to nightfall."

"This is why I like you, always looking at the sunny side. Now, let's go tell these guys we mean business. Apparently, they didn't get the message last year." He clapped his hands together and pivoted toward me. "See you onboard."

Genevieve tapped my shoulder. "It's almost time."

"Thanks," I sat up. "Are you okay?"

"No. But it did feel good to say all of it."

"He deserved it," I chuckled. "But I didn't get a chance to say thank you. I didn't know how I was going to get out of that fight."

She paused. "He shouldn't have acted that way; you deserve nothing but his respect."

"I'm used to it."

"You shouldn't be."

Her words made me pause, but her touch on my shoulder ignited my passions. I wanted to kiss her, to tell her it all be okay, and how I wanted to spend time with her back in London, but I couldn't. Pushing my passion back into my heart, I said, "We should get out of here."

"Yes." Genevieve stepped off, but stopped. She rushed back and kissed my cheek. "You're one of the bravest and most intelligent warriors I've ever met. Never doubt that."

She pushed away from me, but I reached out and snagged her arm. I gently drew her back to me and wrapped my arms around her. When our lips touched, electricity rippled up my spine. I didn't pull away. Neither did she.

Slowly we separated, still in each other's arms. I could have gotten lost in the sparkle of her eyes forever. Breathless, I ran my finger over her cheek. She looked down and bit her lip.

"Good luck," I said.

She touched my cheek. "Godspeed, Alexander."

She slipped out of my arms and ran off.

40
Iron Zulu vs. Milli-train

I stood next to Mr. Singh on the gundeck as the *Sparrowhawk* rose into the sky. Immediately we saw the Milli-train crawling toward us, cutting back and forth through the grass like a predator seeking out its prey.

Mr. Singh conducted the gundeck like a symphony. At his direction, the gun crews rushed around prepping the cannons and manning each Gatling gun.

"What would you have me do, Mr. Singh?" I asked.

He looked at me and pointed to the front room—my room. "Keep the cannonballs coming. First, give me a count of what we have?"

"I'm your man," I said with a salute. "But can we keep an eye on the Iron Zulu, too? It's a superb machine, but I'm worried about Owethu. I know he'll be great, but he's alone down there."

"We will help him all we can."

I leaned a little closer, "When will Genevieve be here, I just left her?"

"No, her father insisted she ride on the Imperial Airship."

"Oh." I blew out

a long breath, trying to force the anxiety of knowing she was with Richard from my chest. I walked off to the front room, but stopped, spun around and said, "Do you just want cannonballs, or should I bring up chain-shot and bar-shot, too?"

"Bring it all. Who knows what we'll need."

"Aye-aye, Mr. Singh." I entered my room, and did a quick check of the ammunition.

The captain's voice echoed out from the copper tube. "Mr. Singh, fire on my mark. Put everything we have on that metal slug."

"Prepare to fire!" Mr. Singh directed the crews. He leaned back and yelled into the copper tube, "All port side guns at the ready, Captain."

The Sparrowhawk tilted to the port side, aiming the guns directly at the Milli-train. As we banked, cannon fire erupted in the distance. Flashes of fire flew out from the top of the train, but nothing hit us … yet. Still the captain didn't fire.

I rushed to the starboard side and looked out. Most of the other airships had lifted off and jockeyed for position around the train. Glancing down at the village, the Iron Zulu stood at ready at the gates. Rows of Owethu's fellow warriors stood behind him, cheering him on. Alongside them, a detachment of British infantry from the Imperial Airship had taken up positions behind a berm. The sight was imposing. I wish I could see Hendrix and Kannard's faces right now.

From the Sparrowhawk, we had the perfect vantage point of the battle lines, the terrain, and even the reinforcement of soldiers setting artillery up on a hill in the distance. Even Alexander the Great would be jealous of this view.

The captain's voice broke through the rushing wind. "Fire!"

Mr. Singh drew his shamshir and pointed it toward the Milli-train. "Fire!"

Both cannons roared to life, spitting fire and lead down at the armored train. As the cannon crew swabbed out the barrel and reloaded, the Gatling gun crew cranked the handle and rained bullets down on the target. The crewmen readied the cannon with the powder charge, ball, and wadding. Then the man with the *botefeux*, turned to Mr. Singh awaiting the next command before touching the slow burning rope to the powder.

Mr. Singh yelled, "Fire!"

The crewman laid the *botefeux* to the powder, and in an instant smoke and fire belched from the cannon, which obscured Mr. Singh, but the shimmer of his blade pierced the veil.

The captain's orders echoed again throughout the ship. "Prepare starboard guns."

Mr. Singh yelled, "Starboard guns ready."

We banked steeply toward starboard, and I grabbed hold of a post to keep from sliding. As we continued turning, through the gunports, I saw the Milli-train charging the main gate of the village. The Iron Zulu held his ground and fired on the metal monster. Fire! Fire! Fire! I repeated over and over under my breath, willing the captain to give the order. But he didn't. Watching the metal monstrosity march forward toward Owethu and the village, I was filled with terror.

Finally, the captain ordered, "Fire!"

Mr. Singh pointed his sword. "Fire!"

The cannon and Gatling gun rained lead down at the train, but the monster kept moving forward. The cannonballs exploded on impact, spitting fire along the iron plating. The bullets battered the hull like hail, dimpling the iron, but not penetrating the metal. Still Owethu held his ground.

"Mr. Singh," the captain yelled, "prepare grapplers. And Mr. Singh, make your shots count. We only get one chance at this."

Mr. Singh ran to one of the grapplers and pointed at me. "Alexander, take hold of the other side."

I ran to the hatch in the floor and yanked it up. Inside lay the grappling gun and coiled cable. In my mind, I flashed over Mr. Singh's lesson on how they worked, but it had been last year. "Unlock it first, right?" I asked.

"Yes, and don't forget to unlatch the cable, too."

I flipped the latch on the gun and freed the cable. Pulling back on short lever, I opened the outer hull and the grappling gun swung out. Using the large circular reticule on top, I aimed it toward the Milli-train. "Which train car?"

"The first car," Mr. Singh replied.

I pulled the trigger and the hooks soared downward with the cable spooling out behind it. Both grapplers pierced the roof of the first car and popped open, securing the lines. Immediately, they pulled taut. The engines of the Sparrowhawk whined under the strain, but the captain didn't give up. I ran to the gunport and looked out. We held the Milli-train just outside the village.

The Iron Zulu still stood his ground in front of the Milli-train. With the beast held at bay by the grappling gun, Owethu had the engine exposed right before him. The Milli-train reared up, pulled back by our cables, like a praying mantis rising up to devour its prey. The Iron Zulu raced up beneath the train, and using its shield to block the legs, he pushed up on the engine. Then with one swift movement, he slammed the Ilkwa into the boiler. Steam rushed out, encircling the Iron Zulu.

The cargo doors toward the back of the Milli-train blew out and two Iron Horsemen jumped out. An inner fire shone through the plates and gears of the steeds, surrounding them in shadowy darkness. The riders, Hendrix and Kannard, cloaked figures, sitting within the backs of the machines, charged forward.

Fear snagged my heart, freezing me in place, again sending a surge of horrid memories rushing through my mind. I took a deep breath and tried to focus on what Mr. Singh needed me to do.

Rushing toward Owethu, Hendrix, the red Horseman of War, raised a giant two-handed sword, a flat sheet of steel with a long handle and cross bar hilt, and galloped full speed. Kannard, the white Horseman of Disaster, raised his cavalry saber and charged alongside Hendrix to the front of the Milli-train. In a single thrust they sliced the grappling lines.

The Sparrowhawk lurched and I tumbled across the deck. I popped up and looked around as the aero-dirigible leveled out. Everyone seemed okay, so I ran to a hatch to check on Owethu. I heard a loud crash and saw a huge dust cloud kicked up as the Milli-train slammed forward. I couldn't see the Iron Zulu in the chaos, but he burst out of the dust and rounded around for another attack.

"The Iron Zulu is fighting both Iron Horsemen." I pointed down below. "We have to help him."

Hunter appeared with the longest two rifles I'd ever seen, as well as the same scowl he always wore. "Captain sent me to help."

"Excellent, but what are those?"

Hunter walked over and knelt next a gunport. "My Kentucky longrifles, Thunder and Lightning. Only these are a bit modified, and I use a different slug. A bit more powerful."

He took a powder horn from his belt and poured a measured amount down the barrel. Next, he wrapped the ball in wadding, and rammed it down. Setting a small percussion cap under the hammer, he set it aside and repeated the process with the second rifle.

Hunter kneeled down and poking the longrifle out the hatch, he rested the barrel in the corner. Sighting down the barrel, he took several deep, steady breaths.

Hunter eased back on the trigger and black powder smoke erupted from the barrel. I watched the bullet hit its mark. But at the last moment, one of the iron plates on the side of Hendrix's steed popped up and deflected the shot. The bullet soared toward Lord Kannard's steed, and when it bounced against its iron plates, the shot ricocheted, striking Hendrix in the bronze plate covering his shoulder.

"Great shot."

Hunter smiled. "I remember how those plates deflected shots from last year."

Both horsemen reared up and looked around for the source of the gunfire. Hendrix aimed at Kannard and roared as his eye sparked with electricity.

In the chaos of the moment, both horsemen forgot about the Iron Zulu, and Owethu shoved his shield under Kannard's steed, thrusting the *Iklwa* into the cannon in its chest. The white horseman of Disaster reared up as the cannons collapsed. Hendrix and the Horseman of War, slammed its hooves against the ground, churning up the grass and dirt around the Iron Zulu.

The Milli-train then began firing on all the airships circling above, including the Sparrowhawk. Two smaller airships plummeted to the ground. Another cannonball exploded out of the train. My heart skipped. It was heading toward us. I turned and ran to the other side of the ship. "Incoming," I yelled as I dove for cover.

The outer hull ripped inward as the cannonball tore through the gundeck and up into the ceiling. Canvas whipped around the twisted frame left in the wake. I looked up and the shot had also gone through one of the room's upstairs and out the other side. I pulled my goggles over my eyes and ran forward for more cannonballs to return fire.

Beams rattled and creaked around me. The Sparrowhawk shook, but thankfully the aero-dirigible didn't list or fall out of the sky. I only hoped no one was injured.

I carried the cannonballs and powder charges out to the gundeck, where the men now fired freely on the enemy below. Smoke billowed through the deck only to be sucked out the gunports and hatches. With my vision limited, I relied on my memory of the obstacles in my way.

Hunter continued methodically loading his longrifles, taking careful and steady aim, and then firing. He'd then set Thunder aside, picked up Lightning and selected his next target. From the slight upturn of the corner of his mouth, I could tell he was enjoying annoying Kannard and Hendrix. I could tell, too, when he'd missed, as he snarled.

Bullets riddled the hull, ripping through the canvas and even the wooden planks. I dove to avoid the searing lead as did the crewmen and Hunter until another swarm passed. He popped up and laughed. "Horsemen found me."

"At least if they're shooting at us, they aren't killing any villagers."

41
The Black Knight Rides Again

Hunter pointed out one of the hatches to the North. "Airships."

"Is it the Templars?" I rushed over and saw several airships racing this way, each adorned with the Templar cross whipping in the wind. "They're here!"

The crew cheered, but Mr. Singh yelled, "Don't get distracted. This fight isn't over."

I nodded and ran to the other side. I stuck my head out an unused gunport between the Gatling gun and cannons. Below, Owethu kept the horsemen out of the village, but the train, which had been forced back by all the aerial attacks, charged once again. Mr. Singh yelled, "Fire!" and the cannons beside me roared.

Upon impact, the blasts merely bounced off the top of the train. Our firepower wasn't enough to stop it, and the Golden Circle was overwhelming our forces on the ground. More soldiers, more airships, and more cannon— would we be enough?

The train again raised its guns toward the Sparrowhawk. Mr. Singh yelled, "Incoming." We all took cover the best we could. The explosion shook the

Sparrowhawk as black smoke drifted into the gunports, but we were not directly hit.

Mr. Singh rushed back to a gunport, and pounded the hull with his fist, "Blasted! They hit the cargo ship."

I rushed up next to Mr. Singh as the largest of the airships, a cargo blimp, plummet from the sky and smash into ground, landing between the train and Owethu. The crumpled wreck smoldered but didn't burst into flames. Turning to Mr. Singh, I asked, "Was that the airship with our armors?"

"Afraid so," Mr. Singh sighed.

"I have to get down to the Black Knight," I said, hoping that it survived the crash intact.

"Apologies," Mr. Singh shook his head. "We can't land. The Sparrowhawk would be too vulnerable."

"What about the grappler?" Not waiting for his response, I ran over to the opening.

"Wait, Alexander, I must inform the captain."

"No time," I loaded another grappling hook into the gun. As I fired toward the crashed airship, I heard Mr. Singh yell into the copper tube, "Captain, Alexander and I are zip-lining down to the armors."

Laughter echoed back through the tube, and I heard clapping.

The hook sank into the ground a few feet from the smoking wreckage. I pumped my fist and I heard Hunter's voice behind me, "Nice shot."

"Hunter, once we're on the ground, retract the line."

Hunter nodded and shook Mr. Singh's hand.

I grabbed the thick leather strapping and wrapped it around me and secured the brass ring to the cable, then handed another to Mr. Singh. Seeing the cable swaying in the wind visions of disaster filled my mind. "This is a bad idea."

Before I could change my mind, Mr. Singh said, "Forgive me my friend." Then he pushed me out the Sparrowhawk.

Hanging tight to the wire, the wind biting my skin, I was thankful I hadn't taken off my goggles.

As I zipped toward the ground, cannonballs and dozens of rounds whipped by me. Only a few feet from the end of the line, I released the strap and slammed into the ground. I rolled several times before crashing into the wreckage. Lying on my back, with the wind knocked out of me, I saw Mr. Singh hurtling down. He waited a moment longer than I had, released his strap, and landed perfectly on his feet in front of me.

"Showoff," I groaned.

"At least I am not lying down on duty." Mr. Singh chuckled as he extended his hand. I grabbed it and he pulled me up.

"Let's find those Iron Knights."

We ran alongside the crumbled airship until we reached the midsection where there was a break in the hull. Climbing through the torn canvas of the outer structure we searched for the armors. I climbed under twisted metal braces, and tossed shattered wooden planks to get deeper within until we saw the Black Knight, the Bronze Knight, and the Iron Templar.

"Over here," I yelled to Mr. Singh.

Ignoring the encroaching fire, I rushed over to the Black Knight and laid my hand against the metal. A flood of memories crashed through my mind. The Tinkerer had fixed the leg and the hole in my shield. I only wished my scars healed so easily.

I opened the chest hatch and climbed inside. I felt

whole again, back in my machine. I reached in the arms and gripped the controls. The power at my fingertips sent a surge of confidence pulsing through me. Igniting the burners to build pressure in the engine, I fired up the armor, and soon smoke belched out of the twin stacks curving along its back.

I knew I should complete a run-through, to make sure the guns were loaded. But there was no time. In front of me, through the web of twisted beams, the Milli-train was charging straight toward me, as if it aimed to plow straight through me.

I battened the hatches and closed the visor and said, "Okay, Black Knight, I know we've been through a lot, but we need to save the village—and survive this day." I raised the arm cannon and aimed it at the train. "By god and my ancestors, please let this work." Pulling the trigger, fire ripped forward blowing a hole through the mesh of the airship. The shell whined through the air and exploded directly on the front of the train.

I cheered and pressed the pedal to move forward. Nothing happened. The treads didn't move at all. I could feel the Black Knight straining against something. The Iron Templar was beside me, took aim at the train, and fired. The round impacted one of the Milli-trains legs, ripping it off.

Studying the Iron Templar, I saw it, straps securing the armor to the deck of the airship, securing it for the flight. We were now trapped. I couldn't use the cannon or risk injury to everyone and anything still in the wreckage. I reached back with the Black Knight's arm and unlatched the sword, a sharpened slab of steel over eight feet long and over a foot thick. Drawing the blade forward, I cut the Iron Templar loose and Mr. Singh crashed through the wreckage and rolled to freedom. I sliced through my own straps, rolled over to the Bronze Knight and freed it from its strapping.

For an instant, I thought of Genevieve and that she should be here taking control of the Bronze Knight. But I couldn't focus on her right now. I pressed the pedal and this time the treads rolled forward. The Black Knight pushed against the beams and wreckage surrounding me and ripped through them like paper. Once free of the debris, I spotted the train ahead of me, again plowing straight toward the village

Mr. Singh's Iron Templar charged the Milli-train, its white tunic with the red cross emblazoned on the chest. Explosions ripped into the ground around me. Dirt and grass rained down on my armor like hail stones. As I moved forward, the Milli-train fired on me, but I continued forward. I had to help Owethu. I lifted my cannon and fired at Lord Kannard, but the steed protected him.

I rolled away as the next set of artillery from the train assaulted me. I looked out the visor and caught a glimpse of the Imperial Airship. Genevieve jumped off the airship. Terror gripped me and I turned in her direction. She was going to plummet to her death. Rodin, too, glided behind her, but didn't even try to slow her. She pulled a handle, and a mass of fabric trailed behind her. A metal canister on her back ignited, shooting fire out behind her. The fabric billowed as the balloon swelled, and Genevieve gently drifted down to the ground. She immediately cut her pack and balloon free, and ran inside the crumbled airship, emerging a few moments later in the Bronze Knight. Now it was a real battle. We finally had an advantage: four Iron Knights against two Iron

Horsemen and the Milli-train.

I spun the Black Knight around, turning my cannons on the Milli-train, in hopes I could keep it from invading the village.

As Genevieve and I rolled across the grasslands, I realized I was a knight. Decked out in armor, I not only had a steed with iron treads, I had a sword, a shield, and a cannon that acted like a lance. My dreams had come true. I may not be an official knight of the realm, but that didn't matter. Like the legendary knight—a commoner, some said—who did not rely on his heraldry, or the prince who defied his king to fight in the tournament, I was the Black Knight.

42
The Heart of a Horsemen

Instead of invading the village head on, the Milli-train formed a circle at its edge. Then it opened fire. With shells exploding around me, I pulled myself up to the visor searching for the Iron Horsemen, but found no sign of either demonic steed.

I dodged the cannon fire, zigzagging my way toward the other Iron Knights. We all fired on the Milli-train's open gunports. The Iron Zulu and Iron Templar then whipped around and fired on the engine, while the Bronze Knight and my Black Knight pounded the cannon cars directly facing the village.

Genevieve rolled up in the Bronze Knight close to the train and as a cannon fired. She raised her shield and deflected the shot back into the train. My cheer was short-lived as a Gatling gun pelted my armor.

Smoke rose out of the center of the village. The Iron Horsemen. They'd slipped past us and attacked the villagers. Knowing most of the villagers had been sent across the river, I felt a moment of relief, but the thick black column of smoke within the village's walls ignited a fiery rage within me. I waved the

Black Knight's cannon and yelled, "Genevieve! The Horsemen are in the city!"

Genevieve stopped. She pointed her cannon at the column and we advanced into the village.

We raced between the huts and crashed straight through the thicket fences, but I grinded to a stop when I saw Chief Zwelethu's dwelling on fire. Thick black smoke consumed the structure.

I opened my visor and watched as the once beautiful archway and building crumbled and deteriorated to ash. I hoped no one was inside. The Iron Zulu then pulled up beside me and Owethu leapt out. He collapsed to his knees, reaching out with his hands.

I opened the chest plate on the Black Knight and climbed out. I hurried over to him and dropped beside him. I threw my arms around him, and he clung to me. "No one was inside," I said, praying it was the truth.

Owethu only exhaled and stood, staring as the flaming roof of his home collapsed into itself.

Genevieve ran up with Rodin on her shoulder. "Owethu, I'm so sorry."

He wiped the tears from his eyes, and a hard expression washed over his face. "Where are the horsemen?"

Genevieve shook her head. "I didn't see them anywhere in the village."

The ground shook beneath us. The three of us looked at each other.

"They're under the village," I said. Part of the flaming roof collapsed into itself, and fell into the ground. I looked at Owethu, "Was there a passage beneath your house?"

"I don't know of one." He ran his hand over his

head. "My grandfather used to say our family protected the Zulu from a great evil, but I thought he meant outside the village."

"We should investigate." Genevieve motioned toward her Bronze Knight.

"What about the Milli-train?" I asked.

"The Sparrowhawk and Mr. Singh will keep them busy." She pointed toward the sky where the airships circled like vultures above the battle.

We ran back to our armors and rolled into the midst of the fire. There we saw that the ground had been torn and ripped asunder, leaving a crater with a large passage leading underground. I wondered why Chief Zwelethu hadn't said anything about the heart. Did he know? I believed Owethu, but as I thought about it, if I were guarding one of the hearts, I wouldn't tell anyone.

Iron Zulu led us into the underground passage. It opened up into a large central chamber supported by thick rock pillars and a forest of wooden beam scaffolding, just like a mine. We rolled past skeletons laid out in alcoves in the passage wall. As we approached a bend in the passage, an orange glow grew brighter.

I opened my armor and slowly climbed out. Peeking around the corner, I saw the two iron steeds at the end of the passage in another large chamber. Colonel Hendrix picked up a rock and pulled it up to his good eye. "Kannard, where is the gold?"

Kannard frantically searched through several urns nestled against one wall. "We're here for something greater."

Hendrix clenched his fist and the rock shattered. "What we need is gold."

"Soon everything will be ours, including the

gold" Kannard said, in a wicked tone. "With the four horsemen's hearts in our possession, we will conquer and enslave the world." Kannard continued to search the area. "I know this is the right place. Look around, you mechanical monstrosity, can't you feel that it is near?"

"With the money we've wasted this year searching for the hearts, I could have reformed the Confederacy."

"There is plenty of gold across your American South."

"I know I buried it." Hendrix snarled, "but we're supposed to be raising funds for the Inner Circle, not playing in the dirt."

Kannard's face flushed red with anger. "I am the Inner Circle! We don't need more of your armored trains or gold. We need four Iron Horsemen with four worthy riders."

The gears of Hendrix's arm whirled as his hand retracted into his sleeve, replaced with its serrated blade, pointing at Kannard. "Four steeds with riders didn't get it done last year. And the boy still isn't willing to join us."

Whoa, he was talking about me. I wanted to shout at them that I would never become a horseman.

"That diseased pirate was not worthy," Kannard thundered. "The baroness, she is worthy, so we have our four horsemen. Now, we just need the last heart."

"My patience ... the Inner Circle's patience, is limited," Hendrix said.

Kannard smashed several of the urns and dug through their contents. Angered at finding no gold, Hendrix kicked the churned-up dirt, catching his foot on a clod. He paused and looked down, then knelt down and shoved his hand into the ground. As he pulled up a large clump of dirt, he again stood, scraping it with the serrated blade of his hand. A green stone. Hendrix gazed at the rock like a wild animal.

When he held up the object in his hand, my stomach twisted in knots. I didn't need my ancestors to tell me I was in danger. I ran back to the Black Knight as Owethu and Genevieve shut the visors of their armor.

Hendrix stepped toward his horse. "Time to go, Kannard," he said as he mounted his iron steed.

"I am in charge and you will do what I say!" Kannard shouted.

I stormed into the chamber. "No matter where you go, a great warrior will always be there to defend their people. And *I* will be there to stand with them."

"Who dares to challenge me?" Kannard twirled around, pointing at my armor.

I took a deep breath and thought about what my heroes and friends would do. The captain would seize the room and keep them busy until he could spring his trap. The baron would attack swiftly and not stop until the battle was over. My father would look for another way, and Grand Master Sinclair would want me to fight with honor. Mr. Singh would never turn from evil, Owethu would defend his home to the end, and Genevieve would be bold, daring, and certain of her actions.

I pushed open my visor so they could see me. "I am the Black Knight! Tamer of Horsemen."

Kannard screamed, "You! Why is it always you?"

Hendrix shook his head, but tipped his hat. "Of course, it's the kid. Wouldn't be anyone else."

Kannard charged toward his iron steed. "I will kill him." As he climbed into the saddle, he pointed to Hendrix and demanded, "Find the heart." Then he saw the stone in Hendrix's hand and charged over to him.

"Give it to me!"

"No."

"Colonel, I demand you follow my orders!"

"The Inner Circle was very clear."

"I *am* the Inner Circle, you fool!"

"Not anymore." Hendrix thrust his large steel sword at the iron steed. The blade slid along the horse's neck kicking up sparks, and plunged into Kannard.

Kannard's guttural cry reverberated through the passage. Hendrix released the sword and Kannard tumbled off the back of the horse. Immediately, Hendrix's reared up his horse on its hooves and crushed down into the iron chest plate of the white Horseman of Disaster. Hendrix turned his mount, reached down, and yanked the urn free. Kannard lay motionless, his iron steed collapsing to scrap metal around him.

Cackling, Hendrix roared past us, firing on the stone columns that held up the ceiling.

Rock and wood tumbled down onto all of us as the entire passage shook. Although Hendrix had three hearts right now, all I could focus on was getting out of here alive. We rolled back toward the entrance. Hendrix exploded from the underground first with a column of dust and debris trailing behind him. We emerged from the passage as it collapsed behind us, only to ride headlong into the Milli-train's concentrated fire.

Hendrix vaulted onto one of the passenger compartments of the train and hopped off. He turned toward the engine and disappeared while the armada rained down its fire.

He stepped up onto the engine and placed the heart in a compartment near the firebox. The Milli-train darkened as shadowy wisps of smoke oozed over its skin and trailed off every surface. A demonic fire burst out of the smoke stack and glowed throughout the open segments of the engine, along with the first few cars. The eerie orange glow snaked its way through the legs and under the cars.

"He put the heart in the train." I gasped, and for a moment was unable to move.

The demonic Milli-train spit cannonballs, trailing huge columns of fire in their wake. Several hit the Imperial Airship, which crumpled and plunged out of the sky, slamming into the grass. Several airskiffs, too, were hit, but the Sparrowhawk avoided the cannon shot and returned fire.

43
Demonic
Milli-train

The Black Knight, the Bronze Knight, and the Iron Templar raced around the Milli-train attempting to divert it from the village. We had to stop them. This was Owethu's family, his home. We had to defend at least what remained.

As I crossed in front of the Iron Templar, Mr. Singh headed toward Owethu. I managed to avoid the gun turrets as they continued to fire at me. I retaliated with my cannon but the round exploded on the iron plates and didn't penetrate its armor.

The Iron Templar fired repeatedly on them, too, but the train avoided each incoming round, swatting them away with its legs as if they were just pesky flies. Drawing the immense longsword, the Iron Templar set its shield arm and charged the train.

Owethu advanced on the Milli-train, too. He fought like nothing I'd seen before. At Eton, he was nice and calm, but now he had a warrior's focus, fueled by passion. His courage ignited a fire within me; I wouldn't stop until his people were safe.

I rolled past Genevieve and stopped. She

looked at me through her visor with a puzzled expression.

"Hit the last car," I yelled. I didn't know if she could hear me, but I hoped she could see me.

She nodded and sped off.

I reversed and turned as twin rounds slammed into the ground in front of where I'd just been. I stepped on the pedal and rushed toward the back of the train. Raising my cannon suspended underneath the forearm of the Black Knight, I focused on the last car of the Milli-train. A hatch flipped open on the train beside me, I twisted the armor and spun as a cannon extended out and fired.

I wouldn't fail. I couldn't fail. This was the moment—the one Alexander the Great looked for in each battle—the one that assured victory. If we demolished, or at least, damaged the train, Hendrix and our enemies would be forced to flee. Either way, we'd win.

Rushing ever closer to the last car, fired again and again, the rounds exploding against the iron. Still, no affect. Pulling a lever in the armor, I dropped the cannon and drew the huge thick-bladed sword from the Black Knight's back. I shoved the steel into the side of the train car, and cut through the iron plating into the legs of the Milli-train, crippling it. Wrenching the sword from the leg, I thrust it back into side of the train with every last bit of power the Black Knight could give me. I pushed forward ripping the blade through the car. Then, Genevieve's Bronze Knight tore up the other side. She raised her cannon and fired into the back of the train. Fire shot through the exposed innards of the last several cars.

The demonic Milli-train charged the village, dragging several damaged cars behind it.

Genevieve and I would never reach it in time, but

we had to try. I raced after toward the engine trailing smoke from the twin stacks angled down off the Black Knights back.

The Iron Zulu rolled into the path of the train. Owethu stopped, set his armor, his shield up, and his spear. Even knowing Owethu couldn't hear me, I screamed for him to move. It didn't matter even if he could hear me, he'd never move. The Iron Zulu thrust its shield forward, anchoring the bottom of the *mgobo* in the ground and using the shield to catch the front of the train. Straining the joints of his armor, with his steam lines bursting, Owethu caught the front of the train and forced it up. In the same motion, he thrust the giant *Iklwa* into the boiler. The Milli-train teetered to one side, but the legs prevented the engine from tipping completely over.

Steam enveloped both vehicles as hot water spewed from the wound. The Milli-train sputtered and limped into the grasslands spitting fire from its tailpipes and turning the land behind it into an inferno.

The Iron Zulu stood stoic in his victory. Like an impenetrable wall.

The Milli-train circled up in the fields like a wagon train. The metal beast spit cannon shot all along its sides, igniting the ground surrounding the crippled train and wicking up the legs. Finally, I thought, we've won. In that instant, however, the pale Horseman of Plague carrying the lady assassin, and Hendrix's Horseman of War leapt over the Milli-train and charged.

"The pale rider is mine," Genevieve yelled as she raced forward to meet the lady assassin head on.

"Colonel Hendrix is mine," I yelled. I barreled toward Hendrix, who cackled from atop his steed.

Owethu and Mr. Singh kept shooting at the cannon sticking out of the side of the train. The fire they drew meant less shells would rain down on the village.

The Horseman of War hurled hundreds of rounds from the dual Gatling guns to pelt my armor. I raised my shield to block the bullets.

Nothing penetrated the Iron Horsemen's iron hides. Their black, haunting shadows clung to every surface, turning day into night. An inner fire within the steeds and the riders seeped through everything in its path, and the iron steed's eyes blazed with demonic light. Their snouts spitting smoke and embers. Something was different. The dark, evil nature of the hearts had somehow consumed the steeds and imbued the riders with hellish speed and strength. Terror tore at me. This new heart must be more powerful—a thought I didn't relish or want to dwell on.

Hendrix reared his steed and slammed the ground with its thundering hooves, tearing up the grassland around me. With only one hand, Hendrix slashed at me with a regular two-handed sword as if it were nothing. He came at me over and over, but I blocked his assault with my shield and countered with the Black Knight's immense steel blade. Still, he parried my sword away, and thrust his own at me, attempting to impale my armor. Again and again, I blocked him with my shield.

As he continued to assault me, a hail of gunfire flew all around me. That's when I saw Zerelda. She'd climbed onto the crippled Milli-train and had trained its guns directly at me. Cannonballs and bullets slammed into my armor, but I couldn't take my focus off Hendrix. If I did, I'd die. I might anyway, if I didn't find a way to stop both Hendrix and Zerelda. I pressed my attacks defending myself with sword and shield.

Suddenly, Rodin landed on my visor, frantically scurrying back and forth. He was trying to tell me something. I opened the visor and he climbed in. Immediately, the small dragon pointed his head toward Genevieve. She was locked in combat with the lady assassin. The pale Horseman of Death sent a constant stream of bullets at the Bronze Knight. But Genevieve wasn't interested in a long-distance fight. She drew the Bronze Knight's sword and charged.

The lady assassin raised a scythe above her pale steed and swiped at Genevieve. She dodged the first attack, then Genevieve wrapped the Bronze Knight's arms around the horseman, locking them together. Genevieve opened the visor and climbed out onto the shoulder of her Bronze Knight. Tears streaming down her cheeks, Genevieve drew her saber and pointed it at the rider. I couldn't hear what they were saying, but I didn't need too. The anguish on Genevieve's face wrenched at my heart.

Genevieve attacked the lady assassin with unrelenting strikes from the back of her machine but the woman drew her rapier and climbed out of the saddle. Still parrying Hendrix's attacks, and dodging the ongoing attacks from Zerelda, I rolled toward Genevieve. Zerelda began firing at Genevieve. Without any regard for the lady assassin. Although I knew I was exposing my rear flank to Hendrix, possibly a fatal move on my part, I put myself between Zerelda and Genevieve and used my shield to absorb the rounds fired by the train. Hendrix, turned and headed back toward the train.

In the barrage of fire that pummeled me, I heard the slamming of iron hooves behind me, and then the crashing of metal echo all around. I cringed and braced myself expecting a massive blow at any moment. Every muscle in me tightened, but nothing came. Instead, I opened my eyes to see Mr. Singh and the Iron Templar slamming the Horseman of War into the side of the train. The Iron Zulu, leaking steam and oil, still fired on the train and swung around to try and help Mr. Singh.

Zerelda stopped firing, as she waited for the Milli-train to settle. I braced myself for more impacts. I'd intercepted everything that would have hit Genevieve, sending dirt and rock raining down on us.

Over the battle, I heard the lady assassin yell, "Genevieve, I don't want to kill you. You have no idea what is happening."

"Lies," Genevieve screamed.

Their swords clashed repeatedly behind me. I wanted to turn around, but Zerelda, who had raised her sword, would momentarily lower her wicked cutlass and give the signal to fire again.

"The Templars are not the great organization you think they are." The lady assassin said.

"I won't listen to you," Genevieve screamed as she attacked again.

"But I am your—"

"You are not my mother! You are evil."

The lady assassin lunged at Genevieve and locked her sword with Genevieve's. "You have no idea who I am, or why I have done what I have. I didn't want to hurt your friends, but I had no choice."

"I don't want to hear it." Genevieve's fury erupted. "My mother was a great swordsman and an honorable warrior. You're nothing but a cheap imposter."

Their fighting intensified just as Zerelda lowered her sword and the train began firing again. One large cannonball slammed into my shield and dented it. Rodin jumped and flew off the chest plate he'd been clinging too. He curled up around my shoulders. My shield wouldn't hold up much longer, but I couldn't stop defending Genevieve.

The glint of light reflecting off Genevieve's silver saber shone through my visor as the sword soared past and stuck into the ground. I whipped around to see if she was okay, and found her with her arms held out in surrender. The lady assassin's sword aimed at Genevieve's throat. I went to raise the barrel of my cannon, but I'd already cut it free.

Explosions ripped all around me. I looked up and saw the airships. Our allies had arrived. They'd hurled cannon fire at the train, and in turn, Zerelda turned the train's cannons toward the fleet.

Hendrix and Mr. Singh stopped fighting momentarily and looked up at the airships. More dotted the horizon, as the Templar Air Corp arrived. Hendrix reared up on his steed and slammed down the horse's hooves with the force of a terrible earthquake, kicking dirt and rocks into the air. The ground around Mr. Singh and Owethu was ripped to shreds, and then, just like at Agincourt, their treads became mired in the loose earth and the ground gave way beneath them sending them plummeting into the caverns below.

Hendrix, now back on the Milli-train, turned and waved his hat. The train reared up on its legs and a demonic hiss pierced the valley as the Milli-train wiggled its back end like a rattlesnake, breaking the engine and about ten cars away from the back of the train. The train, now unimpeded by the damaged cars, scurried off to the north over the mountains.

With Hendrix and the onslaught of fire from Zerelda fading into the distance, I turned back to Genevieve. Rodin flapped incessantly inside of my armor so I threw open my visor to let him fly free. I scanned the surroundings for her, but didn't see her. The Bronze Knight stood empty next to a scrap pile, the remains of the pale horseman. Not a good sign. I rolled over to the armor.

Where is she? I opened the chest hatch of my Black Knight and jumped out. I searched the area, but she was gone. Only her saber remained, sticking up amid the tall grass. Frantic, I yanked it out of the dirt and held it out as if it would lead me to her. "Genevieve!" I screamed, looking around frantically. Then the world slammed down on my shoulders, and I fell to my knees. Rodin screeched, his cry piercing the air as he flew off, heading for the Milli-train. *The train.* Genevieve had to be on the train. The Golden Circle had her.

I clutched her sword and sobbed. "I'm so sorry, Genevieve! I failed you."

44
Alexander's Decision

Shuddering hard and forcing myself to breathe, I remembered Owethu and Mr. Singh. I rose out of the torn earth now soaked with tears and ran back to the Black Knight. I sped over to the hole they'd plunged into and sprang from my armor.

Racing to the edge, I peered over and saw Owethu smiling up at me. *They're safe!* He raised his hand. I waved. He and Mr. Singh sat on top of the Iron Zulu, not too far from the surface. I dropped to my stomach and reached down to give them a hand up.

"Where is Genevieve?" Mr. Singh looked around and then slowly turned to me.

I wiped my nose on my sleeve and looked at my friends. "The Golden Circle."

Within moments, the Sparrowhawk landed, and Eustache ran up to make certain we were uninjured. After he was satisfied, he set about securing the scene, as all around us crewmen climbed out of crashed airship wreckage, and Zulu soldiers rushed forward to capture the remains of Hendrix's men scattered amidst the remnants of the damaged train cars.

The Duke and

Richard, both in torn, soiled garments, and slightly singed by fire, walked down the gangplank. The baron, with the captain and Sinclair, followed.

This was the moment I dreaded. The baron scanned the fields now bathed in the last light of day. I knew he was looking for his daughter, and it crushed my soul to be holding the answer. I gripped Mr. Singh's shoulder and extended a hand to Owethu, "I have to tell him."

Both nodded and I walked off, my shoulders weighted down more with every step.

The baron, the Duke, and Richard gazed at me as I approached them. Seeing only me, the joy on their faces quickly faded into puzzlement, and then horror as they saw I carried Genevieve's saber.

"She's gone," was all I could muster before breaking down into tears.

Obviously not entirely comprehending, the baron asked, "Where is my daughter?"

"She was fighting her mother when I last saw her."

The baron gripped his cane so tightly I thought he might break it. He stayed silent, but his jaw clenched.

The Duke's eyes narrowed, hate filling his eyes, but as he started to speak, Sinclair pulled him off. "Your Grace, we need to send word immediately."

Richard snarled and stepped toward me. "You imbecile. You've killed her!" I snapped him an *are-you-crazy* look and he backed off.

Captain Baldarich placed a hand on the baron's shoulders. "They don't have much of head start, and the Sparrowhawk is in good shape, barley a scratch on her, so we should find them in no time." He winked at me.

The baron nodded. "Name you price, Sky Raider."

"I wouldn't do that to an old friend." He clasped

the baron's arm. "But I insist on taking the kid."

"Richard?" The baron asked with a puzzled expression.

"Oh, no." The two men looked at me and then at Richard who, instead of protesting, stormed off. Baldarich turned to me. "I don't want to think about what Mr. Armitage will do if we don't take him. He'd probably build wings and learn to fly."

"When can we leave?" the baron asked, which surprised me. I thought he'd not want me anywhere near him since I'd not protected Genevieve from harm.

"As soon as I give Heinz the orders."

"Good." The baron nodded and walked over to the Duke and the Grand Master.

Baldarich approached me. "So, lad, how you doing?"

"Not good, but I like your plan."

"I thought you might." He tussled my hair, and it was hard to keep the scowl on my face. "Can you live without that armor for a bit? You're pretty deadly in it."

"The Tinkerer says, it's not the armor but the man inside that matters. Captain, even after this is all over, I'd like to join your crew for a while, if you'll have me."

He paused staring at me, as if sizing me up. "You wouldn't be the youngest I've ever brought on board, and you have a bit of resume, and an in with the captain, the boatswain, and my engineer." He extended his hand, "Welcome aboard, Mr. Knight."

I smiled and shook his hand. Rodin flew up and landed on my shoulder. He folded his wings and nestled down. Looking tired, he curled up against the back of my neck.

We turned around as Mr. Singh and Owethu walked

over. Baldarich grabbed up Mr. Singh and hugged him tight. "Glad to see you without any major scratches. Prepare for departure. Oh, and we got a new crew member."

The weary Mr. Singh snapped his head up, his torn turban almost slipping from his head, "Aye-aye, Captain." He saluted and hurried up the gangplank.

Owethu shook my hand. "Thank you, my friend. Without you, my family and my village would have been lost."

"Thank you. You stood by my side against a terrible evil."

"I am sorry about Genevieve. She will be fine. She is as strong as any warrior in real life or legend. I'm certain you will find her, but if you need me, send word, or Rodin,"—he stroked the dragon's back—"and I will come."

"*Kuhle kakhulu*," I said. "I am returning to learn your language."

"I look forward to that day."

The baron returned with the Duke and Sinclair. He patted his shoulder, calling for the dragon, but Rodin stayed on my shoulder. The captain nodded to the men and boarded the Sparrowhawk. Sinclair took my hands in his. "Good luck, lad."

"Thank you, sir." I stepped off and stopped. "Please tell my father where I'm going, that I'm sorry, and he can ground me when we meet again." Sinclair nodded.

The baron and I walked up the gangplank and the crew reeled it in after us and closed the cargo door. The baron stopped me in the corridor. "Alexander, you said Genevieve was fighting her mother earlier. I take it you believe it is her now."

"It's why she took Genevieve and didn't kill her." I looked at him. "You should have explained to Genevieve who she was. She had a right to know."

The baron stared off into space for a minute then said, "I never told her who her mother was before we met. I realize now I should have."

"And I realize now that the Inner Circle wants Genevieve, just like they want me." I looked down at her saber. "I won't stop until she's free."

"Alexander, I—"

"Baron, apologies for my abruptness, but I don't care. I'm certain I will be blamed for her capture. I'm surprised you will even speak to me. My father, most certainly, will say I'm reckless. The Duke will say I'm rebellious. I don't care what either of them say. I don't care that Genevieve is betrothed to Richard or that we can never be part of the same world." I locked eyes with him. "Mark my words, I will find her. I will rescue her. Nothing will stand in my way."

Alexander Armitage will return
in Iron Lotus

Alexander's Sketchbook

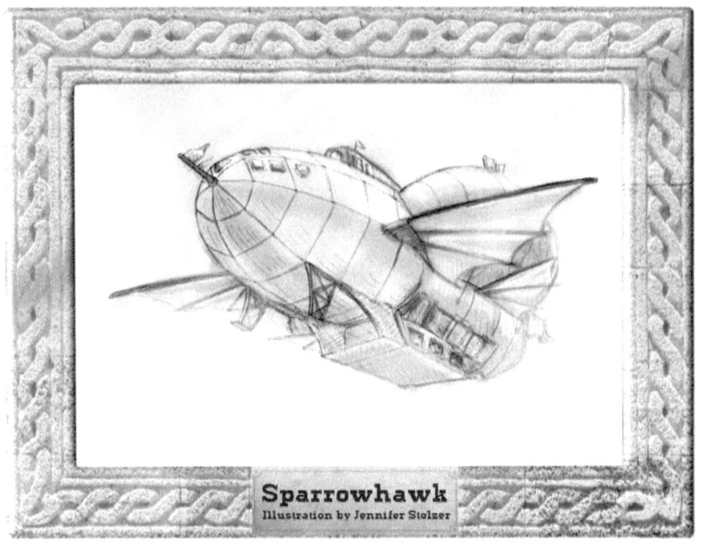

Illustrations by Jennifer Stolzer

Acknowledgements

I want to start by thanking my critique partners the word weaver Cole Gibsen, and the sci-fi siren T.W. Fendley. They are amazing authors, and I highly recommend their novels. Mine are immensely better because of their efforts.

Thank you to Jennifer Stolzer who creates the illustrations for the Sparrowhawk and the rest of Alexander's Sketchbook.

I wouldn't be where I am without St. Louis Writers Guild, and though I recently stepped down as president, I am thrilled that it will not only continue, but will thrive! Literary communities are important to every writer, so I also need to thank the Society of Children's Book Writers and Illustrators for everything they do.

I love all book stores, but I would be remiss not to mention Emily and the staff of Main Street Books in historic St. Charles for all the support! Drop by and you might find secretly signed copies of my books. Support your bookstores and the libraries; they are the gateways to infinite adventure.

Shout out to the Write Pack… those cool writer cats.

I must pay homage to the Zulu, a culture I have admired for many years. I only wanted to honor their great nation, and wish I could have showcased them more.

Lastly, thank you for joining us on this adventure.

For 2022
A book dedicated to my family seems appropriate right now. I've haven't seen so many of them recently, and can't wait to see them all once again. Shout out to my aunts, uncles, cousins, and they're kids. I hope you all are doing well.

Of course, I have to thank my wife for all her support.

To my mother as well, she reads everything I've written.

Stay healthy!

Brad R. Cook

BRADRCOOK.COM

About the Author

Brad R. Cook
Author and Historian

I see things that never were and say, "Why not?"

Brad R. Cook, is the author of historical fantasy, and award-winning short stories. He began as a playwright, dipped into the corporate writing world, and served as co-publisher and acquisitions editor for Blank Slate Press. He currently serves as Historian of St. Louis Writers Guild after three and half years as President. He learned to fence at thirteen, and never set down his sword, but prefers to curl up with a centuries' old classic.

bradrcook.com
@bradrcook

More Stories by Brad R. Cook

<u>Books</u>

Iron Horsemen
Book I of The Iron Chronicles

Behind the Iron Door
Steampunk Short Stories

Steamtree
The Airdrainium Adventures

The History of St. Louis Writers Guild
Celebrating a Century

<u>Short Stories</u>

A Clockwork Heart
The Dragon Slayer
Doomed Flight of the Majestic
Touch the Stars
The Secret of Knotbridge Hill
The Legend of Spring-Heeled Jack

Find them at BradRCook.com
Order online or from your favorite local bookstore.